AN ARTFUL DECISION

HOLLY NEWMAN

All rights reserved.

No part of this publication may be sold, copied, distributed, reproduced or transmitted in any form or by any means, mechanical or digital, including photocopying and recording or by any information storage and retrieval system without the prior written permission of both the publisher, Oliver Heber Books and the author, Holly Newman, except in the case of brief quotations embodied in critical articles and reviews.

PUBLISHER'S NOTE: This is a work of fiction. Names, characters, places, and incidents either are the product of the author's imagination or are used fictitiously. Any resemblance to actual persons, living or dead, business establishments, events, or locales is entirely coincidental.

An Artful Decision Copyright 2024 © Holly Thompson

Cover art by Dar Albert, Wicked Smart Designs

Published by Oliver-Heber Books

0 9 8 7 6 5 4 3 2 1

CHAPTER 1
MRS. SOUTHERLAND

The knock on the parlor door stopped their laughing reminiscences.

"Enter!" Mrs. Southerland called out, setting her teacup down, her cheeks rosy and her eyes twinkling from shared laughter. She was a stout, older woman of some five-and-sixty winters.

Gwinnie set her cup down as well, then blotted the corners of her mouth with her serviette.

She and Mrs. Southerland sat together in the Pomona-green parlor of Mrs. Southerland's House for Unfortunate Women, for their Friday afternoon discussion of the week's activities.

For the women who called Mrs. Southerland's house their home for a time, it was their day for shopping with the coins they'd earned for their diligence in lessons; for others, it was their time to be household staff in the hopes they would learn all that was proper for a maid in a great house. Mrs. Southerland did not run a simple charity house. The unfortunates who found their way to her door and were admitted entry, worked hard to learn lessons that would send them on to other profitable endeavors far out of the stews of London. Those who did not wish to learn lessons or gain a profitable endeavor other than the baud houses, were given clean clothing, a few coins, and wished well on their way, wherever that might be.

Sometimes Gwinnie thought that heartless; however, if this rule was not kept, they would not have accommodations enough for the women who truly needed assistance. That was not acceptable.

Today, Polly Petrie held the role of housemaid. When she opened the door, she crossed her foot too far back as she attempted a curtsy and wobbled, then righted herself.

Gwinnie smiled. The young woman tried hard to learn everything they taught. Sometimes too hard. Gwinnie vowed to work with her next week on her curtsy.

"Pardon, Mrs. Southerland, Miss Knolls, there is a gentleman come to visit." Polly rubbed her hands down the front of her maid's apron as she spoke. A common habit, judging by the streaks Gwinnie saw.

"Who is it?" Mrs. Southerland asked gently.

Polly looked in the corner of the room, her brow furrowed. Then she looked at Mrs. Southerland. "I forgets..." she admitted.

"Well—" Mrs. Southerland began.

"But I gots 'is card," Polly said suddenly, pulling it out of her apron pocket. A wide smile lit her rather plain face and revealed a missing front tooth. She handed the card to Mrs. Southerland.

"Thank you, dear. But do try to remember the names of callers, that could be important in any future position you may hold. Visitors don't all carry cards— though they should, to my mind," she said as she glanced down at the card. "Oh, it's Mr. Martin, Miss Knolls." She looked over at the maid. "Please show him up and bring a refresh of tea and a cup for the gentleman."

Mr. Lewis Martin of Bow Street appeared at the door to the parlor holding his hat and gloves in his hands, still bundled in his scarf and heavy greatcoat against the January cold. Gwinnie compressed her lips against a laugh. More reminders for Polly. She should have taken his outdoor wear. Sometimes the poor woman had a mind like a sieve. Gwinnie vowed she would make her into a good maid— somehow.

"Mr. Martin! What brings you here?" Mrs. Southerland enthused.

He nodded toward Gwinnie. "Lady Guinevere Nowlton's father requested I escort her home."

Gwinnie frowned at him for using her real name and title. At least she and Mrs. Southerland were alone in the parlor. "It's Miss Knolls, and I thought father was sending Jimmie— not that I need an escort, as I've been coming and returning from here on my own for well over a year with nary an issue."

And not that anyone was liable to give her trouble, she thought, given her giantess size and the subdued attire she wore as Sarah Knolls, solicitor's daughter and teacher for the women here at Mrs. Southerland's House for Unfortunate Women. It was the guise she wore to be accepted by the residents. A duke's daughter would scare them into silence and resentment.

Mr. Martin placed his hat and gloves on a table and unwound the gold knitted scarf from around his neck. "He sent word to me this morning that he'd received another threat."

"Another one?" Gwinnie clarified.

"Yes, and after reviewing it, I advised him to take it seriously. This one appears to target the entire family."

Gwinnie grimaced, then waved a hand in the air. "But that doesn't explain why you're here. Ever since he's been receiving these threats, he's had the footmen, Jimmie or Stephen, escort me. Which is perfectly ridiculous as the threats have been against him, not me, and I don't look like a—" She stopped abruptly before she said 'duke's daughter' when the parlor door opened again to admit Polly, walking backward, carrying a full tea tray.

She couldn't see where she was going. Gwinnie, from across the room, saw Polly's heel catch at the edge of the rug. Gwinnie gasped. Luckily, Mr. Martin was near enough to grab Polly before she fell with the tea tray and its contents all over herself.

Gwinnie and Mrs. Southerland exhaled sighs of relief as Mr. Martin righted Polly and steadied the tray.

"Thank you, Mr. Martin," Mrs. Southerland said. "Polly, now do you understand why we always instruct you ladies to carry the tea tray before you and not walk backward into a room? You can't see where you are going and that is how accidents happen."

"Yes, ma'am. Sorry ma'am." Polly lifted a packet off the tea tray. "This come for yous as I brung the tea from the kitchen."

Gwinnie pressed the heel of her hand against her forehead at Polly's diction, but did not correct her. She and Mrs. Southerland would have to have a discussion about the young woman soon.

"Back to why you are here," Gwinnie said to Lewis, as Mrs. Southerland read the letter.

"Jimmie sprained his ankle," Lewis told her.

"Again? I don't think he let it heal properly from last month's incident," Gwinnie said.

"I believe he is very conscious of his duty to your father."

Gwinnie shook her head, her lips compressed in a sharp line.

"Oh, gracious," she heard Mrs. Southerland exclaim. "This is good news. I must, I must..." She looked around the room, then when her eyes settled on Gwinnie, she stood up excitedly. "Excuse me a moment."

She turned toward her desk set between the windows and dug out a pencil and a stack of paper she had in her desk. She jotted a quick note, then folded the paper she'd written on before returning her writing supplies to the desk.

"I must run a quick errand," Mrs. Southerland said, her cheeks flushed, her eyes shining. "You wore your short cape today, correct? Might I borrow it for a few minutes, I'm too excited to run upstairs to fetch my heavy coat."

"Of course," Gwinnie said, looking at the older woman curiously. She'd never seen the white-haired, grandmotherly looking woman this excited. She looked years younger. "But what has happened?"

"This is such good news! I'll tell you all about it on my return. Mr. Martin, sit please; you can stay a few minutes more before you take Miss Knolls away, can't you? Have some tea," she said, her hands waving excitedly.

Mr. Martin laughed. "I should be delighted to. I detect you have received good news?"

"The best." She hugged her arms across her ample chest. "And you should learn all about it on my return. This is so exciting!" she enthused. "I shall not be long," she promised as she rolled out of her chair. She shook out the skirts of her burgundy-with-black, pin-stripe bombazine dress. She settled her fichu with its tatted lace trim, made by a woman who'd been a resident a year ago, around her decolletage, and scurried out of the room, rocking side to side, calling for Polly as she went.

Mr. Martin and Gwinnie looked at each other. "That is the most unusual reaction to any communication I have ever witnessed," Gwinnie said.

"So I gather," Mr. Martin drawled, smiling after Mrs. Southerland, then he turned his brilliant, smiling blue eyes in her direction.

Suddenly Gwinnie felt a trifle uncomfortable alone in Mr. Martin's presence. She felt aware of him in a way she had never had before.

While Mr. Martin stood tall, by society's standards, he wasn't quite as tall as she. Few men were. Yet, there was a presence about Mr. Martin that made him seem taller to her. He had an easy, relaxed manner for all his upright posture and a deceptively relaxed smile that reflected in his always-twinkling blue eyes. He was not a man easily read, as some of the gentlemen of Gwinnie's acquaintance were wont to be. He didn't use pomade on his blond waves to control them, unconcerned for the wild disarray. Not at all what she had come to consider the manner of a Bow Street Runner. And that made her curious— and her heart beat faster.

"So, what should we talk about," she asked, her low voice unusually gruff.

"Music?" he suggested.

"Unfair, you know my weakness," she told him with a little laugh. She poured tea into a cup for Mr. Martin and handed it to him.

"When did you start to play the violin?" he asked.

Gwinnie soon found herself avidly recounting her journey into music. Mr. Martin was a good listener, asking just the right next question to have her talk more. Finally, she wound down, laughing at herself for her enthusiasm for her topic.

"Now you know all about my weakness. But I don't know any of yours. Confess, do you have a weakness?" she asked teasingly.

"Crime," he stated succinctly.

"All your life it has been crime?" she asked.

He cocked his head to the side for a moment. "Well, no," he conceded. "Law preceded crime in my interests. For a time, I studied law at the Inns of Chancery."

"You were going to be a solicitor?"

"My father thought it a good vocation for me. I should have preferred to be a barrister; however, they did not accept me."

"Whyever not?"

He laughed. "Something about being born on the wrong side of the blanket."

A bright red blush suffused her cheeks. Gwinnie didn't know if she was mortified that she'd asked a question that would lead to that answer or mortified that he'd answered truthfully! But Mr. Martin would. He could play a role, as she understood he'd done at her grandmother's house last year, but in other matters, he was a forthright and truthful man. She'd always liked that about him in their past meetings.

Mr. Martin laughed, and Gwinnie's cheeks grew warmer.

"Please don't be embarrassed, La— Miss Knolls," he said easily. "My father had gone to get a special license to marry my mother when I unfortunately decided to enter the world earlier than anticipated. I long ago decided the fault is entirely my own," he said with another of his wry, self-deprecating laughs.

"Nonsense!" Gwinnie protested. "Couldn't they have gotten married on his return and just fudged the dates a little?"

Mr. Martin sighed and shook his head, then ran his fingers through his blond waves. "Not in my mother's and father's circumstances." A melancholy look flashed across his face, then was gone, replaced by his normal wry smile.

Gwinnie wanted to ask more questions, to learn about his parents' circumstances, but she didn't wish to embarrass herself or Mr. Martin further. To still her ready tongue, she picked up her teacup and nearly drained it. What else could they discuss? Maybe the young boy who'd been with him at Versely Park?

"Grandmother said you had a young man with you when you were at Versely Park."

"Daniel. I've taken him in. The boy is amazingly intelligent, the kind of intelligence that could get him into immense trouble as he gets older if someone doesn't channel him in the right way. In my naivety, I vowed to attempt to do so. I don't know how successful I will be— Sometimes I wonder who is teaching whom."

"Where did he come from?"

"He was— still is, if I don't keep him busy— a mudlark, leading a gang of mudlarks. Cheeky devil," he said laughing and shaking his head. "Got your grandmother's housekeeper to have a footman's outfit made for him."

Gwinnie laughed. "I heard about the boy in his footman outfit. Where is he now?"

"At one of Soothcoor's schools. His request."

"He requested to go to school?"

"As I said, he's too int—"

Bloodcurdling screams came from the back of the house. Mr. Martin jumped up to run toward the sound. Gwinnie felt her blood pounding in her chest as she followed after him. At the door, he stopped.

"Stay here," he ordered.

"Not likely," she countered, brushing past him. Her heart climbed into her throat.

The screams had changed to shrieks. They heard *"Mrs. Southerland! No! Mrs. Southerland!"*

Gwinnie picked up her skirts and ran faster down the short flight of stairs to the servants' area and the backdoor.

Polly stood frozen in front of the door, staring at it as they heard someone fumbling with the lock. Gwinnie pushed Polly aside. Then the door flew open, two young women fell forward to land in the entry.

The women immediately saw Gwinnie. "Oh, Miss Knolls! Miss Knolls!" they cried, grabbing onto her.

Gwinnie's mind raced in a whirlwind of fear and confusion.

Mr. Martin brushed past the women, not waiting for their words.

Gwinnie tried to set them aside and follow Mr. Martin, but they clung to her.

Polly stood against the wall like an animal too frightened to move.

"Mrs. Southerland," one of the women gasped out. "She's dead!"

"Her throat's cut!" said the other.

Gwinnie recognized the women as Georgia Marke and Harriet Warden. She looked over their shoulders. Mr. Martin was squatting down before a woman's body. In the afternoon's rapidly fading light, she saw a froth of burgundy with black pinstripe over a white petticoat.

Mrs. Southerland.

Gwinnie's blood ran icy in her veins as she realized the truth.

The women were crying, sobbing, clinging to her. Mrs. Southerland would wish her to take care of the living. A few tears leaked down her cheek. *Now was not the time!* her mind screamed. She pulled herself together.

"Polly!" Gwinnie snapped at the frozen woman. "Where are Mrs. Albert and Miss Wooler?" The housekeeper and the cook should have been there at the back door before them, Gwinnie thought as she guided the sobbing women down the short flight of stairs into the kitchen.

"Th— the Thirsty Pig," Polly stammered. "Fer their Friday nip," she explained. "Is it true? 'Bout Mrs. Southerland."

"I know as much as you," Gwinnie retorted. "Put water on, then find Cook's calming leaves."

"Yes, Miss," Polly said, galvanized into action.

Gwinnie saw one of the women wipe her nose on her sleeve. "Miss Warden! Where is your handkerchief?"

The woman jumped. "Here, Miss," she said, fumbling into her reticule that still hung from her wrist.

"Use it, not your sleeve," Gwinnie ordered. She felt like a monster for reprimanding the woman, but she knew giving instructions would help calm them.

"Miss Knolls, may I speak with you?" said Mr. Martin from the backdoor landing, his voice the opposite of hers, soft and calm.

"Yes, yes, of course," Gwinnie said, stepping out of the kitchen and closing the door behind her, glad to be away from the others.

"What happened?" Gwinnie asked, as she climbed the short flight of stairs to where he stood. "Did she fall?" She heard Miss Woolsey say her throat had been cut, but hoped she'd been mistaken in the growing shadows.

Gone was the handsome and smiling man from the parlor. Mr. Martin grimly shook his head. "Throat slit."

Gwinnie closed her eyes momentarily as she shuddered. "Here!" she said, shaking her head, her mind warring with disbelief. "Here, at the back door?"

He nodded. "I need to get the coroner. Will you be fine here until I return?"

Gwinnie looked back at the kitchen, wanting to be anyplace but here. She straightened. "Yes, I'll be fine," she said firmly, more to herself than Mr. Martin. "And when the women calm down more, I'll ask questions as to what they've seen."

Mr. Martin reached out to squeeze her arm. "I know I can count on you. I'll return as soon as I can."

On another day, another time, she would have been

shocked by his touch. Today, she welcomed it. Her thoughts swirled, thinking of the residents. Some were emotionally fragile, and none of them trusted men. The coroner would want an inquest. There would be men about. She had to protect the women, she fiercely decided.

"There will be other women returning from their Friday free afternoon..." she said.

"I've locked the back gate. That should force them to come around to the front."

She grasped Mr. Martin's arm before he could turn to leave. "Soothcoor—do you know if he is in town? He needs to be here."

"He is at his stepmother's estate, Appleton. I'll send word to him— I assume you will be staying here for the night?" he said.

"I can't leave the women alone," she said.

He nodded. "I'll get word to the duke you'll be staying here."

"Thank you."

He started to climb the short flight to the ground floor, but turned back to Gwinnie. "Where is the housekeeper?"

"Down the way at The Thirsty Pig," Gwinnie said disgustedly.

"What is her name?" he asked.

"Mrs. Albert."

He nodded. "I'll send her back here."

"She's with Miss Wooler, the cook."

He snorted inelegantly. "I'll send them both back."

"Thank you," Gwinnie said again, softly this time, her eyes filling with tears.

Mr. Martin swore, then came back down a step and pressed his clean handkerchief into her hand. Without another word, he turned to climb the steps to the ground-floor landing and headed out the door.

Gwinnie turned back to face the closed back door. Throat slit, he'd said. She shivered. She couldn't fathom that. And Mrs. Southerland exuded such happiness not thirty minutes past. It didn't make sense.

She had to see her.

She turned again and walked slowly toward the back door. Her hand shook as she grasped the door handle. *She had to see her!* Slowly, she opened the door. Evening darkness now claimed the small yard behind the house. She couldn't see color clearly. Gwinnie thought that a blessing. She stepped closer to her friend and mentor. She lay on her right side and back, her right arm pinned beneath her. Her throat cut from one side to another. It looked deeper on the right, but that could have been for how she fell.

Blood saturated Gwinnie's cape and spread across the ground. The cape had been a gift from her brother Lancelot from a trip he'd made to Austria to attend the Congress of Vienna. It had been a beautiful, heavy, gray wool half-cape, embroidered with white flowers and green trailing vines and leaves along the edges.

Gwinnie clenched her trembling hands into fists, desperately trying to hold back the flood of tears threatening to overwhelm her. She hoped the cape had kept Mrs. Southerland warm on her errand. And what had been her errand? Why was she returning through the rear door and not the front?

She felt the tears flow down her cheeks before she realized she was crying. She swiped at her cheeks, then turned back to the house. She hoped Mr. Martin returned quickly with the coroner. She couldn't bear the idea of Mrs. Southerland being out here on the ground all night.

Perhaps she should get a quilt...

Don't be silly, Guinevere! she chided herself, crying harder. She wanted to sink down on the stoop before Mrs. Southerland's body and wallow in misery. But Mrs. Southerland wouldn't approve. As she'd told Gwinnie many times, the women here saw Gwinnie's height as strength and they looked up to her for her strength.

Gwinnie needed to be strong now for the woman who lived here, even though she, herself, felt tiny and lost. This was no time to wallow. She straightened and returned to the kitchen and those who needed her.

CHAPTER 2
THE THIRSTY PIG

Mr. Lewis Martin shoved his arms into his coat sleeves as he ran down the front steps of Mrs. Southerland's townhouse. It was not fully dark yet, though heavy, charcoal-gray shadows ate up the roads, and the nighttime chill had already descended upon the streets. The lamplighters had begun their rounds but hadn't made it down by the townhouse. He could see tiny bright specks glowing to his right at the other end of the street. He turned left and hurried up the street's slight rise to where it met the main road, and he rounded the corner to where *The Thirsty Pig* pub stood.

He didn't want to leave Lady Gwinnie— as he thought of Lady Guinevere Nowlton— with the body of Mrs. Southerland and a house of emotional young women who had already seen enough horror in their lives without having their haven impacted with horror.

He thought the duke's daughter was a remarkable woman. He'd met her the night after the Duke of Ellinbourne's engagement ball to her cousin, Miss Ann Hallowell. He'd come to Malmsby House at the behest of Lord Aidan Nowlton and the Dowager Duchess of Malmsby. They requested his services to investigate Lord Candelstone's gunshot wound during the ball. He questioned everyone in the household about what they saw and heard during the ball, before he sought out the guests and questioned them as well.

She had been practicing with members of her musical quartet. She played the violin. It was obvious she was the leader of the musicians.

She was a tall woman, over six feet and therefore taller than him, with a voluptuous body, a voice lower than most women, and a cloud of deep-red hair casually tied up in a loose knot, tendrils framing her face. It was the kind of hair a man longed to run his fingers through. She welcomed him into her midst with a warm smile that spread into a pair of beautiful brown eyes, and a deep laugh. Unlike her brother, her facial freckles were lighter and fewer, her skin a light alabaster with a pale rose glow.

He'd been surprised to learn she was not married, that she devoted herself to her music and her charity work with women who'd been abused within society and cast aside. Despite himself and his years of ignoring any of the glittering trappings of the ton— for they could be as guilty of crimes as anyone— she intrigued him.

In the weeks and then months since he first became involved with the Nowlton family, he'd found it harder and harder to ignore the Junoesque beauty. Regrettably, he knew he could not become involved with a duke's daughter. Though his father had been an earl, he— as he'd told Lady Gwinnie— was baseborn. But he appreciated her intelligence and humor and enjoyed the mild friendship that had evolved between them. With her brother now married, he'd encouraged her to shift her teasing and joking to himself and Mr. Hargate, the London solicitor who managed the Earl of Soothcoor's charity projects. They'd come to understand their roles in her life as guards and friends for the lonely woman.

With the duke's interests and investment in new inventions, cottage craft workers and small factory workers worried for their livelihood. There were threats against the duke and his family for his support of the inventions. Lady Gwinnie ignored the threats to her, as she did not feel they were real. Lewis and Mr. Hargate did not think they should be ignored. Thus, he had come to Mrs. Southerland's that day to escort Lady Gwinnie home, no matter how she railed at the intrusion into her independence. She did not believe, with her height and size, that any man would dare to try to harm her. Lewis did not want to have to prove his point following an attack on her person.

He pushed open the door to the brightly lit and warm pub and scanned the crowded room for the two employees of Mrs. Southerland. The wintry weather did not keep people from going out; however, it did encourage their hunkering down in a warm pub. He knew Mrs. Albert better than Miss Wooler and would have to count on their being together to help him to identify her.

"Mr. Martin!"

Lewis turned to see the publican, Tobias Watney, hailing him from over by the bar. He lifted his hand in acknowledgement and walked over to join the man. He needed to speak to him as much as he needed to speak to Mrs. Albert and Miss Wooler.

"Pleasure or business," Mr. Watney asked when he reached him.

"A most unfortunate business," he said.

Mr. Watney screwed up his face in disgust. "Robbery?" he asked.

Lewis shook his head. "Murder."

"Murder, eh?" he said, as he passed a mug of ale to Lewis.

Lewis nodded. "Mrs. Southerland," he said.

The publican nearly dropped his mug. "Mrs. Southerland!" he exclaimed. He shook his head. "What's our city coming to? This is a nice neighborhood. Not ton, but no Seven Dials neither. What happened?"

"Set upon almost at her back door."

Mr. Watney whistled through his front teeth as he shook his head.

"Do you have a cool room below stairs where we might keep her until an inquest can be arranged? I'd hate to have those poor women live with her body in their midst, let alone a company of men traipsing into their home."

"For Mrs. Southerland, of course! I'll have my boy Jamie set it to rights so you can have her brought here."

"I am much obliged to you, sir.'

"Nonsense. She was a good woman. Did good work."

"Thank you. Do you know where I might find Mrs. Albert and Miss Wooler? I need to notify them so they can return to the townhouse."

"Yes, yes." He stepped away from the bar and pointed to the back wall. "They're in the second-to-last booth."

Lewis looked where he pointed and nodded. He drained his beer and set it back down. "I am obliged to you again."

Mr. Watney shook his head. "Nonsense. In this neighborhood, we all do what we can for each other."

"That's not what I've heard," said Lewis. "I hear there is one neighbor here who would be happy to see Mrs. Southerland's establishment leave the area."

Mr. Watney shrugged. "Mr. Jeffrey Simmons. Full of hot air, like in those balloons. If it is not one thing to complain about it is another. One day, one of his complaints is going to carry him away much like those balloons."

Lewis laughed and clapped the publican on the back. "Thank you. I needed that laugh tonight. I'd best be off to see the ladies."

"I'll warn Mabel if she hears screams it won't be from you causing physical pain."

"Thanks— I think," Lewis said as he turned to walk to the back corner of the pub.

"Mrs. Albert," he said cordially, as he came to a stop by their table. "Forgive the intrusion."

Mrs. Albert squinted at him, then put her glasses back on. She'd only taken them off for a moment to clean the lenses.

"Mr. Martin?"

"Yes ma'am. You are needed back at Mrs. Southerland's. There has been an incident."

"An incident," Miss Wooler repeated.

An Artful Decision

He turned toward her. "Miss Knolls needs your assistance."

"Miss Knolls?" she repeated, confused.

"Where is Mrs. Southerland?" Mrs. Albert asked, the quicker of the two women.

"Mrs. Southerland has met with an unfortunate occurrence," he told her seriously, his hands clasped behind his back.

"Yes?" the women said.

"She's deceased."

"Dead!" screamed Mrs. Albert.

All around them conversation stopped. Lewis looked around to see everyone looking in their direction.

Miss Wooler grabbed his arm. "What? How? I don't understand."

Lewis frowned. "I don't have time to explain it to you. I need to fetch the coroner and Miss Knolls will need your aid with the other young women as they return to the house from their free afternoon." He disengaged his arm from her grip. "Will you return to the house?"

"Yes, of course," Mrs. Albert said, rising to her feet. She grabbed her coat and put it on. "Come, Jessica."

"Thank you." He turned to leave, and they trailed after him.

"Mr. Martin," Mrs. Albert said, as he held the pub door open for them and they stepped out into the wintry night. "Can you at least tell us how she died— it will be hard for us to immediately support Miss Knolls if we don't know how she died when we arrive."

"She'd gone out on an errand to meet someone, and on her return, she had her throat slit," he said baldly.

"No!" the women cried out.

"Yes. Excuse me I must go." He strode away from them before they could ask any more questions.

~

GWINNIE HAD JUST COME BACK into the house when she heard the front door slam shut.

"Where is she?" Mrs. Albert yelled.

"What happened?" Miss Wooler shrilled.

They clattered down the half-flight of stairs to the back door.

"Let me see!" insisted Mrs. Albert, reaching around Gwinnie for the door handle, Miss Wooler crowding against her.

"No!" Gwinnie said, blocking the door.

"But—" Mrs. Albert protested.

"No," Gwinnie repeated. "A Bow Street Runner has gone to fetch the coroner."

Mrs. Albert compressed her lips and stepped back, forcing Miss Wooler back. "You mean that handsome blond man who told us Mrs. Southerland had been killed is a runner?"

"Yes."

"We've seen him here before," Mrs. Albert said.

Miss Wooler nodded. "I thought he was sweet on you, that he's your courting gentleman."

Gwinnie laughed lightly. "Hardly," she said. "He's shorter than me," she tossed out in a wild explanation on seeing Mrs. Albert's eyes narrow, hiding her insecurities.

Miss Wooler made a dismissive sound as she put her hands on her hips.

"Lord Soothcoor asked him and that solicitor, Mr. Hargate, to keep a watch on goings-on here— for the safety of everyone," Gwinnie hastened to explain, feeling a twinge of guilt, for tonight she felt unaccountably drawn to Mr. Martin.

"I'll be betting that's on account of the threats made by the gentleman down the street." Mrs. Albert nodded wisely.

Gwinnie blinked. "What gentleman? What threats?" she asked, looking hastily from one woman to the other.

"Mr. Simmons," Miss Wooler said. "He don't like Mrs. Southerland's House for Unfortunate Women being here. Says it brings down the neighborhood."

"And him just moving in not eight months ago. We been here over three years now," Mrs. Albert said.

"Hmm," was all Gwinnie replied. She would tell Mr. Martin and the coroner for sure, but something about the way Mrs. Southland was killed did not seem to Gwinnie like it would be as vicious if it were over dissatisfaction with a charity home on the same street.

"Miss Wooler, I know meals aren't typically served on Friday night, but could you see what you could get the girls to eat and drink to help calm them? Mrs. Albert, I just heard the front door open, I'm sure that is more of the young ladies returning. I depend on you to take charge of those returning now, carefully explaining the situation— and *no one* is to go out this door," she emphasized, pointing to the door behind her, "but the coroner and Mr. Martin."

"I can't say I know what the situation is to tell them," Mrs. Albert retorted. She drew herself upright. "But I'll look after the women. It is what Mrs. Southerland would have wanted."

Miss Wooler nodded.

"Such is my thought as well," Gwinnie said, breathing out a sigh of relief that they hadn't given her too much of a bother.

Miss Wooler turned toward the short flight of stairs down into the kitchen and Mrs. Albert trudged back up the stairs to the ground floor, her shoulders slumped, her footsteps heavy. Gwinnie sagged against the wall for a moment, then drew herself up as Mrs. Albert had done.

She needed to send notes to the earl— and to her father. She gathered her skirts in her hands and ran up the stairs after Mrs. Albert. She slipped by the woman talking softly to the two recent arrivals, one of whom had sunken onto a step leading to the first floor. Gwinnie went into the parlor. Mrs. Southerland had a small desk set between the long windows that looked out on the street. Her favorite chair to the left of the intricate desk.

Gwinnie sat on the delicate Hepplewhite chair before the desk and stared out the window. She could almost see the march of shadows across the street and the houses opposite. The last of an orange haze sat just above the houses, then it, too, disappeared. Tears now ran down her cheeks, unchecked. She already missed Mrs. Southerland, a surrogate mother to her as much as to the young women she welcomed into her home. She helped Gwinnie feel comfortable with her height. She showed her she had value far beyond being a duke's daughter. Gwinnie had hated her oversized body since she'd been twelve and that year grew taller than her twin, Lance.

She'd tried dieting on bread and water for a month to reduce the curves that came with the height, but that only made her sick and weak. Her mother constantly told her that her size had nothing to do with fat. Gwinnie hadn't believed her until she fainted in church. Her father became quite stern with her and ordered her to eat. She continued to grow until she stood six feet two inches, her bones large and her body covering them in curves.

Mrs. Southerland had helped her to be at peace with her body. Mrs. Southerland with her ready smile and sage advice— a mother to many lost women— bringing them home, encouraging them to love themselves no matter what their life experiences had been.

The last orange in the sky disappeared. Gwinnie turned up the lamp and lifted a section of the desktop up to reveal a stack of paper and pencils. Mrs. Southerland eschewed ink and quills, saying she couldn't write with ink without getting her fingers smudged with ink. She preferred pencils.

Gwinnie removed the paper from the desk and selected a pencil. She stared at the paper stack a moment as she considered what she could say to Lord Soothcoor. Her hand hovered over the paper when she noted the indentations on the top sheet. Deep indentations from a hand pressing down, writing quickly. She remembered Mrs. Southerland jotting down something before she left.

A sizzle of excitement traveled through her. If they knew where she'd gone, they could get a clue as to who killed her. She opened the desk again to find the small knife Mrs. Southerland used to sharpen her pencils. She took it out and carefully scraped it against the graphite while holding the pencil over the paper. Tiny amounts of dark gray floated down to the paper under her hand. She gently rubbed the tip of her finger across the paper to transfer the graphite to the sheet. Her excitement jumped when she saw the graphite was doing what she'd hoped, illuminating the writing.

She hurriedly continued scraping the pencil. In her excitement, she pushed too hard. The graphite broke.

"*Bloody hell*," she muttered to herself, then bit her lower lip, embarrassed by her expletive, though no one stood by to hear.

She lifted the desktop open again to pull out the small metal wax stamp. Moving the broken graphite piece to another sheet of paper, she used the stamp to grind the broken piece into powder. When it was as fine as she could make them, she picked up the paper and let the graphite dust slide off to the paper with the handwriting imprint. With the tip of her finger, she carefully smoothed the graphite across the page.

My darling, yes! I have p ayed for his. I don't know wheth r t lau or cry. Take this note to butler at venor Squa . He'll s th t e. Foll i n ucti

The more she wrote, Mrs. Southerland's hand pressure eased. The impression disappeared save for an occasional letter. Nothing that Gwinnie could make out.

She sat back on the delicate chair.

Whom was she addressing as darling? Gwinnie knew Mr. Southerland died four years ago. It was after his death— at the encouragement of her sister-in-law— that Mrs. Southerland had approached the Earl of Soothcoor to ask if he would fund this house.

She carefully set the original paper with its impressions, and her graphite smudge document aside, then pulled out clean paper for her notes.

Dear Father,

I will be staying at Mrs. Southerland's establishment tonight. There has been a murder here and...

No. To baldly state there has been a murder without context would have her father rising in protest. She crumpled the paper and tossed it into a beautiful, filigreed iron bin beside the desk. She brought another sheet of paper toward her.

Dear Father,

There was an incident at Mrs. Southerland's this afternoon. I feel I should stay here with the ladies to help sort it out.

This one followed the first into a crumpled mess in the bin. It was so mealy-mouthed and evasive!

She breathed deeply, determined to be accurate, concise, and non-emotional.

Dear Father,
Mrs. Southerland has...

Rapping at the front door had her set her pencil aside with relief.

She hurried through the parlor and down the stairs just as Mrs. Albert was coming up the stairs from the kitchen area.

"Do not worry, Mrs. Albert, I'll get this," she told the woman.

CHAPTER 3
THE CORONER

Dr. Ignatius Brogan was the coroner for this area of London, an area that included Covent Garden, but he lived closer to society Mayfair, in a middle-class neighborhood situated on its edges. Lewis walked to Oxford Street to hail a hackney carriage to take him there.

Riding in the carriage, his mind went back to thinking about Lady Gwinnie. He disliked leaving her at Mrs. Southerland's, even though she was a woman who always exuded confidence. He wondered what her father, the duke would say, or her uncle, Lord Aidan Nowlton would say, if they knew he'd left her there. Their worry and subsequent intrusion into her life had driven her to hide most of what she did from them. She'd achieved the privacy she craved against her uncle Aidan, but not the duke. To his credit, the duke came to understand she did not like him hovering over her, so he watched over her without intruding by setting himself and Mr. Hargate as guardians. More like watchdogs, he thought. He smiled as he held back a sudden urge to bark.

He found she was on his mind a great deal. He admired her. He knew her extreme height for a woman held her at a disadvantage among the men who wished for a more petite and fragile dance partner, let alone a life partner. Aidan had told him she often sat along the sides of the ballroom with the wallflowers if she and her quartet were not providing the music for the evening's dancing. He couldn't fathom how society gentlemen could overlook her. If ever he should marry, she was the type of woman he would wed. Luckily, he didn't think he would ever marry, so he need not be disappointed in his search for her twin in his class— Not that he had a class. Those who were base-born seldom did. He'd been raised in an earl's household, had a peer's education, yet could never be one. He was out of place in the world.

The carriage pulled up before Dr. Brogan's townhouse. Lewis jumped out and quickly paid the driver. With the coming of night, the temperature dropped. He ran up the steps to bang the knocker.

A footman answered the door.

"I must see Dr. Brogan immediately," Lewis told the man as he handed him his card.

"*Who is it, Samuel?*" Lewis heard from behind the footman's broad shoulders.

"Lewis Martin, from Bow Street," Lewis called out before the footman could answer his employer.

"Mr. Martin! Samuel let him in," Dr. Brogan said.

The footman started to step back as Lewis brushed past him to face Dr. Brogan who stood at the base of the staircase. The doctor was obviously doing well for himself, judging by his townhouse. A large crystal chandelier blazed with lit candles. Most houses did not have such ornate fixtures in the entry hall, nor did they light all the expensive beeswax candles if they did. It took a moment for his eyes to adjust.

"There has been a murder," Lewis said.

"I assumed as much by the way you push Samuel aside," the doctor said drily.

Lewis dipped his head as he gritted his teeth at the doctor's tone. "I believe you know the victim. Mrs. Southerland."

"Hilda Southerland! Where? What happened," Dr. Brogan demanded, taking a step forward.

Lewis was glad to hear the casual, sarcastic tone disappear. "Slit throat, at the back entrance to her home. She had gone out on an errand and was returning when she was attacked. No one heard anything. She must not have had time to call out or fight her attacker."

"Who found her?"

"Two of the residents returning from shopping."

"Has the body been touched?"

"No."

"Good. My wife and I are planning to attend the theater tonight as the guests of Lord and Lady St. Ryne. We can go to Mrs. Southerland's house first so I may see for myself the corpse and the situation. My wife will wait in the carriage. She is used to it— Samuel," he called out to the footman. "Find Reginald Gedney and have him meet me at Mrs. Southerland's House for Unfortunate Women. He should know where it is on Green Street off Soho Square."

"Yes, doctor," the footman said.

"I leave all investigation to the coroner's office investigators before the inquest," Dr. Brogan said, addressing Lewis.

"Of course," Lewis said. He did not care for Reginald Gedney. In his experiences with the man, he found Gedney lacked diligence. But it wasn't in the purview of Bow Street to investigate murders unless specifically requested. Murders were the responsibility of the coroner's office— as much as that truth irritated him.

"I need to get back," Lewis said, turning to go.

"Ride with my wife and me. My carriage should be out front by now and I know my wife is waiting for me in the parlor. We can leave immediately." The doctor crossed the hall to open a door. "Margaret, we can leave now. I shall have to make a stop first."

Mrs. Brogan came through the door. "This is becoming a habit, Ignatius. Perhaps we should invest in a second carriage that I might go ahead to our evening entertainment."

"I know, and I'm sorry my dear. However this one is important, I fear. Mrs. Southerland has been murdered."

"Oh no! Mrs. Southerland?! Those poor young women who depend on her! What will they do? Are they there alone now? Perhaps I should stay with them!"

"No, you will not!" said Dr. Brogan.

Lewis stepped forward. "Mrs. Albert, the housekeeper, and Miss Wooler, the cook, are there along with Miss Knolls," he assured her.

"Oh, good evening, Mr. Martin. I didn't see you there. You must have brought the news to Ignatius."

"I did."

"And he will be in our carriage as we go to her house. You can ask him more on the way, as I know you are full of questions. Come, let's be in on our way."

Lewis sat with his back to the horses, facing the Brogans and, as Dr. Brogan subtly warned, Mrs. Brogan was full of questions.

"How did she die?" Mrs. Brogan asked Lewis.

"Margaret, that is my job to determine!" Dr. Brogan objected.

Mrs. Brogan waved her hand dismissively toward her husband. "As officially you shall. Mr. Martin?"

Lewis looked between Dr. and Mrs. Brogan. The doctor gave him a slight nod. "Her throat was slit."

"Slit! Where did this happen?"

"At the back door to her townhouse. She had gone out for a quick errand and was returning. Whoever slit her throat must have come upon her stealthily, for not a sound of a scuffle or scream was heard inside the house."

"You were there?"

"Yes, I'd come to escort Miss Knolls home at the behest of her father. Mrs. Southerland requested we remain until she returned from her quick errand— an errand she appeared quite excited to go on."

"I know who Miss Knolls is," the doctor said. "Why would she need a Bow Street agent to escort her home?"

"There have been threats made against the duke and his family for the duke's investment in new inventions. As his daughter is the only one of his children in London right now, he has asked for protection for her. He knows she will not take precautions. She doesn't believe anyone would go after a woman as tall as she is."

"Wait," Mrs. Brogan interrupted, "are you saying this Miss Knolls is Lady Guinevere?"

"Yes, but please do not bruit it about. I think her disguise when she visits Mrs. Southerland's has been a protectant. That includes Mr. Gedney. Beg your pardon, Dr. Brogan, however, Mr. Gedney is known for loose lips when he's had a bit to drink, and I imagine this bit of news could be exciting gossip to share, and that may not be to Lady Guinevere's advantage."

"No, not at all," agreed Mrs. Brogan.

Dr. Brogan frowned and compressed his lips together tightly. "I have spoken to him about his drinking habits. He has made promises. However, in light of the threats to the duke and his family, I believe we can allow Miss Knolls to remain Miss Knolls."

Lewis let loose the breath he was holding in. "Thank you."

The carriage drew up before Mrs. Southerland's house.

"I'm coming in, too," Mrs. Brogan said, following her husband as he descended from the carriage.

"Margaret!"

"I come here every other Tuesday with Mrs. Grant. The girls know me."

Lewis stepped onto the pavement with them. "She could be a benefit. Her presence may allow me to take Miss Knolls home. I can return to answer any questions Mr. Gedney has."

Dr. Brogan shook his head but then said *yes* and the three of them hurried up the steps and knocked on the door.

After a moment, Gwinnie opened the door. He felt something loosen in his chest that it was she who opened the door and not either of the women he'd roused from the pub.

"Miss Knolls," he said, as he edged through the open door, "this is Dr. Brogan and his wife, Mrs. Brogan. I caught them on their way to the theater. Dr. Brogan is the coroner for all of Mayfair."

"Thank you for coming so quickly, Dr. Brogan!— Oh! Mrs. Brogan!" Gwinnie looked sharply at Lewis, her eyes panicked and questioning over Mrs. Brogan's presence.

"I am happy to meet you, though not under these circumstances. Please come in," Gwinnie smiled faintly at the couple, recovering her surprise. "Thank you for coming on short notice and when you were on your way to entertainment. I'm so sorry for the diversion."

"Nonsense, Miss Knolls, I am used to having plans changed unexpectedly. Where is the deceased?" Dr. Brogan said heartily.

"This way," Lewis said, gesturing toward the stairs down toward the landing.

"Margaret, please keep Miss Knolls company while Mr. Martin and I investigate."

"Certainly, Ignatius," his wife said serenely. "Miss Knolls?"

"This way, please," Gwinnie said helplessly. Reluctantly, she led Mrs. Brogan back into the dimly lit parlor. She'd wanted to be in attendance when Dr. Brogan viewed Mrs. Southerland's body so she could hear anything he might say that he observed.

"I'm sure Mr. Martin will tell you all my husband says," Mrs. Brogan said.

"Am I that obvious?" Gwinnie asked.

"To others, probably not; however, I am married to the coroner," Mrs. Brogan said wryly.

Gwinnie's thin smile reappeared.

"So tell me, why does Mr. Martin address you as Miss Knolls?" the woman asked, as they both sat down.

Gwinnie hung her head for a moment, then looked across at Mrs. Brogan. "So you recognize me?"

"I would have, for you are a rather distinctive person in society, but I learned who you were in the carriage on the way here, based on my husband's conversation with Mr. Martin," Mrs. Brogan said.

Gwinnie made a sour face. "Yes, unfortunately, but not to these young women, and they are why I am here. I don't believe they would pay attention to Lady Guinevere Nowlton in the way they might to the solicitor's daughter, Miss Sarah Knolls. I'm here to teach them. I cannot appear to be way above them. Sarah, as a supposed solicitor's daughter, is more approachable a person for them to get lessons from."

Mrs. Brogan nodded. "I supposed I can understand that," she said, nodding. "I come here every other Tuesday with Mrs. Grant. Do you know her?"

Gwinnie shook her head.

"Her husband is a banker with Mouton's Bank. She likes to talk to them about money, and how saving pennies helps and sewing them into hems protects their savings. She says in London, many more women may be mugged and their reticules stolen. If they have funds in their hems, they are not left completely destitute and starving, and they may pick themselves up and not be devastated and hopeless."

"That is true. Does she practice what she preaches to the women?"

Mrs. Brogan laughed. "Oh, yes! Sometimes her gowns get so heavy that her maid complains, and then she grumbles and moves some of the money into her husband's bank."

"I like to talk about hygiene," Mrs. Brogan continued. "Dr. Brogan believes many illnesses may be avoided with proper hygiene. We talk a great deal about the compromises they may have to make in the big houses they find work in, where hygiene for the staff is not prioritized and how to do the best they can in those households."

Gwinnie smiled and shook her head. "I knew others came to help these women, but I didn't know who. You are to be commended."

"Well, dear, we go by different names, too, more for Mrs. Grant's protection."

"I can certainly see why Mrs. Grant would!"

They heard footsteps on the stairs.

"Are they done already?" Gwinnie said, rising to her feet.

"It doesn't take long for a preliminary review," Mrs. Brogan said. She rose to her feet as the parlor door opened to admit the gentlemen.

Lewis closed the door quietly behind him. He looked

over at Gwinnie. "Dr. Brogan and I agreed, we need to get you out of this house as soon as possible."

"But we discussed this earlier, before you went to get Dr. Brogan, and you agreed that I was going to stay here tonight and you would notify my father," she complained.

"I did not consider the ramifications of you being here when Dr. Brogan's investigator arrives and wants to question everyone here. He'll want to question you, too, and then your carefully constructed persona will be destroyed. It will harm your relationship with the women here at a time when perhaps they require Miss Knolls the most. I will escort you home and then return to answer any questions on your behalf, since I was here the entire time the events unfolded. Your testimony will not be required."

"But they need familiar faces with them, besides just Mrs. Albert and Miss Wooler," she protested weakly. She looked at each of them for support.

"It's all right," Mrs. Brogan said softly, as she lightly touched Gwinnie's arm. "I'll stay here while Mr. Martin escorts you home."

"I couldn't leave now!" Gwinnie protested again. "The young women are so distraught and frightened. Frightened of an inquest with men coming in and out of the house."

"I have arranged for her body to be carried to The Thirsty Pig. Mr. Watney has offered his cool room and is readying it now," Lewis said softly, trying to comfort her fears. Lady Guinevere was more shaken than he'd ever seen her.

"Good thinking, Mr. Martin," Dr. Brogan said. "This is not an appropriate location for an inquest."

"You need to get out of here before the coroner's office inquiry agents arrive."

"Take my carriage," Dr. Brogan offered. "It can bring you back here all the faster."

"My cape!" Gwinnie exclaimed.

Immediately, Lewis remembered the cape Mrs. Southerland wore, now soaked in blood. "You can wrap up in one of the blankets thrown over the back of the sofa in the parlor," he said.

"What is wrong with her cape?" Mrs. Brogan asked.

"It is a short, hooded cape. Mrs. Southerland borrowed it to go on her errand," Lewis explained. "— We must consider if someone mistook Mrs. Southerland for Miss Knolls," he said grimly. He picked up a black-and-yellow plaid wool blanket from the back of the settee.

Gwinnie snorted. "Hardly. It may be my cape, but I am a foot taller than Mrs. Southerland."

"All things must be considered in the case of a murder, my lady," Dr. Brogan said.

"Hush!" Gwinnie hissed out. "It's Miss Knolls."

Lewis draped the heavy blanket around her shoulders. "Come, Miss Knolls," he said, taking her arm and leading her out the door. The wind had picked up outside.

"All right, all right," Gwinnie said, grumbling, holding the blanket around her. She climbed up into the carriage.

"You do know I will want to know all that is said, all that is discovered!" she told Lewis, as he settled across from her. He knocked on the carriage roof to tell the driver to proceed.

"I know. There are some things you can do tonight to assist. Send notes to Lord Soothcoor and Mr. Hargate, Sr., the solicitor who handles Mrs. Southerland's legal papers. They need to be notified as soon as possible. Do you know if Mrs. Southerland had any family?"

"I know her husband is deceased," she said. She paused. "There is something else. Remember that note she wrote after you arrived?

He nodded.

"She wrote in pencil with a heavy hand. The imprint of some of the note passed through to the paper below. I used graphite shavings to make it come forward," she said, as she pulled the note from between the buttons of her pelisse. "I have not had an opportunity to study it yet. I heard this carriage draw up, and I folded this paper to keep it safe."

"Why did you feel the need to do so?" he asked.

She shrugged. "I don't know." She held out the note to him.

He took the note from her, noting the fine trembling of her hand. Lady Guinevere was not as calm as she tried to display. "You know her murder is out of my jurisdiction. I cannot investigate unless I am specifically requested and am offered funds for my efforts. It is in the hands of the coroner and his investigators."

She stared at him, biting her lower lip as she pulled the blanket up higher around her shoulders. "I shall see that the Duke of Malmsby engages your services if the Earl of Soothcoor cannot be reached before the inquest," she said. "He's at Appleton right now, you said?"

"He is, and that is less than ten miles away."

"Still, getting messages to him and back will take time, whereas my father is here," she stated as the carriage pulled up at Malmsby House.

He spread his hands in a shrug.

"Maybe you will get paid by both!" she said with a trembling, forced brightness.

He shook his head as a footman opened the carriage door.

Gwinnie jumped down from the carriage before Lewis or the footman could help her alight.

"Hello, Stephen," she said to the footman. "Is Father at home this evening?" she asked briskly. The cold wind pulled at the blanket wrapped about her and chafed her cheeks. She shivered.

"He is, Lady Gwinnie."

"Good. Close the carriage door, Mr. Martin needs to be on his way," she said over her shoulder, as she ran up the stairs and pushed open the heavy oak door before Stephen could get before her.

"The Earl and Countess of Norwalk and the Dowager Countess are with him," Stephen called after her as she was halfway up the stairs.

Gwinnie paused. "Helena and Adam are here? Jolly good! No wonder Father sent Mr. Martin for me. I'd best get changed before I see them, then," she said, glancing down at her plain attire. She turned and ran up the stairs, not stopping on the first floor, but hurrying up to the second-floor bedrooms.

CHAPTER 4
THE NORWALKS

She threw open her bedroom door. A lamp on the table near the window cast a warm glow on the other side of the room where Rose sat alone, knitting a blue jacket for a church foundling.

Rose stuffed her needles and the garment into a canvas bag at her side and got to her feet. "Mi lady!" she exclaimed, coming toward her. "I was gettin' that worried for you. Your father expected you hours ago," she said. She wrung her hands in front of her gray dress with white cuffs and collar.

"I've been here all even' waitin'," Rose said.

"Thank you, Rose! There were extenuating circumstances for my delayed appearance," Gwinnie said carefully.

"Your father has been askin' after you every thirty minutes." Rose took the black-and-yellow blanket from around her shoulder, frowning at it. She folded it up and laid it on the settee.

Gwinnie winced. "I understand. But he never told me he was expecting company tonight or that I was expected to join him."

Rose nodded. "I know, mi lady, but he's been in a rare takin'. What kept you so long? We expected you by five o'clock!" Rose said.

Gwinnie drew her brows close together and squeezed

her eyes tight. She'd kept her control all evening—now a sudden onrush of tears threatened to fall. "Mrs. Southerland," she began in a cracked voice.

She couldn't hold the tears back any longer. They streamed down her cheeks. She looked up, valiantly sniffing against the emotions that held her, that had her face contorting. She closed her eyes as sadness swamped her.

"What do you mean? Why are you crying?" Rose demanded anxiously. She pulled a handkerchief from the sleeve of her dress and stepped forward to place it in Gwinnie's hand. She rubbed Gwinnie's back as one would rub the back of an inconsolable child. The irony was not lost on Gwinnie. She needed to explain.

"She's dead!" Gwinnie whispered. She collapsed onto her dressing table chair, then leaned her elbow on the dressing table and covered her eyes as she wept.

"What? No! Oh! Mi lady!" Rose exclaimed. Abandoning maid-to-employer decorum, Rose clasped her in an embrace, her head against Gwinnie's.

Gwinnie allowed herself to accept her maid's comfort. She raised her hand and placed it atop Rose's shoulder.

"Thank you," Gwinnie murmured, as she strove to pull herself together. This wasn't like her. She was stronger than this. She would be stronger. The last time she had bowed to sorrow had been when her mother died, long ago now. She lifted her head up, straightening her spine. She looked in her mirror at Rose behind her.

"She was murdered this evening as she returned home from an errand. And the worst of it?" She laughed harshly. "I don't know if the intended victim was to be her or me."

"What?"

"She said she had to go out for a quick errand and asked Mr. Martin and me to stay until her return. And she asked to borrow my half-cape, as it was downstairs. You know, the gray embroidered one with the hood, and tassel off the back of the hood? The cape that only fell a little past my waist?"

Rose compressed her lips. "Yes. I know it well. It is a

favorite of your Sarah Knolls person." She rummaged on the dressing table, then lifted a bottle and held it up before Gwinnie.

Gwinnie nodded. Lavender water. Rose waved it before her. Gwinnie let the delicate, calming scent engulf her.

When her tears ceased, Gwinnie wiped her eyes and nose with her handkerchief. She worked on leveling her breathing. "I said yes, of course, when she asked to borrow it. While short on me, I knew it would be long on her and keep her warm. While she was gone, Mr. Martin and I sat in the parlor discussing random topics. He is an easy man to talk to; however, sometimes I still find it difficult to think of what to say to him." She frowned. "He is very erudite."

"Erudite?" Rose repeated, a curious look on her face.

A slightly watery laugh escaped Gwinnie. "I'm sorry, excuse me. I find him highly knowledgeable and well-read. Most odd, I would think, for a Bow Street Runner, not that I have met many runners," she admitted.

Rose laughed, "I would think that would make it easier for you to hold him in conversation." Rose went to the wardrobe to find a dress for Gwinnie to wear downstairs.

"Yes, so would I. I don't know how to *be* around Mr. Martin. I believe I am a bit in awe of him," Gwinnie said ruefully.

"Awe?" Rose asked, looking back over her shoulder at Gwinnie.

Gwinnie cocked her head as she considered the word. "He has a beautiful mind, and I think I am too prejudiced to appreciate him."

Rose laughed again as she pulled the dress out. "I think the duke would consider this one of life's lessons, I certainly do."

"To be sure! But as a result, I don't know how to be around him." She relaxed in the chair.

"Well, he is not here now; howsomever, your cousin and her husband and his mother are below. Are you feeling better now? You should make your curtsy."

"Yes, you are correct," Gwinnie said.

She looked at the dress Rose had picked for her. A pale-green, figured satin. Simple yet elegant. Gwinnie approved and allowed her maid to help her into it.

"Thank you, Rose," she said when she was dressed. "Wish me luck getting out of Father's displeasure."

"The news you bear will stop the scold, mi lady."

Gwinnie nodded. "I hope so." Then she frowned. "No, that is a selfish thing to say!" She draped a pastel-yellow and peach sheer shawl loosely about her shoulders. "I would wish Mr. Martin to swiftly capture Mrs. Southerland's murderer so we might put her to rest, as she deserves."

"Yes, Lady Gwinnie. That is to be wished," Rose said, bowing her head.

Gwinnie nodded and headed down the stairs.

She tentatively opened the parlor door. Inside, she saw her cousin Helena and her husband Adam, the Earl of Norwalk, sitting next to each other on the sofa. Adam's mother, Lady Norwalk, a woman near her father's age, sat on a winged chair near the fireplace, and her father in the flanking chair. The group appeared to be having an easy discourse.

Gwinnie quietly let herself into the room; however, her stealthy approach did not hide her from her father.

"Gwinnie! Where have you been? I expected you back here more than two hours ago," her father said, setting his drink down on the table next to him and rising to his feet. Adam turned his head to look in her direction, then rose to his feet as well.

"I beg pardon, Father. There was an unfortunate incident at Mrs. Southerland's this evening."

"So unfortunate that you are several hours late in returning home?"

Gwinnie took a deep breath. She looked at her father, her gaze steady as she wondered what was going on behind his dark, unfathomable gaze. "Yes, I am afraid so."

She steeled herself, but he surprised her.

He stared at her for another moment, then nodded.

He sat down again. "*Hmph.* Come, take a seat. Have you eaten?"

"No, Father," she admitted, as she took another of the chairs drawn up near the sofa.

"You've been crying," Helena observed, as Gwinnie walked further into the light.

She nodded. "Before I came down to join you," she said, determined to keep any more tears at bay.

The duke rang for one of the maids. When one appeared, he asked that food be brought for Gwinnie.

Gwinnie started to protest, but the look on her father's face stopped her.

"I invited your newlywed cousin, Helena, and her new spouse, the Earl of Norwalk, along with his mother to dinner tonight. I realize I did not give you any advanced notice; however, I assumed Mr. Martin would bring you home in plenty of time. That did not happen. Now," he said, leaning back in his chair, "what has happened?" he asked, his voice kind now that he, too, could see evidence of her past tears.

Gwinnie clasped her hands tightly in her lap, her knuckles white. She rocked back and took a deep inhale. She turned to her father. "Mrs. Southerland was murdered this evening," she said baldly.

"Murdered?" her father repeated, his bushy, dark brows pulling together. He leaned forward in his chair.

The Norwalks looked between each other, then intently at Gwinnie.

Gwinnie compressed her lips and nodded. Again, taking a deep breath before speaking, she paused. "She had gone out on an errand and was returning home when someone attacked her from the back—" Gwinnie raised her hand toward her neck, "and slit her throat!" she said, her voice wobbling as she mimicked the motion across her own throat. She held tight against the tears.

The Dowager Countess gasped and instinctively raised a hand to her neck.

"Any idea why?" her father asked.

"No." Now that she got the worst out, she slumped in her chair. "And there is worse," she said slowly. "... She was wearing my short cape when she was attacked," she finished with a clipped voice.

The duke shook his head. "That should not be a concern for you. She was much shorter than you. No one could mistake you two," her father assured her.

"But what if an assassin was only given a description of the cloak? It is very distinctive," Gwinnie said, sitting forward in her chair.

The duke considered her statement for a moment, his expression darkening. "You make a point worth considering," he granted, nodding toward her. "However, I can't imagine anyone describing you without mentioning your height. No, I believe the killer murdered whom they intended. The question is why."

"Mr. Martin told me this case falls under the jurisdiction of the coroner's office, that he cannot be involved in the investigation."

The duke sniffed, drawing his brows together again. "True. I take it you do not trust the coroner's office to do a creditable job for the investigation?"

"No, I don't. Mr. Reginald Gedney will be in charge of the investigation, and the sense I received from Mr. Martin is he does not trust Gedney to do a good job."

"I have some knowledge of the man and would agree," her father reluctantly said.

"You could hire Bow Street to investigate under a separate contract," Gwinnie suggested slowly, her eyes bright though she tried to temper her excitement.

Her father looked at her, a half-smile pulling at his lips. "And I take it that is what you wish me to do?"

"Yes, please. I know the Earl of Soothcoor would hire him; however, the earl is at Appleton and word would not get to him and back before tomorrow evening. Bow Street needs to be engaged for the inquiry before the inquest on Monday at The Thirsty Pig."

"The Thirsty Pig? Why there?" the Dowager Countess asked with a laugh.

"It was the closest place with a room of a size for an inquest. I did not want the inquest to be in Mrs. Southerland's house. It would be too unsettling for the women living there. It is not uncommon for inquests to be held at pubs and inns."

"And who is this Mr. Martin?" the Dowager Countess asked. "It sounds like you know him quite well."

"Is he a suitor?" Helena asked brightly.

Gwinnie laughed lightly. "Not hardly," she denied, but with a slight pang in her chest, she refused to acknowledge.

"Mr. Lewis Martin is a Bow Street agent who is a friend of my brother Aiden. He has helped us on a few occasions in the past year," the duke explained.

"And he is one of the guards you have set on me," Gwinnie said, disgruntled, folding her arms over her chest. "He and Mr. Hargate."

"Why have you seen the need to set a guard for Lady Guinevere?" the Earl of Norwalk asked.

"Please call me Gwinnie, as the rest of the family does," Gwinnie said to him.

"I'll answer for Gwinnie," Lady Helena said, as she looked affectionately at Gwinnie. "Because my dear cousin has never believed she needs looking after."

The duke held up his hands. "One subject at a time. We will start with the death—"

"Murder," interjected Gwinnie.

"Murder," her father said slowly, "of Mrs. Southerland."

"Should you like us to leave?" the Dowager Countess asked. "We can finish our discussion at a later time."

The duke turned to her. "No, please stay, and you will see why in a moment." He turned back to his daughter. "I have some knowledge of Mr. Gedney, and I, too, would not trust the man. Unfortunately, Dr. Brogan inherited him when he took over as coroner, and as he is considered a senior investigator, he cannot get rid of him unless he does something egregiously wrong. I agree Mr. Martin should investigate."

Gwinnie jumped up a little in her seat, her eyes brightening. "Then you will authorize him?"

"Yes." The duke nodded.

Gwinnie jumped a little again and clapped.

"— In the morning," her father temporized.

Gwinnie slumped in her chair. "Morning? But he should be authorized now before Mr. Gedney makes a mess of everything and...and...I don't know, terrorizes the women there."

"Didn't you say Mr. Martin was there when Mrs. Southerland was found?"

"Yes."

"Then he will be invited to the inquest. Two reasons. First, as an onsite witness, and second, in his role of protecting the facility. I trust Mr. Martin to play those cards appropriately," the duke said.

"But—"

"Inquests are generally held late in the morning or early in the afternoon. I'll send a note to Mr. Martin to come here and talk to us," the duke said, pointing first to Gwinnie and then to himself, "tomorrow morning so we may strategize an investigation before the inquest."

"You'll include me?"

The duke frowned. "Yes, of course. You were as much of a witness as Mr. Martin, maybe more so, but we can't have you get directly involved. We must use Mr. Martin as the intermediary."

"Why can't I be directly involved? If it is about the disguise I use as Sarah Knolls, I've been thinking about that. I'm willing to let that go to discover the murderer."

"Well, I'm not," countered her father, "and that brings me to the second subject that involves you and why I wished you here this evening," he said repressively, "and for the conversation I wish to have with the Dowager Countess of Norwalk and of course her son and wife."

"What is that, Your Grace?" the Dowager Countess asked. She was a regal-appearing woman, but without the haughtiness usually associated with a regal appearance.

"Arthur, please," the duke said, smiling at her. "I believe if we are all going to be working together, I'd rather it be on a first-name basis than with any infernal formality," he said gruffly.

The countess lifted one well-formed, dark eyebrow.

She turned her head slightly, then nodded. "All right, Arthur, and I am Charlotte."

Gwinnie had only briefly met the Dowager Countess of Norwalk and her son, the Earl of Norwalk, her cousin's husband, during the Ellinbourne wedding in Surrey last month. There had been so many people about, and during the social events, her quartet provided the music, so she hadn't had the opportunity to socialize. Not that she wanted to socialize, for it always brought well-meaning observations that she should be married next. And sly questions as to any suitor waiting to ask for her hand.

The duke leaned forward, resting his elbows on his knees. He laced his fingers together save for his pointers which he kept straight, touching at their tips like a church steeple.

"Charlotte and I have been in communication for several months now, as we share an interest in technology. I am fascinated in how things work and what benefits they can bring to our nation and our lives. She has a financial interest in inventions. She wants to determine if they are worth investment and promotion."

Lady Norwalk nodded. She tilted her head slightly to listen closely, for the duke was not talking particularly loudly.

"I have shared information with her, and she has shared information with me. We see the potential for working together, and with her Gentleman's Trade Club — which, by the way, I believe is a clever use of our well-educated second, third, and fourth sons, rather than them becoming wastrels."

"And I hope in the future, our daughters as well," the Dowager Countess said.

The duke looked toward her and nodded. Then he turned back to them to continue. "You recall the Luddite riots."

There were murmurs of *yes* and nodding heads in the room. He nodded as well.

"They were only the beginning. The forerunners of dissatisfaction and fear with inventions and new technology. And who can blame them?" he asked, spreading his arms wide. "Unscrupulous industrialists are looking for ways to speed production and decrease expense, and they see the only expeditious way to cut expense is to cut their skilled craft workers and offer machine employees half their skilled workers' wages." He shook his head. "As much as I love inventions, it tears at me to see a gleeful waste of talent and resources. Unfortunately, people like me are seen as at the forefront of destroying lives."

"No," protested Gwinnie.

He shook his head. "I'm afraid it is all too true, and it is why I receive threats against my life for what I do."

"Threats, Your Grace?" the Earl of Norwalk asked. He frowned and slowly turned his head to look at his mother. She sat stoically listening.

"Yes, threats, very pointed threats. But lately, the threats have taken a particularly nasty turn. The missives I have received have suggested retribution toward my family is not out of the realm of possibility. In fact, Gwinnie was mentioned as a target, as she is the only one in town with me at the moment, and that they should know this is worrisome."

"Me? Why should they threaten me? What have I got to do with industrialization?"

"You don't, not in any active way. However, you do in the manner of being my daughter. That is the nature of the threats received and that I have shared with Mr. Martin and Mr. Hargate."

He looked at the Dowager Countess. "I am concerned, Charlotte, that you will also receive such threats."

The Dowager Countess compressed her lips, silent for a moment. "I already have," she finally admitted.

"Mother!" exclaimed the earl.

The duke grimaced. "I'm sorry."

"Why are you sorry? You didn't do anything other than have the same interests as I."

"Have they threatened any others in your family? Your son, your daughter-in-law? Her expectant child?"

She shook her head. "Not really, not in specific terms."

"But in pointed inference," the duke said.

She shrugged. "I suppose you could call it that." Her lips and eyes tightened.

"Mother! Why didn't you tell me?" objected the Earl of Norwalk. "You can't go around hiding things like this from me. I am not my father!" he finished, practically yelling.

She closed her eyes, a crease appearing between her brows. "It all seemed so farcical."

"Your Grace, what do you suggest I do to protect my family?" the earl asked.

"At this time, all I can tell you is to remain vigilant. As I must divert Mr. Martin to investigate Mrs. Southerland's death, or Gwinnie will give me no rest."

Gwinnie winced. What her father said was true.

"Mr. Hargate will continue his investigation. As a solicitor, sometimes these rebels will talk to a solicitor. I will also ask him and Mr. Martin if they know of anyone we might bring into our circle for protection."

The duke straightened in his chair. "At this point, I'd rather keep it quiet. It has occurred to me that this could all just be threats as well, threats without teeth, as they say. Or maybe a competitor is striving to drive me away from something I am considering, so he might get to it first."

He spread out his hands to shrug. "Frankly, I don't know. There may be more to it than I can ever imagine. What I do know is I do not wish to be chased away, but neither will I endanger my daughter nor any of my family."

Gwinnie stood, her mind in a whirl. "I'm sorry to leave you all now, but I desperately need to think. The murder, the threats...this has been a great deal to take in. If you'll excuse me?" she asked, knowing she was rudely running away. So many emotions swirled inside her, trying to overwhelm her. She refused to let that happen.

"Of course, my dear," said the Dowager Countess.

"Take care of yourself," her cousin Helena said to her.

"I will. That is why I need to leave. So much happening..."

"I will send that note to Mr. Martin tonight and see you in the morning," her father promised.

"Thank you." She curtsied to them and left the parlor.

Gwinnie touched her hand to her head and closed her eyes for a moment before going down the stairs to the music room. She grabbed a candle from the entrance hall and went into the dark room. She spent so much time in this room, she knew its layout without the need for the candlelight; however, she took it to light a branch of candles set on a sideboard along the wall. She walked toward the little stage in the center of the room where her quartet practiced. They'd be practicing again soon, with the season approaching.

She'd left her violin in here the other day, something she seldom did. She took her violin out of its case and ran her hands over the smooth surface. She removed the bow from the case lid and set the instrument's base under her chin. She tightened her bowstring, then drew the bow across one string and then another, to check for its sound, making minor adjustments to the pegs as she did so.

She knew she was being rude not to visit with her cousin and her new husband. Helena had always considered herself a misfit, as Gwinnie did. At least she had been able to find her 'fit.'

Gwinnie let her thoughts go. She took a deep, cleansing breath and began playing, letting the music fill her, overflow, and then cradle her... It calmed her body. She played mindlessly at first, bits and riffs from one composer to another, then found herself playing Bach. Mrs. Southerland always liked Bach.

Feeling the music, Gwinnie smiled as she allowed one lone tear to roll down her cheek. She played on.

CHAPTER 5
MRS. SOUTHERLAND'S REPLACEMENT

Gwinnie heard the rustle of her blue-green silk bed curtains. She knew that was Rose coming to wake her. Gwinnie steadfastly kept her eyes closed. Maybe Rose would go away. She didn't want to face the day. Mrs. Southerland was gone. All that was left were memories, each one a bittersweet reminder of the love and guidance she had lost from her mentor and dear friend.

"I know you are awake, mi lady. I saw your muscles tense. The duke said to tell you Mr. Martin would be here in an hour to discuss investigating Mrs. Southerland's death. He said you wanted to be included," Rose said, as she fastened the open bed curtains in place.

Gwinnie lay there a moment longer, feeling a gaping void in her heart. But lying in bed wouldn't heal the void. She'd made a silent promise to herself last night that she would work to uncover the truth behind Mrs. Southerland's murder. A steely determination replaced yesterday's heavy lethargy of sadness with its threat of tears.

No more tears. She was stronger than that, and she owed Mrs. Southerland more than a maudlin champion for her murder investigation.

She threw her heavy covers to the side, then sat up on the edge of the bed. She pushed her thick, red braid back over her shoulder and stood up.

"Might I have a coffee this morning as I dress?" Gwinnie asked Rose. "I was up late playing my violin."

"I thought you might want coffee this mornin', mi lady. I requested it before I came up here. A tray will be here shortly," Rose said, as she picked up Gwinnie's robe and helped her into it.

Gwinnie smiled. "You take such good care of me. Thank you," she said. She walked to the window and looked out at the street and the square beyond. "It looks like it could rain or snow, the clouds look so heavy."

"Probably rain," Rose said, as she made the bed. "It's warmer his morning."

Gwinnie turned to look at Rose. "You went out this morning all ready?"

Rose nodded as she fluffed a pillow and put it in place. "I— I needed to walk and think a bit, after— after your news of yesterday."

Gwinnie walked swiftly over to Rose and touched her gently. "I'd forgotten you were one of her first students."

Rose visibly swallowed. "Yes, mi lady." Her eyes glistened. "I know you will do all you can to find her murderer. As that is who you are."

Gwinnie laughed slightly. "Yes," she admitted.

"I want to help," Rose said with firmness. "It is not right that she be dead. Not right at all. I am angry at God right now for taking her—"

"Oh, don't say that!" Gwinnie protested.

"I know that isn't right. I need to focus my anger on whoever took that dear lady from us."

Gwinnie nodded.

"And you know I can go places you can't," Rose added, giving Gwinnie a sly look. "I still know people from days long past."

There was a knock on the door.

"Come in!" Gwinnie called out. She turned back to Rose. "I hope that won't be necessary, but I will speak to Mr. Martin," she promised as the maid, Mercy, brought in a breakfast tray.

Rose motioned the girl to set it on a table by the window. "Come and eat, Lady Gwinnie. It will likely be a busy day."

"That is fer certain," said Mercy as she set the tray down. "Mrs. Hunnicutt has us runnin' every which way, what with the dowager duchess arrivin' today."

"Grandmother is coming to visit?" Gwinnie asked.

"Yes, mi lady, and on that account, I could scarcely get a moment to brung your tray till Cook said sumpin' to Mrs. Hunnicutt."

Gwinnie laughed. "Phillipe is about the only person who will stand up to her." Phillipe had been her grandmother's cook at Versely Park before she brought him to London during one of her visits and he never left.

Mercy nodded. "He were right determined you get your tray. Said you needed sus— sus— sumpin, I cain't remember the word."

"Sustenance," Rose said.

"Yes, that were it. I'd best get back downstairs," Mercy said, smiling brightly.

"Thank you, Mercy," Gwinnie said. She crossed to the table and sat down.

"Did you know my grandmother was coming?" Gwinnie asked Rose after Mercy had left.

"No, mi lady," she said, as she straightened the room.

Gwinnie began to eat.

"What dress would you like today?" Rose asked, as she crossed to the wardrobe.

"I think the blue one. And could you find me a black ribbon to wear about my arm?"

"Yes, that would be a fine idea. You might have one long enough in your hair ribbon box. I'll check there."

It wasn't long before Gwinnie finished her breakfast and felt much the better for it, and Rose had her dressed in her long-sleeved blue gown that had a print of small yellow-and-white flowers over it. And Rose did find a black hair ribbon that they were able to tie around Gwinnie's arm right below the puffed top portion of the sleeve.

"Let's keep my hair like we would do for Sarah Knolls, more sedate."

"Yes, mi lady," Rose replied, as Gwinnie sat down at her dressing table.

"I wonder why Grandmother is coming?" Gwinnie mused as Rose brushed her hair. "She can't have heard about Mrs. Southerland yet."

"Because the Norwalks have come to town?" Rose suggested.

"Most likely. But she will soon learn of Mrs. Southerland, and I'll admit to some concern as to what she will do. You know how she is. She meddles in everything."

"Won't the duke keep her under control?"

"He will certainly try, but trying and doing are different things where Grandmother is concerned," Gwinnie said. She picked up her bottle of scent from the dressing table. *Lilies of the Valley.* "I must talk to him about her and what her presence means to the investigation of Mrs. Southerland's death and the threats he's received. I don't believe Father has any interests in the machines that threaten Luddites, so they are not likely to come from that direction." She lightly applied the scent. She didn't wear a scent every day, but today the urge pleased her.

"It may not matter, mi lady," Rose answered. "They may not understand that and just be against any machines. Especially them steam-powered, dirty, noise-makin', giant machines."

Gwinnie laughed. "Rose, now you sound like a Luddite."

"No, mi lady, but you have to admit they are noisy and messy."

"Right now, but that will change with time as more new things are designed."

"*Humph.*"

Gwinnie laughed harder.

～

Mr. Martin was already with her father when their footman opened the library door for her.

"Good morning, Father, Mr. Martin," Gwinnie said, striding purposefully across the room to sit in the other chair in front of her father's desk. Both men had risen when she entered, which Gwinnie found annoying. She made a face and waved at them to sit. "Please, it's just me, Gwinnie," she reminded them.

"Nonetheless, you are a lady," Lewis countered.

"Sometimes," she admitted, tossing her head.

Her father laughed. "I'm glad to see you in better spirits this morning."

"I have to be, I heard Grandmother is coming to visit. Seriously, I decided on waking that wallowing in sadness does not help Mrs. Southerland, nor would she approve."

"I'm gratified to hear that," said her father in his rumbling voice, the tone of which Gwinnie quite liked over his *'Father'* voice.

"My mission is to discover who killed her and see there is retribution," she told them.

"Mission?" her father repeated.

"I knew there was something else to that first statement," Lewis said with a sigh, looking at the duke, his lips twisting in a wry smile.

The duke's bushy brows drew together in a condemning 'V' shape, then he raised one brow in a manner Gwinnie envied. She couldn't do that. "Gwinnie, you will leave the investigation to Mr. Martin," said her father sternly.

"I did not say I would not," she countered, squirming to sit upright in her chair.

"Or that you would," Lewis said *sotto voce*.

Gwinnie turned to glare at him. "There is much I can do. Just this morning I discovered— or I should say, I was reminded— that Rose, my maid, was one of Mrs. Southerland's first students and first successes."

"You think she might know more about Mrs. Southerland's background?" Lewis asked.

"Yes, as she was present while Mrs. Southerland organized the charity," Gwinnie said. "And, as she told me, she can go into parts of London I cannot."

"I will grant you that, and if that is what you mean by *help*, I won't complain," Lewis said, nodding his head in her direction.

"See that you keep your help to that level," her father admonished. "Soothcoor has a replacement going to Mrs. Southland's today to take over the institution temporarily until a permanent replacement can be found."

"That quickly?" Gwinnie asked.

"Do we know who this person is?" Lewis asked.

Her father nodded. "Miss Millie Southerland, Mrs. Southerland's sister-in-law."

"What? I didn't know she had a sister-in-law; she never mentioned her," Gwinnie said.

"While her husband was alive, they were all very close. They drifted apart after Mr. Southerland died, Soothcoor tells me," her father explained.

"Where did he find her?" Lewis asked.

The duke laughed wryly. "She was the housekeeper at Soothcoor Mansion."

"I don't understand," said Gwinnie, frowning.

"Soothcoor's stepmother lived in Soothcoor Mansion for many years and Miss Southerland was the housekeeper. Now the Dowager Countess of Soothcoor wishes to make Appleton her principal residence, and Soothcoor intends to sell Soothcoor Mansion; she needs to find a new position."

"Why didn't she go with the staff to Appleton?" Gwinnie asked.

"There was already a housekeeper installed at Appleton— this all has happened quite recently," her father explained.

Lewis had been sitting with his arms crossed and two fingers resting against his lips. "Why is he selling it?" Lewis asked

"He and his wife want something smaller."

"I can understand that," said Lewis, nodding and relaxing back in his chair. "Soothcoor is not a pretentious man."

"Exactly. Anyway, Miss Southerland has been maintaining the London house for several weeks, waiting for decisions to be made. Now she needs to find another position. She suggested to Soothcoor that she could temporarily take leadership of Mrs. Southerland's charity while she looks for another housekeeper role. From my understanding from the note I received with Soothcoor, the idea appealed to him, one less immediate problem for him to resolve, so she is moving in today."

"This is all very sudden," said Gwinnie. She worried her lower lip between her teeth. "I hope she is kind like Mrs. Southerland was. I would have thought he would have Mrs. Albert take over leadership as she has been there from the beginning."

Lewis shrugged. "I would agree with you, but it looks like his need to have Soothcoor Mansion emptied was greater than his concerns for the charity. Probably seemed like a natural fit."

Gwinnie sighed. "And it well might be a good fit. I shouldn't judge without meeting the woman."

"No, you should not," said her father gruffly.

"I should like to go meet her," she said brightly, nearly bouncing out of her chair.

The duke laughed at the abrupt change in tone from Gwinnie. "I'm sure you would. But not until she has had time to settle in. You might be too much for her to take in until she has been there a day or two."

Lewis laughed.

"But I could help," Gwinnie protested.

"Mrs. Albert and Miss Wooler will provide her with the support she needs. I do not want you going there until after the inquest. I'm sure all the women will have questions about the inquest, and I believe they would be more relaxed with you providing the answers than a stranger," her father explained, and Gwinnie owned she could not refute him.

Mr. Harold appeared at the door. "Excuse me, Your Grace, but there is a Mr. Edmunds here to see you."

"Oh blast, I forgot entirely about the man coming, what with everything going on."

"Shall I request he return another day?" asked Mr. Harold.

"No, he had to journey over an hour to see me today — Gwinnie, please take Mr. Martin to the parlor. I need to see Mr. Edmunds. He is an inventor, and I am particularly interested in his invention for farming."

"Of course." She stood up to leave. "But we will be in the music room instead. I know Mr. Martin plays the pianoforte."

The duke laughed as Lewis rolled his eyes and displayed a *'what's a man to do'* expression. He dutifully followed Gwinnie out of the room.

In the hall stood a nervous-looking, robust gentleman in an ill-fitting suit. He held the brim of his hat in two hands and kept turning the hat around by the brim. Gwinnie encouragingly smiled at him as they passed him.

The music room was opposite the Lady Margaret Parlor and faced the terrace at the back of the house. She pushed open the white double doors to the music room, then looked back at Lewis.

"Brr! It is cold in here! I should call a footman to get the coal stove lit."

"I can take care of that," Lewis countered, as he walked over to the coal stove.

"Do you mind accompanying me while I practice?" she asked him, as he shoveled coal into the stove.

"My lady, it is a brilliant idea," he answered. He pulled a tinder box from the mantel and lit a punk, carefully feeding it into the stove. "If the music room doors remain open, there should be no hint of impropriety," he said, turning back to her.

Gwinnie laughed. "At my age, I don't worry about that." She took her violin out of its case and plucked some strings, then ran her bow over a string, stopping to adjust its tuning peg.

Lewis frowned. "You should be concerned," he said. "Forgive my bluntness, but you are a beautiful, desirable woman that age has no bearing upon."

Gwinnie smirked. "I did not take you for a flatterer, Mr. Martin."

"Lady Guinevere," Lewis began seriously. He took her hand in his. "I have long admired you, and if my circumstances in life were different..." He broke out his cheeky smile, his clear blue eyes twinkling. "... and if I were a taller man, I should request permission to court you and call you Gwinnie," he finished seriously.

Gwinnie looked down at their clasped hands. The moment he'd touched her, she felt a wave of reaction through her body, a tingling awareness of the man. Her breath came faster. She looked into his beautiful blue eyes. The weight of unspoken desires hung heavy in the air between them, a thread waiting to be pulled.

Why now, why him? she asked herself.

She could not deny the pull. It quivered in her chest. She'd felt it for months— since she'd first met him, if she were honest. Since he'd first played the pianoforte in this room.

Maybe that was why she'd suggested playing music today. But he was right. Their circumstances were different. She was a duke's daughter, and that had always hung heavily on her shoulders.

"Mr. Martin, I—" Gwinnie began, a warm blush on her cheeks.

Lewis let go of her hand. "My intent was not to discommode you, my lady, but to tell you to always consider propriety." He stepped away from her. "What shall we play?" he asked, moving toward the pianoforte.

"Oh! Umm, let me see what music I have that includes pianoforte," she replied, pulling herself together. She laid her violin aside and walked over to her music cabinet and ruffled through some pages before pulling out a score for pianoforte and violin. She handed the pianoforte sheets to Mr. Martin and took the violin music to her stand, just to the right of his instrument. She fetched her violin as Mr. Martin read over the sheet music she'd given him.

"I'm not familiar with this piece. Let me run through it once, first."

"Certainly, I need to check the tuning on my violin anyway," Gwinnie replied.

They played for an hour, hardly speaking to each other save for a discussion of the next music selection. They played until they heard multiple voices in the hall.

Gwinnie laid down her violin and went to investigate, Lewis following behind her.

CHAPTER 6

THE DOWAGER DUCHESS OF MALMSBY

"Grandmother!" Gwinnie exclaimed when she came out of the music room to see what all the noise was about.

Lady Vivian Nowlton, the Dowager Countess of Malmsby, held out her arms to Gwinnie.

Gwinnie ran to her, hugging her tiny grandmother to her chest.

Until the feathers on her hat tickled her nose.

"Oof, I'm going to sneeze!" Gwinnie warned, as she took a couple steps backward. She jammed the handkerchief she kept up her dress sleeve over her nose and waited. The feeling subsided.

"That hat is a menace," Gwinnie told her grandmother.

Her grandmother patted the side of her head. "I think it gives me stature," she said regally. The Dowager Duchess of Malmsby was known for her playful nature. Her once red hair had given way to white hair with her years; however, her dark-brown eyes still had the sparkle and liveliness of youth.

Gwinnie gave a snort of laughter at her grandmother's affected air.

"Don't you think my hat gives me stature, Mr. Martin?" the Dowager Countess asked when she spied him at the end of the hall by the music room door.

"Certainly, Your Grace," Lewis said, walking up to her, smiling. He took her hand in his and kissed her knuckles as he bowed.

"Oh, enough of that, young man. But why are you here? And why were you in the music room with Gwinnie?" She wagged an eyebrow at him.

"I was requested to be her accompanist when the duke threw us together while he is in a meeting with another gentleman," Lewis said.

"Adhering to the niceties of society? So sad," she said, shaking her multi-plumed head.

"Oh, Grandmother," Gwinnie said, gently batting her arm.

Her grandmother pursed her lips impishly as she smiled at her.

"May I take your coat and hat, Your Grace?" said Mr. Harold, appearing suddenly at her side.

"Yes, I suppose that would be best," the duchess said, loosening the bonnet ribbons and lifting the hat off her head to hand it to the butler, then unbuttoning her coat. "Mrs. Morrison, where are you?" she sang out.

"Here, Your Grace," the duchess's companion said from over by the stairway. "I was speaking to Mrs. Hunnicutt about our rooms and the items you brought with you for your comfort."

"Well, meet us in the Lady Margaret Parlor when you are done," she called over her shoulder. She tucked her arms through each of Mr. Martin's and Gwinnie's and walked them to her parlor. "And you two will tell me what is going on. Something is, I know it. I sense it."

Gwinnie smiled wanly at her grandmother. "You are correct, Grandmother. We've had a troubling few days. Father has been receiving threats for his interest in inventions, and a dear associate of mine has been murdered."

"Murdered!— No, don't say anything more yet. Let's go into my favorite room. If I have to hear bad news, that is the room to be seated in to hear it... with a glass of sherry in my hand," the dowager duchess said firmly.

The Lady Margaret Parlor, across from the music

room on the ground floor, had been designed by the dowager duchess's mother-in-law fifty years ago, yet had stood the test of time to be as bright and comfortable in 1817 as it had when first created. Pink, white, and gold ornamented the walls. All the furniture was upholstered in shades of pink, white, and green stripes or floral motifs. It suited the dowager duchess.

"It's cold in here!" the duchess complained as they walked into the room. "Harold!" she called out through the open door.

"Yes, Your Grace?"

"It's cold in here," the duchess complained. "And where is my sherry service?"

"Apologies, Your Grace, we weren't expecting you so early."

The duchess's frown disappeared, replaced by her impish smile. "We did make good time getting here, didn't we," she said gleefully.

The butler agreed and apologized again.

She waved his apology away. "We are early, but if we can get the fire lit to warm the room, we can wait on tea and sherry…"

Mr. Martin crossed to the fireplace with its coal stove and began to feed coal into it.

"What are you doing, Mr. Martin?" demanded the butler.

"Getting the fire going," he returned. He turned his head to look up at the man. "I just did so in the music room and performed this task many times at Versely Park," he assured him, reminding them all of the time he went undercover at the duchess's country home to discover who was threatening her.

The duchess laughed and clapped her hands together. "Thank you! You were the best footman I ever had."

"Are you suggesting I missed my calling, Your Grace?" he asked with a smile, as he stood up and wiped his hands on his handkerchief.

"You are a man of many talents. Perhaps that is why

you make a good Bow Street agent," the duchess returned. "Let's sit down while the room heats up and we await fortification."

The duchess sat down on the pink-striped sofa. She took her shoes off and drew her feet up beside her. "Gwinnie, would you hand me the dark, rose-colored shawl?"

Gwinnie picked up the large shawl and helped her grandmother drape it over herself. "My feet are freezing. I did not wear the right footwear for the journey," the dowager duchess said. "But sit, sit! Why are you both still standing about?— Oh, Mr. Martin, please place one of the armchairs nearer to the fireplace along with that little table over there." The dowager duchess pointed to the pieces she wanted moved. "Those will be for Mrs. Morrison. She won't admit it; however, her arthritis has been paining her in this cold weather."

Harold returned with the sherry decanter and glasses and set them on the table next to the duchess.

"That was quick, have you been hiding the sherry in the entrance hall?"

"No, Your Grace. I took this sherry service from the music room across the hall."

"My sherry?" protested Gwinnie.

"My apologies, my lady, but it was the closest and quickest way to get Her Grace her sherry."

"And that was a smart idea," said the duchess. "I appreciate your quick return. Would you pour glasses for us?"

Harold did as the duchess requested and passed the glasses around.

"Pour another for Mrs. Morrison and leave it on the table by the fireplace," she instructed, then turned to Gwinnie. "What is going on?"

"What makes you think things are going on?" Gwinnie asked, sipping her sherry.

"The Norwalks did not return straight to Devon but came here. I thought that odd, as Helena discovered she is increasing while they were at the Ellinbourne estate for Ann's wedding to the duke. They decided to remain there a few weeks to lessen the chance of losing the babe, and now they are in London."

"I believe that was at Father's insistence. Mr. Martin could explain better," Gwinnie said.

Lewis looked at Gwinnie with a doubtful expression but did explain to the duchess about the threats the duke had received and— they had recently discovered— the Dowager Countess of Norwalk had as well.

"And you say the threats extended to their family members?" she asked, surprised.

"Yes, Your Grace."

"And the first casualty of these threats might have occurred," Gwinnie said sadly.

Mrs. Morrison came into the room, walking quietly to the chair by the fireplace.

"What do you mean?" Gwinnie's grandmother asked.

"Last night Mrs. Southerland was murdered while wearing my Austrian short cape."

"Mrs. Southerland from the charity house?"

"Yes. They— they slit her throat!"

"No!" said the duchess.

Glass broke against the hearth stone. "I'm so sorry," said Mrs. Morrison, going on her knees beside the hearth to pick up the glass pieces. Her hands shook.

"Mrs. Morrison— Josephine! Leave it!" the duchess said. "The maids will get it."

Gwinnie rose and went to Mrs. Morrison's side to encourage her to sit again. "Did you know Mrs. Southerland?" Gwinnie asked her softly.

"We come from the same village. We were friends. We've kept in touch over the years," Mrs. Morrison said. "Whenever the duchess came to town, Hilda and I would visit for an hour or two."

The duchess shook her head ruefully. "I didn't know Mrs. Southerland's first name, and I'd often heard you mention your friend Hilda. I never heard your friend's last name. I didn't connect them."

"What we don't know is if Mrs. Southerland was the intended target or a random target. And if she was an intended target, was the person going after her, or Lady Guinevere."

"But our Gwinnie is much taller!" protested the duchess.

"Yes, but Mrs. Southerland was standing on the stoop, which would have made her a little taller, and we don't know if the assailant would have had a good description of Lady Guinevere, if she was his true target," Mr. Martin said.

"You are saying, she might have been the intended victim, or Gwinnie might have been the intended victim. I can see where that would have my son tied up in knots," the duchess said. "Quite frankly, it is tying me in knots as I think of it! Mr. Martin, what are you doing to protect my granddaughter?" the duchess asked in a strong, demanding voice.

"Grandmother, please!" said Gwinnie.

"Please what?"

"I don't think I was the target. I don't know why Mrs. Southerland might be; however, I can't see anyone confusing us— even in the dark and it wasn't full dark when the attack occurred," she said.

"Near enough in the alley," Mr. Martin said.

Gwinnie scowled at him. "Consider, it would be difficult to grab someone taller, as I am likely to be."

"Difficult, perhaps. Not impossible. Your height cannot protect you. You need to get this past that beautiful, thick, red hair of yours and into your brain, and understand this point: Your height is not a protection," Mr. Martin said, leaning toward her. "And she *was* standing on the stoop which would make her a few inches taller."

"She was? I didn't—" Gwinnie stopped. She wasn't supposed to have gone outside to see her body. She bit her lower lip.

He looked at her with one of his sideways wry smiles. "I knew you would go to see her body even when I instructed you not to."

"I did keep anyone else from going outside," she said petulantly. She plucked at the folds of her dress, head down. She looked at him through the veil of her lashes as she tried to hide a slight smile.

Mr. Martin grinned at her.

The duchess looked from one to the other, her lips pursing. "I see," she said.

"I felt I owed it to her," Gwinnie defended, turning to face the duchess. For some reason, looking at Mr. Martin always made her smile. He had such an expressive face. They were having a serious conversation. She should not be smiling!

The duchess took in an audible deep breath. "We have determined— theoretically— Mrs. Southerland could have been confused with Gwinnie. We return to my question, Mr. Martin. What are you doing to protect my granddaughter?"

"Lady Guinevere is used to going about the city with just her maid, Rose. When she is dressed as Sarah Knolls, she would go out unaccompanied. In both guises she would walk."

"I like to walk," Gwinnie put in.

"Now when she is out, she is escorted by one of the duke's footmen. The only reason I was with her the other night is the duke had received another note that morning threatening the family. He requested I take over the escort responsibilities at least for that night. We are discussing hiring permanent guards."

"I didn't know that!" Gwinnie exclaimed.

"It is that serious?" the duchess asked.

Lewis nodded, his lips compressed for a moment. "We think so."

"Then he should stop messing with these newfangled machines and go back to his Arthurian studies," declared the duchess, flopping back against the cushions of the sofa.

Both Gwinnie and Mr. Martin laughed.

"That suggestion would fall on deaf ears," Gwinnie declared.

The duchess frowned and shifted on the sofa. "I know," she finally said. "Now where is my tea?"

"I'll ring," Gwinnie said. She started to get up when the door opened to admit Stephen with the tea tray.

"Ah, finally! Put it on that table," the duchess instructed, pointing to the table near Gwinnie's chair. "Granddaughter, would you pour, please?"

"I would be delighted to." She poured for her grandmother first. "Cook has provided some of his treats. Would you like one?" Gwinnie's hand hovered over the tarts, one of the sweets she knew her grandmother loved.

"Yes. The tart would be nice," the duchess said. "You know me too well," she said, with a warm smile for Gwinnie.

Gwinnie prepared the tea for Lewis and included a lemon bar.

"It appears you know Mr. Martin well, too," observed her grandmother.

Gwinnie instantly blushed. "As much as he has been here lately," she said sourly. "I'm surprised he doesn't have a room assigned to him!"

"Daniel is coming home tomorrow," Lewis said, speaking of his ward, Daniel Wrightson, the mudlark he'd taken in following the investigation with Sir James and Lady Branstoke into the kidnapping of Soothcoor's young nephew. He and his gang had been instrumental in saving young Christopher Sedgewick's life.

"Got himself sent down from school?" the duchess suggested with a smile.

"Not for bad behavior. A group of boys were running on the ice to get speed then trying to slide on the soles of their shoes. He hit a rut and down he went. Broke a couple of ribs and sprained his wrist."

The duchess chuckled and nodded.

"The doctor says he needs to rest and stay quiet. He is a natural leader and wants to be in the thick of activity. The school suggested he come home to rest as they can't keep him down. My man will watch him, but he'll have his challenges."

"That young man certainly had my Versely Park housekeeper wrapped around her finger."

"He won't wrap Lindsay around his finger— I hope," Lewis said, a brief frown creasing his brow.

Gwinnie and the duchess laughed.

The click of the latch on the parlor door had them all turning to see the duke enter.

"Hello, Mother," he said, crossing the room to kiss the duchess on her head and clasp her hand briefly. He looked over at Lewis and Gwinnie. "Sorry for the interruption. Mr. Edmunds is a bundle of nerves, worried someone will steal his ideas or blow up his prototype. And I'm not even certain the machine is worth investment."

"What did you tell him?" his mother asked.

"I told him truthfully that I do not think it is ready for investment yet. I also told him that was the best news I could give him at this point, as it will likely turn the would-be Luddite followers away from interest in him for a time."

"Does this new group have a name?" The dowager duchess swung her feet to the floor and gestured to the duke to sit next to her on the sofa. Gwinnie rang the servants' bell to have the teapot refreshed.

"No one has stepped forward to claim leadership. They are highly secretive," he said, sitting next to her.

"I do not like this, Arthur," she said severely. "Gwinnie and Mr. Martin have told me of what happened to Mrs. Southerland."

"I do not believe someone killed Mrs. Southerland mistaking her for Gwinnie," he said, waving a hand dismissively

"But you do not *know* that," his mother said archly.

"No," he sighed, "I do not."

"The family needs protection," the duchess declared.

The duke compressed his lips, obviously thinking.

"And I will not be able to be here tomorrow," Lewis reminded him. "However, I have arranged for Tom Cott to come here in my place. He is a veteran of the 88th Foot under Lieutenant-Colonel John Wallace, and now is involved with pugilism exhibitions."

The duke lifted his head. "Organizing, or as a fighter?" he asked.

"Fighter. Lately, he's been winning more than he loses. He's a big man, but has the demeanor of a mild-mannered person until the fight begins."

Gwinnie giggled. "And that's why he wins!" she suggested.

"You might consider him for a permanent guard position," Lewis said slowly, knowing the duke did not want a guard.

"You are that concerned for the rebellions against technology?" the duke asked.

"I am, Your Grace," Lewis said on a long exhale.

Mercy quietly brought in a new teapot during the discussion. Gwinnie prepared her father's tea and handed it to him.

Gwinnie watched her father closely as he frowned and thrust his lower lip forward almost like a pout. "I don't like to back down from ignorant ruffians," he said.

The duchess laid a hand on his arm. "They are frightened, Arthur," she reminded him. "They are frightened you will take their livelihoods away from them."

The duke relaxed. "I know. How can I prove to them it will not?"

"On your properties and in your factories, I know you will see that your people are protected because, as a duke, you consider those who work for you as a kind of extended family. It has been drilled into you as part of your heritage. Others do not have your conviction, and you know you can't keep what you invest in solely for your use. Others who make use of the technology will exploit people."

"So, what would you have me do?"

The dowager duchess, Gwinnie, and Lewis looked at each other. "I'd say," Gwinnie began slowly, "ask them for their suggestions and also tell them of all you have seen. What would they like to try? Tell them the goal is to increase yields, to make them more productive to benefit them and yourself."

Her father frowned. "I'd need to discuss this with

An Artful Decision

Lady Norwalk," he said. "They are with the Galboroughs today. She and the Earl and Countess of Norwalk are intending to be here after services tomorrow."

"I will be sorry to miss them," said Lewis.

"I think we can convey your concerns to them," Gwinnie said.

~

LEWIS APPROACHED The Thirsty Pig early that evening with curiosity and suspicion. He hadn't expected an invitation from Mr. Gedney to be waiting for him on his arrival at home after spending most of the day with the Duke of Malmsby and his family.

Mr. Gedney and he did not often cross professional paths, as Mr. Gedney dealt with death, and Lewis's Bow Street mandate was anything other than death that would pay Bow Street and himself. However, Lewis knew of him. The man did not have a good reputation for being a diligent investigator. If the perpetrator was not immediately obvious, he would accuse the nearest person who "might" have a cause, or simply declare the death "murder by misadventure" or something of that ilk.

Lewis had told him his knowledge of the events of that evening. What could he want to discuss with him before the inquest? To concoct matching stories? What was there to concoct? Someone killed Mrs. Southerland.

It did bother him to consider the murderer may have mistaken the victim, but he didn't believe in that story, even if it still warranted investigation. He did not want to consider Gwinnie as the intended victim. In his dreams — nightmares— following the discovery of Mrs. Southerland's body, it was Gwinnie's face he saw with a slit throat, her red hair fanned out around her beautiful face with its unseeing eyes.

He didn't like that he could bring up that vision so easily, either.

A good-sized crowd filled The Thirsty Pig when

Lewis arrived. Inside, it was loud, hazy with smoke, and smelled of spilled ale.

Maude came by after delivering drinks. He stopped her. "Have you seen Mr. Reginald Gedney here tonight?"

She pointed to the far front corner of the taproom and scurried off. Lewis walked in that direction, twisting and turning through the crowd. He was halfway to the corner when he saw him at a small table by a front window. Lewis elbowed his way through more people to get to Gedney. He turned the chair opposite the man around and dropped into it, resting his arms on the chair's back.

"You wanted to meet?" Lewis asked, trying to talk loud enough to be heard over the din of the other patrons, but not so loud as to draw attention.

Gedney nodded. "What do you think happened to Mrs. Southerfield?"

Lewis frowned. "Southerland," he corrected. "I told you what I saw and heard."

Gedney waved his hand. "Yes, yes. I know what you said. I'm askin' what you think."

"Why?"

"You Bow Street types have a different way of perceivin' things."

Lewis stared at him, wondering what he was getting at. "We don't deal with death like you do," he acknowledged.

"I'm not talkin' about that," Gedney said gruffly. "Who do you think done it?"

Lewis shook his head. "I don't know," he said wearily, for suddenly he felt drained of life.

"Can I get you sumpthin'?" Maude asked from by his elbow.

"Another ale," Gedney said.

"Coffee," Lewis said.

"Coffee on a Saturday night?" Gedney asked with mock dismay.

"It's been a long day," Lewis admitted to Gedney.

"Well, I'll tell you what I think happened," Gedney said.

Lewis nodded, then dropped his chin on his folded hands as he listened.

"Friday's the day those women go shopping, and the housekeeper and cook come here. With the house empty or nearly empty it's a prime invitation for a robbery. You should know that, seein' as you're with Bow Street. I think someone was in the backyard when Mrs. Southerland came into the yard and they killed her," Gedney said. He downed the rest of the ale. "Where is that barmaid with our drinks?"

Lewis lifted his head. From what he'd known and heard of the man, this was his classic murder resolution. Simple, no work for him. Lewis frowned. "Why kill her? Why not just rob her?"

"Afraid she could identify them," Gedney replied promptly.

Lewis rubbed the sides of his face with his hands. He was tired. Too tired for Gedney's nonsense, but he had to hear him out for the sake of the inquest on Monday. "But he hadn't done anything other than be in her yard. Maybe he came just to shelter from the wind," Lewis suggested.

"And got startled and killed her," Mr. Gedney said, nodding. "Some of these street types, they are not right in the head. I find they are often the ones that commit the murders."

Lewis began to wonder how many of the damaged veterans Gedney accused of murder and saw hang. He had no proof this happened; however, the mere possibility it could, made him want to see Gedney out of his position with the coroner's office.

"If it wasn't for the murders they do, I'd have more compassion, but I seen too much," Gedney continued, as if he were trading professional tips, not noticing Lewis's frown.

"So, what are you going to advise Dr. Brogan as the cause of death for the death certificate?" Lewis asked, though he felt he knew.

Maude came back with Gedney's ale and Lewis's coffee. Lewis handed her some coins. Maude held her hand out to Gedney.

"What, you're not going to cover for me?" Gedney asked Lewis.

"No."

Gedney grumbled and reached into his waistcoat pocket for money. He slapped it into Maude's hand.

"What is your verdict?" Lewis repeated when Maude left.

"Death by misadventure by person or persons unknown."

Lewis picked up the cup. He could tell by the smell he may regret the coffee. "The Earl of Soothcoor will not like that verdict," he calmly told Gedney.

Gedney laughed. "Just because he funds the place doesn't mean he is interested in it. I doubt he'll even be at the inquest. I heard he's not in town."

Lewis sipped his coffee. It was weak. He wondered how many times they'd brewed these grinds. "The Duke of Malmsby sent him a letter informing him of what happened."

"What's he got to do with this case?"

Lewis set down the coffee mug. "What has your investigation revealed?"

"Nothing. No one saw anything. No one was around. Like I said, death by misadventure— This Miss Knolls who you took away before I arrived, will she be at the inquest?"

"Yes. I believe her father is intending to bring her. Will you continue investigating until the inquest on Monday?"

Gedney shrugged. "If something comes up, certainly — So, you don't support my verdict."

"No, but what does that matter?" Lewis asked. "I'll give my testimony. I doubt Dr. Brogan will ask for my opinion."

Gedney nodded, with a slight, self-satisfied smile. "True enough. Still, it would be good if you could see your way to my way of thinking."

Lewis set the coffee mug on the scarred table. "I'd

have to talk to more people and turn over more rocks before I could do that." He sighed and ran a hand through his hair. "As it is, I don't think it was her being in the wrong place at the wrong time. Good luck to you," Lewis said, as he rose from his chair.

Gedney nodded and sipped his ale. Lewis thought he looked annoyed. He wondered why the man thought he would back him, and why he felt he needed the backing. Wasted meeting and deplorable coffee. He left The Thirsty Pig to find a hackney to take him to his home. He had more important things to think about right now.

Tomorrow Daniel would return. He'd need to figure out how to keep the lad quiet. *That* would be a challenge.

CHAPTER 7

DANIEL COMES HOME

Gwinnie was coming down the stairs Sunday morning when Jimmie answered the front door to a large, Black man wearing a greatcoat over a neat, plain suit with a silver-and-green figured waistcoat. He held a bowler hat in one hand and a portmanteau in the other.

"Tom Cott to see His Grace, the Duke of Malmsby," he said crisply, with a slight country accent, Gwinnie thought. "I've been sent by Mr. Lewis Martin."

"We've been expecting you, Mr. Cott," Gwinnie said from behind Jimmie.

"You must be the Lady Guinevere Lewis told me about," he said, smiling.

"I am. Jimmie, please let the man in and go tell my father Mr. Cott is here."

"Yes, my lady," Jimmie said, limping away on his still-healing sprained ankle.

Gwinnie stared after the young man for a moment. She shook her head. She'd heard his foot had slipped off the curb and twisted when he jumped out of the way from three running and yelling street urchins pushing a stolen tinker's cart. "He needs to stay off that ankle for another few days or he will hurt it worse."

"Now that I be 'ere, perhaps the lad'll 'ave that opportunity," Mr. Cott said.

Gwinnie liked his calm demeanor. Though a big man, he did not speak with a big voice. It was one of those voices that sounded like it was more accustomed to laughing than yelling. His dark brown eyes shone with comfort. He was not as tall as she, but his broad shoulders and barrel chest had the impression of great size.

"You can leave your portmanteau, your coat, and your hat here," Gwinnie told him, pointing to the footman's alcove.

"Thank you, my lady," he said, bowing to her.

Mercy ran down the stairs. "His Grace says you are to come up to join him for breakfast."

"Where is Jimmie?" Gwinnie asked.

"His Grace says as how he was to stay off that foot and if he wanted to do something he was certain Mr. Harold could give him silver to shine."

Gwinnie and Mr. Cott laughed. She heard his humor rumble out of him.

"I 'ave already eaten," Mr. Cott said. "I could wait 'ere, until His Grace finishes."

"Nonsense," Gwinnie said. "I'm sure a man of your stature could eat several meals a day. Besides, my father likes to hold meetings over breakfast. Keeps them more informal, he says. You will see, he is not a formal man. Forget all you think you know about dukes," she said with a laugh.

She led him up the stairs to the breakfast parlor. "Father, this is Mr. Cott, the gentleman Mr. Martin talked to us about yesterday."

The duke rose and held out his hand to the man. Mr. Cott paused, uncertain, then placed his hand in the duke's. "Glad to have you with us," the duke said. "Sit—what would you like, coffee or tea?"

"Tea," he said softly.

The duke waved to Mercy to serve him.

"I hear you are a veteran of the 88th Regiment Foot."

"Yes, Your Grace."

"That was a good regiment. The newspaper always was saying how many times the 88th routed the French."

Mr. Cott grinned. "They didn' like our bayonets."

"That's what I've read. And now you are a pugilist?"

"Yes, I'm tryin' to save money to buy in as a tenant farmer, or become a yeoman farmer, if I'm lucky."

"Do you have experience with farming?"

"Yes, Your Grace, my family were wage labor for a large tenant farm in Yorkshire."

The duke nodded. "I like that you have goals. Good goals for our country."

Mercy served Mr. Cott a plate full of breakfast items. Gwinnie thought his eyes got as round as saucers.

"Go ahead and eat, Mr. Cott. I don't know all that Mr. Martin has told you, so I will just start rambling about the family and the possible challenges ahead of us that may need your help."

"Thank you, Your Grace."

The duke spent the next twenty minutes while Mr. Cott ate talking about his interest in inventions and what they could do for the nation, and the pushback he was getting from those who were afraid the new machines would take away their livelihoods.

"There will need to be some retraining, of course, but I don't see the number of workers being reduced. I do respect their fears but not the pushback. Change is inevitable. It is how we react to the changes that determines the outcomes. I'd like to train people to be ready for change."

Mr. Cott laughed. "I'm sure that is not as easy as it might sound."

"No, it is not."

Mr. Cott nodded. "My father would be one of those filled with fear for losing his job, particularly as a Black man. Don't think he'd be a rabble-rouser though— that's not his nature, but he would worry and pray."

"Unlike your father, there would be people only too happy to cause problems."

"I see that, Your Grace," Mr. Cott said, nodding.

"I have received letters threatening me and my family."

Mr. Cott frowned. "So Mr. Martin said. Said I'm to 'elp protect everyone."

The duke nodded. "I warn you, however, my mother, the Dowager Duchess of Malmsby, and my daughter here, can be stubborn."

"Never say so," protested Gwinnie.

"Don't give into them," the duke said firmly, looking intently at Mr. Cott from under his dark, bushy brows, his lips pressed in a firm line.

"Father!" protested Gwinnie. He ignored her.

"But the next group of people I would tell you of are the Norwalks," the duke continued. "The Dowager Countess of Norwalk likes to fund inventors and their inventions. She has also received threats, but she insists on ignoring them. I'd say she is more stubborn than my mother and my daughter combined."

"You cannot be serious," Gwinnie said, her eyes flaring.

Her father glanced in her direction, then back at Mr. Cott. "I am. They will be here this afternoon so you will have the opportunity to meet them."

Mr. Cott touched his napkin to his lips. "Might I 'ave a tour of the property?" he asked.

"Excellent request, Mr. Cott. I will have Mr. Harold, our butler, give you a complete tour. Afterward, we will go over the plans for the next few days." He rang for the butler.

"Thank you, Your Grace."

"If you are serious about the danger," Gwinnie said after Mr. Cott left with Harold, "one man— no matter how broad his shoulders are, or how many pugilistic exhibitions he's won— can protect us all."

"I know. I'm hoping the presence of an escort will show we are not as vulnerable and make these miscreants think twice before taking action. In addition, I have been thinking steadily of what we discussed yesterday. Maybe I am rushing too fast. Working with Mr. Edmunds yesterday made me realize these inventors are starting to see money signs in their eyes when their inventions are not perfected yet."

An Artful Decision

"So, you are saying we need to talk to Lady Norwalk? Maybe persuade her to hold off on her funding for a while?"

"Yes. And what would be the most appropriate under the circumstances, would be for them all to return to Devon at this time."

Though Gwinnie had been looking forward to spending more time with Helena— they so seldom got to see each other— she agreed with her father. Oh, bother!

∼

"FINALLY, I'VE FOUND YOU!" Gwinnie's grandmother said later that afternoon as she walked into the music room. "I almost didn't think to look for you in here, as quiet as it was. What are you doing?" she asked, as she crossed the room.

"I'm going through the quartet music I have. I need to make decisions as to what we will play when the spring social season gets underway."

"Can't you just do what you did last year?" Her grandmother sat on the small blue armchair near the fireplace, near where Gwinnie sat on the floor, sheets of music surrounding her. The light-blue-painted room was not filled with the comfortable furniture that decorated other parlors in the house. Other than the one settee and two armchairs, the furniture consisted primarily of chairs for listening to music.

Gwinnie scrunched her face up. "I could, but I don't like to. It is better for us to practice new pieces. It keeps our playing fresh— though there are a few hostesses for whom a repeat of last year wouldn't be amiss. They have no appreciation of music other than something society says should be part of a party." She looked down at the music she had in her hand, shook her head, and pushed it aside.

The duchess leaned back in her chair, a pensive smile on her face. "I hadn't considered the work you go through for balls and your little concerts."

Gwinnie smiled as she nodded. "It is work, but I

enjoy it, almost as much as I enjoy teaching the women at Mrs. Southerland's."

"You like working with these women more than your music?" the duchess asked. She looked quizzically at her granddaughter. "When did that happen? For years, music was all you talked of."

Gwinnie looked up at her grandmother as she laughed. "And I still love music. But my love for music is for me, like when I played the violin on the ramparts of Baydon Castle when I was there last year, the wind whipping through my hair." She hugged herself at the memory, an impish smile on her lips. She looked back up at her grandmother. "I don't care if I play for anyone else's enjoyment— and I certainly dislike it when no appreciation for the music is shown by those I play for." Her smile fading. "That it is taken for granted."

She paused and tilted her head to the side as she thought. "But the women I teach, they so much want to help themselves. They want to rise above whatever circumstances have tossed them into misery. If you could see their faces as they listen, soaking up the words I say to them, you would understand," Gwinnie explained, her face glowing with her enthusiasm. She felt a trifle embarrassed at her enthusiasm and returned her attention to her music sorting.

The duchess rang the servants' bell as Gwinnie continued her task.

She hadn't really thought before about her changing attitude toward her music. It was just something she had done since she was a child. Was she tired of music? She didn't think so; however, what she told her grandmother stirred something within her. For her, music *was* personal. She loved it. She did not love the inattention of people when the quartet played, or the rude hostesses who dictated what they played and desired the same pieces repeatedly.

Now she had a quartet whose members depended on her to get them opportunities to play and get paid for doing so. If she didn't negotiate the jobs, they might starve.

Gwinnie's brow creased as she went through another stack of music. She felt trapped. She hadn't articulated the feeling for herself before now, but there it was, hitting her in her heart. But she couldn't abandon the quartet!

"*Please serve tea in here?*" she heard the Duchess ask the footman who answered the bell. Gwinnie looked up. She'd almost forgotten her grandmother was in the room with her. She felt guilty for ignoring her.

"Certainly, Your Grace," the footman said.

"We could have gone to the Lady Margaret Parlor for our tea," Gwinnie protested.

Her grandmother waved her hand. "I am comfortable where I am, and you are well into your task. Here works as well as the parlor across the hall," she said airily.

Gwinnie neatened her piles of music into two types: music to be retired for a time and music to play this year, and opened the French-painted music cabinet to put the music away. She smiled when she realized the piece of music that had ended up on the top of the keep pile was one she and Mr. Martin had played that morning.

That was fun.

"Did you know that Mr. Martin plays the pianoforte?" Gwinnie asked her grandmother as she slid the music in place and shut the cabinet door.

"No! Does he play well?"

"Very well. I learned that when Uncle Candelstone was shot. He came to interview the quartet about that night. The group was nervous. I think he played the pianoforte to get the musicians to relax around him."

"If he did, he would be highly knowledgeable about people," her grandmother said.

Gwinnie nodded. "I think he is," she said, a hint of wonder in her voice. She then smiled at her grandmother with a hint of mischief. "And I made audacious use of him this morning to accompany me as I played one of the new pieces I am considering. Father had a visitor and asked that we wait until his visitor was gone to finish our conversation, so I decided to put the time to good use."

The maid, Mercy, came in with the tea, followed by

the footman returning the music room's sherry service—which Gwinnie was delighted to see returned.

Gwinnie poured the tea, making it like her grandmother preferred.

"Mr. Martin seems to have become quite useful to the family," her grandmother said as she accepted the teacup and saucer from Gwinnie.

"Yes. This may sound odd; however, I feel he understands us." Gwinnie tilted her head as she smiled. She turned back to fixing her own tea.

"What do you mean?" her grandmother asked, leaning forward toward Gwinnie.

Gwinnie sat in the armchair nearest her grandmother. "Our manner of being in society. Our sense of humor. Our interests," she said easily. "We aren't like many in the ton are, caught up in their importance and, because of that, afraid to step out of the tightly constrained box of their heredity." She looked up at her grandmother again. "Gracious, consider, a duke's daughter playing the violin as part of an evening's entertainment? A duke's heir writing lurid gothic novels? Another son becoming a physician?— And we must not forget the duchess who likes to play practical jokes," Gwinnie said pointedly, staring at her grandmother.

"Nonsense, I haven't played a practical joke in months," protested the duchess, straightening.

Gwinnie laughed.

The dowager duchess pursed her lips. "I must tell you, Mr. Martin reminds me of someone, and every time I try to think of who it might be, it slips away," the duchess complained, pursing her lips together.

"Maybe what I learned the night Mrs. Southerland was murdered, might help you to recall," Gwinnie said, suddenly anxious to know of Mr. Martin's family. "We were chatting together, having tea, and awaiting her return. He said it is his fault he is base-born. He was born early and his father had not yet returned from procuring the special marriage license he'd gone after."

"Interesting," her grandmother said. She cocked her head, smiling.

Gwinnie swore she could almost see her grandmother thinking, so pensive was her smiling expression. She believed her grandmother had a glimmer of an idea as to who Mr. Martin's family was.

"Did his father raise him?" her grandmother asked suddenly.

"Yes, and from what I understand, his father thought he should have a career as a solicitor, but he became more interested in crime. He is different from what one would consider a Bow Street agent. He is well educated, and he plays the pianoforte brilliantly."

The duchess leaned back on the sofa. Her smile grew brighter. "I had no idea, though I might have guessed."

"You know who his family is?" Gwinnie asked. "Who?"

Her grandmother waved her hand airily but did not answer Gwinnie. Instead, she said: "I knew I liked him from the time he was at Versely Park during the threats to the Michelangelo sketches."

"I consider him a friend," Gwinnie confessed to her grandmother.

The Dowager Countess looked at her granddaughter. She nodded and smiled broadly. "And so you should."

∽

Lewis sat in his study situated in the front of his small house when the Earl of Soothcoor's carriage arrived.

Lewis laid down his quill. Daniel was home. Then he laughed at himself for referring to Daniel being home. He'd taken in the boy as his ward less than a year ago. He'd settled in nicely, and now Lewis could not imagine the boy not being part of his life.

He grinned, Daniel had only been at school two weeks, and he'd missed the scamp. But he couldn't let him know that. He dismissed his smile. He had to have a serious look when he greeted the boy, for he was only home because he'd gotten into mischief and injured himself.

When he got outside, Lord Soothcoor was gingerly

helping the boy descend from the carriage. Daniel's left arm lay in a sling. He stood stiff and straight, no doubt due to the tight wrapping of his ribs.

Lewis bowed to the earl. "Thank you, my lord, for bringing Daniel back to London."

"I had to come anyway to attend this inquest for Mrs. Southerland," he said. "Do you know who killed her?"

"No, my lord. Mr. Gedney of the coroner's office is leading the investigation."

"Does he have any good leads?"

"No. I was just organizing my notes when you arrived. The Duke of Malmsby has hired me to take over the investigation if there is no solid suspect from Mr. Gedney's actions."

Soothcoor frowned and nodded. "We'll talk later. The horses shouldn't be standing in this cold after the drive here," he said. He climbed back into his carriage and signaled his coachman to drive on.

"Lord Soothcoor tol' me he was comin' back to Lunnon for Mrs. Southerland's inquest. I never met that lady; who was she?" Daniel asked.

Lewis picked up the portmanteau the carriage footman had set down beside Daniel, and placed his left arm under Daniel's right to help him up the stone steps before the house.

Daniel tried to shrug away from him. "I don't need no help," he declared.

"Maybe not," Lewis said. "My hand beneath your elbow steadying you ensures that."

"I'm not an infant," Daniel complained.

They climbed the stairs to the door. "No, you are an idiot for using your shoes as skates on the ice."

"It worked!"

"Until you fell," Lewis reminded him as he opened the black-painted front door.

"Yeah, yeah."

"Mr. Martin," said his man, Philip Lindsay coming into the entrance hall. "Can I be of assistance?"

"Take his winter wear, then ask Mrs. Fullerton to meet us in Daniel's room. You go on up with Daniel's portmanteau. I want everyone to hear what the rules are to be for Daniel's recovery so there can be no wheedling," Lewis said strongly, looking down at Daniel as they walked to the stairway that would take him up two flights to his bedroom.

"I'd never," Daniel said stiffly.

Lewis stared at him; his lips compressed in a disbelieving smirk.

"I could have stayed at school. I didn't have to come home," Daniel said.

"If you had followed instructions, that would be true. I understand you rarely remained in bed as the doctor requested."

"I feel better, nothin' hurts as much as it did."

"Daniel, cracked and broken ribs are serious. They could have punctured your lungs. And as damaged as they are now, there could be more damage if you don't allow them to grow back together."

Daniel made a disgusted face.

"The fact it doesn't hurt as much is good. We'll have Dr. Brogan check on your ribs and your wrist this week. I do wish Dr. Nowlton was in town, though."

"Is he the brother of that tall, pretty lady with the red hair?"

"Yes. Lady Guinevere Nowlton. I didn't know you knew her," Lewis said, as they reached the second floor.

Daniel side-eyed him. "I know you're sweet on her," he said slyly.

"I like her. She's a friend, as much as a Bow Street agent and a duke's daughter can be friends. That's not courting sweet," he said.

"I used to see her down near the docks afore I moved in with you. But she wasn't dressed like no duke's daughter."

"Hmm," was all Lewis could manage to say to that, but his mind flooded with thoughts of all the times she had undoubtedly put herself in the line of trouble. He led Daniel over to a chair by the desk in the room. "Sit," he said. He took off Lewis's shoes.

"Here's Daniel's portmanteau," Lindsay said, coming

into the room. "Mrs. Fullerton will be up in a moment. She is preparing something for Daniel to eat."

Lewis nodded. "Find a nightshirt in there." He carefully removed Daniel's sling, then pulled his bad arm out of the jacket, then the other.

Immediately Lindsay opened the bag and pulled out a white muslin nightshirt.

Lewis had Daniel stand up, then pulled his shirt over his head. "Mr. Lindsay, help me get this nightshirt on him and his pants off. I'd like to have him in bed before Mrs. Fullerton gets here." He examined the bandage around Daniel's chest, satisfied it remained tight and would prevent improper movement.

"See if we have extra pillows we can use to prop him upright."

"Oh, we do, Mr. Martin," Mrs. Fullerton said, coming in the room with a tea tray. "In the linen closet near your room."

"I'll get them," said Mr. Lindsay.

"Now then, Young Master Wrightson, I baked an apple pie today when I heard you were coming home. I thought you would quite enjoy that your first day back and stuck in bed. And the tea I made special for you with plenty of milk and sugar, just like you like it."

"Wonderful! Thank you, Mrs. Fullerton," Daniel said. He lunged forward to grab the plate only to stop suddenly with a pained look on his face. "I keep forgetting," he said, his voice tight with pain.

"Which is precisely why you were sent home from school," Lewis said.

"Here are pillows to support you while you sit up," Mr. Lindsay said, coming into the room.

"I'll get these situated," Mrs. Fullerton said, taking them from the man and carefully placing them behind Daniel to support him. "When you want to lie down you must tell one of us so we can help you. I imagine all the jolting about in the carriage today has not done you any good," she said.

"Excellent point, Mrs. Fullerton," Lewis said.

"Do you need me to stay the night?" she asked.

"No, your family needs you home."

"Oh posh," she said. "They's old enough to takes care of themselves. But if you need me, you let me know and I can make arrangements."

"Thank you, Mrs. Fullerton."

"But I believe you and Mr. Lindsay here, needs to see young Daniel stays quiet. Not easy for him. Look how easily he forgot and went after the pie I brought and grimaced in pain. Master Daniel, did you bring any schoolbooks home with you?" the housekeeper asked.

"Yes," he said, with pathetic resignation.

"I thought you liked school," Lewis said.

"I do, I just don't like reading *The History of Britanica* right now."

Lewis laughed. "I wouldn't either. Is there anything you would like to read?"

"One of those gothic novels!"

"Is your reading up to that level already?"

"Yes," he said proudly. "Head of the class."

"What a clever boy you are," said Mrs. Fullerton.

"Too clever, sometimes," Lewis said drily. "I'm not a gothic reader, but I do have one given to me by its author. I'll bring that up to you, otherwise you will have to wait until Lindsay or Mrs. Fullerton can go to the subscription library tomorrow. I will be busy with the murder inquest."

"Who's the author?"

Lewis grinned. "I can't tell you. The book says *Anonymous* on it."

"Well, I'd best go look to dinner," Mrs. Fullerton said. "If you be needing anything from me, just tell Mr. Martin or Mr. Lindsay."

"Yes, ma'am," Daniel said.

"Lindsay, if you would, stay here with Dan while I get the book for him and my writing supplies. I can use his desk to finish organizing my notes. I'll stay with him this afternoon. I want to get a sense of how he is."

"Understood, Mr. Martin. And if he and I leave our bedroom doors open tonight, I shall hear him from my room across the hall should he need anything."

"Yes, I was wondering if I should set a pallet up in his room; however, I think what your suggested will work better."

~

"Mr. Martin?" Lewis heard from the darkened corner of the room where Daniel lay in bed.

"Yes?" Lewis answered. It was getting late, and he should be seeking his own bed, but once he'd started his notes and letter inquiries in Daniel's room, it had just been easier to continue at his small desk.

Daniel would recover from his injuries. Lewis knew he felt overly concerned. Somehow, the lad had gotten under his skin, just as Lady Guinevere had. At least he could take care of young Daniel. He wished he could take care of Gwinnie, as he would love to call her.

"You need a stool," Daniel's almost disembodied voice said from the shadows.

Lewis turned toward him. "A stool?"

"Yes. You need a courting stool. For Lady Guinevere," he said seriously.

Lewis laughed.

"So you can kiss her," Daniel continued.

He'd obviously been thinking about this for a while. "A fact of society is gentlemen born out of wedlock can't kiss a duke's daughter," Lewis said, the idea of kissing Lady Guinevere's full, lush lips flashed in his mind, and he found himself yearning for her.

"Why not? You're a man and she's a woman."

Lewis choked out a little laugh. "I wish it were that easy... You should be asleep. Sleep will help the bones knit together faster."

"I know. I was just lying here thinking," Daniel said. "Mr. Martin?"

"Yes."

"Thank you for taking me in."

"I enjoy your company. And I think you should call me Lewis, not Mr. Martin."

Daniel was silent for a moment. "Goodnight, Lewis."

"Goodnight." Lewis gathered up his writing and turned out the oil lamp on the desk. "Remember, if you need anything during the night, you have only to call out to Mr. Lindsay."

"Yes," said a sleepy voice in return.

Lewis stood at the doorway looking toward Daniel, then left the door open and went downstairs to his rooms.

CHAPTER 8
GWINNIE'S STRATEGY

The footman, Stephen, let Lewis into Malmsby House at 9:00 a.m. Monday morning. "Is His Grace available?"

"In the breakfast room, sir. He said if you arrived, I was to bring you there. Follow me, please."

"Thank you, Stephen."

Lewis had met and learned the names of all of the Malmsby House staff last June, after the betrothal ball for the Dowager Duchess of Malmsby's granddaughter, Anne Hallowell, to Miles Wingate, the Duke of Ellinbourne.

He'd been called in to investigate the shooting of Lord Candelstone during the ball. It was a flesh wound caused by a small-caliber bullet from a petite gun such as a woman might carry. It was during that investigation that he'd formally met Lady Guinevere Nowlton, or Gwinnie, as she preferred to be called. He had known who she was before that, as her father had hired him and others to be guards to keep an eye on her from a distance. She believed she was too tall and broad-shouldered for any man to want to hassle her. Her father, not wishing to squelch her confidence, quietly arranged for discreet guards.

But he didn't formally meet her until he walked into the music room that next afternoon, where she was practicing with her quartet for an upcoming performance. He'd been entranced by her ebullience, wit, and talent. She stood half a head taller than him, her dark red hair coming loose from their pins as she furiously played solo, the other musicians watching her. To this day, he didn't know why he did it; however, he walked over to the pianoforte and began accompanying her. She looked over at him in surprise, then her face exploded into the biggest grin, and they played together until the end of the piece.

Since that afternoon, they'd been friends of a sort—as much as a Bow Street agent and the daughter of a duke could be friends.

"Mr. Martin has arrived, Your Grace," Stephen said from the breakfast parlor door, reclaiming Lewis's attention from his memories.

"Welcome, Mr. Martin! Come in, please, and join us for breakfast," the duke said. With him sat Gwinnie. He pointed to the seat to his left. His daughter sat to his right. Lewis made his way around the table.

"Coffee," he told the maid standing there waiting. After his cup was filled, she set a full breakfast plate before him.

The duke touched his napkin to his mouth and leaned back in his chair. "I sent a letter off to Soothcoor Saturday morning and heard back from him last night. He plans to be at the inquest today."

Lewis nodded. "I know," he said with a smirk. "He is in town now. I saw him briefly yesterday when he brought Daniel down from school."

The duke looked at him with curiosity. "What are you thinking that you smirk?"

"I met with Mr. Gedney Saturday night. He assumes the earl will not appear at the inquest. Based on my conversation with him, he will make the motions of investigating. He said he intends to instruct Dr. Brogan to render a verdict of death by person or persons unknown."

"Really," the duke drawled. He looked toward his

daughter. "That will not do, not do at all, will it, Gwinnie, my dear?"

She took a sip of her coffee. "I should protest it if I were at the inquest; however, as women are not allowed, it will be up to you gentlemen to see that doesn't occur."

"Not correct," her father said. He laced his hands together over his stomach. "Women are not allowed as part of the jury; however, they may come as witnesses."

"However, you are partly correct, from Mr. Gedney's standpoint," Lewis said. "He does wish Sarah Knolls to come to the inn prior to the inquest so he may question *her* then. He'd rather not have her before the jury."

"Why?"

Lewis shrugged. "To corroborate my statement, I suppose. But he doesn't know where Sarah Knolls lives, nor her real identity," he said.

The duke looked at Gwinnie. "Am I to understand by your appearance this morning that you intend to go as Lady Guinevere Nowlton and not as Sally or Sarah Knotts, or whatever name it is you gave yourself?"

Gwinnie laughed. "Sarah Knolls. Yes, I intend to go as myself. Grandmother convinced me that to try to tell a truth while one is living a lie is not proper."

"I will be going with you," the duke said. "I intended to go anyway in case Soothcoor does not make it in time." He looked over at the maid. "Mercy, request Stephen to fetch me the paper I have on my desk."

The maid curtsied and left the breakfast parlor. "I have prepared a paper to formally request your services to investigate the death of Mrs. Southerland."

Lewis bowed his head slightly. "I was intending to do so anyway. Mr. Gedney will not give her the attention she deserves. He thought her house was a brothel, not a charity house. I informed him otherwise. I don't know if he believed me."

"A brothel," Gwinnie protested.

Her father laid a hand on hers. "Calm yourself, Gwinnie. There are better ways to get one's point across than using a loud voice. Ways that may have a more lasting impact," he finished as he patted her hand. He smiled.

"Oh! You are planning something!" she said. Her expression lightened, and she smiled happily at her father.

He nodded. "Perhaps. We shall see how it plays out before running in with battle cries."

"Should Grandmother be pleased?" she asked.

He gave a shout of laughter.

Lewis looked at them both, confused. "I am missing something, I know."

"Stay around the Nowlton family long enough and you won't be."

~

"You are wearing heels," Lewis observed to Gwinnie when she came downstairs for their trip to The Thirsty Pig.

"Yes."

He frowned. "Now you are a full head taller than me. Unfair," he complained, but with an appreciative eye. A battlefield Valkyrie!— or for him, Freya. Come to demand Mrs. Southerland's rightful respect, as they did for the dying heroes of war, taking them to Valhalla.

She laughed. "I am making a statement that I cannot make if I walk in on my father's arm, as he and I are not so different in height, so I have determined I must walk in on your arm."

Lewis laughed. "If we weren't friends of a sort, I should take that as an insult that I am to be used, however, I appreciate the jest. You are taller than me without the heels. Why the extra height?"

"Subtle intimidation."

Lewis sighed. "And I suppose your bonnet will add even more height, like your grandmother's bonnet did when she arrived?"

She beamed at him. "Of course! Oh, come now, I know it won't bother you. You are playing with me."

"As you, I believe, intend to play with Mr. Gedney."

Gwinnie tilted her head from side to side and gave a little shrug. "Merely the first salvo to unsettle him. I leave the rest to Father. He wants him out of the coroner's office."

"And he will be out, one way or another," came the deep voice of the duke, as he too descended the stairs. He looked Gwinnie up and down. He nodded. "Very different from your Miss Knolls attire."

She smiled. "That is the intention," she said, as she accepted her bonnet from Rose. As Lewis surmised, it was a poke bonnet with a tall poke accented with pheasant feathers.

"Mr. Cott," the duke said, "please try to keep the others here until we return."

"Yes, Your Grace," the big man said, bowing with an amazing gracefulness for his size.

"Come," the duke said to Gwinnie and Lewis, gesturing to the door. "Let's be on our way."

Stephen hurriedly opened the door, then ran down before them to assist them into the ducal carriage.

"You are displaying the ducal rank prominently," Lewis observed, as the coach started toward The Thirsty Pig.

"I did not like the attitude you reported displayed by Mr. Gedney toward Mrs. Southerland and her establishment," the duke said.

Gwinnie nodded. "Those women who find their way to Mrs. Southerland's, and who participate as they should, deserve a chance to better their lives. Their past need not influence their future if they work hard enough. And they do!"

"I don't think Mrs. Southerland's murder has anything to do with her establishment," Lewis said idly, as he looked out the coach window. "I would imagine her past has more to do with it."

"Why do you say that?" Gwinnie asked.

He shrugged as he turned back to look at her. "I think she would have offered more information before she left. Remember how giddy she was?"

Gwinnie nodded.

"Typically, she's quite serious about her establishment, and the work she's doing."

"Soothcoor told me when she approached him," the duke said. "She was nervous but had everything thought out. His interests three years ago lay primarily in the children. It wasn't until she approached him that he expanded his activities to include women."

"I didn't know that," Gwinnie said slowly. "I assumed he'd come to her with the idea."

The duke shook his head. "No. And he smiled at the memory when he told me— and you know how seldom he smiled before he married the widowed Mrs. Montgomery."

"She certainly has removed his epithet of the 'Dour Earl'," Lewis observed.

Gwinnie and the duke agreed.

A moment later, the carriage drew up before The Thirsty Pig. The duke went on ahead into the building as Lewis assisted Gwinnie to step down out of the carriage and offered his arm to escort her inside. He had to repress a smile as the friendly, ebullient Gwinnie faded away, replaced by Lady Guinevere Nowlton, a queenly woman.

"Thank you, Mr. Martin," she said austerely in her low voice. She disengaged her arm from his and walked over to where her father was greeting the publican.

Lewis looked around and spotted the spare, angular form of Mr. Gedney. Mr. Gedney saw him as well and waved him over to him.

"Is that Soothcoor?" Gedney quietly asked him.

Lewis laughed lightly as he shook his head. "No, that is the Duke of Malmsby and his daughter, Lady Guinevere Nowlton."

"Why are they here?"

"Two reasons. If the earl does not arrive, the duke will stand in at the inquest for his interests in this case."

"There was no communication sent to the earl."

"I believe the duke sent a messenger to him Saturday."

Gedney frowned. "Why is the duke involved? What business is this inquest to him? Did you go to him?"

"No, his daughter did."

"His daughter? I don't understand. What game are you playing, Mr. Martin?"

Lewis spread his hands out. "Me? None."

"Where is Miss Knolls? You were supposed to bring her today so I might question her before the inquest."

Lewis bowed his head slightly. "And I did." He turned toward where Gwinnie stood with her father. "There stands Miss Sarah Knolls." He gestured in her direction. She turned just then to see him, and he bowed to her. She started to walk toward them.

"Martin!" Gedney ground out. "You'll not make a May game of me."

"Lady Guinevere is Miss Knolls. That is what the women at Mrs. Southerland's house know her as."

"Mr. Martin is correct," Gwinnie said coolly. She looked down at Mr. Gedney as she held out her hand to him.

Confused, Mr. Gedney briefly took her hand in his.

"I am Miss Knolls when I am at Mrs. Southerland's."

"Why?"

She raised her chin, her expression haughty. "I should think that would be obvious. It is so the women will be more comfortable with me teaching them."

"Teaching them?" he repeated.

"Proper speech and etiquette, primarily." Her expression hardened as she looked down on him. "Not what you insinuated to others that they were taught!" Anger flared in her eyes, her voice louder. "That you should even dare make that statement judges you poorly, sir, and I address you as *sir* with considerable reservations," she finished with a drawl. She cast another haughty sneering look at him then left them to return to her father's side.

Lewis rocked back on his heels. "I guess she told you!"

"Boot-licker," Gedney sneered at him.

"No, just one of her guards," Lewis returned, watching her. *Bloody hell, she was glorious!* Then he turned back to Gedney. "Use your head, man. Do you think the duke would allow his daughter to go about her charity work in all parts of London alone?"

To Lewis's amusement, Gedney's mouth worked against what he wanted to say. Finally, he said: "You should have said something Saturday night. You should have immediately said who Miss Knolls was."

Lewis shrugged. "Was not my secret to share." He walked back toward Gwinnie and the duke.

The door to the pub opened again to admit the Earl of Soothcoor, followed by Dr. Brogan. Dr. Brogan went immediately to talk to Mr. Gedney.

Gwinnie curtsied to the earl. "Good to see you, my lord."

"Have you grown?" he asked.

She laughed and surreptitiously lifted her skirt a bit to show the height of her heel while raising a finger to her lip with the other hand to shush him."

Soothcoor shook his head. He held his hand out to the duke. "Good to see you, Malmsby. Thank you for your note Saturday."

"Nasty business," the duke said, as they shook hands.

"Agreed. Any clues to who would have done this?"

"Not that I am aware of, but perhaps Mr. Gedney will be able to provide more information at the inquest. If not, I have retained Mr. Martin to pursue the investigation."

Soothcoor nodded. "As I was intending to do." He looked back at Gwinnie. "Lady Guinevere, you will be glad to know I have brought Mrs. Southerland's sister-in-law to take over the establishment temporarily. She does not want to do it full time— nor do I wish her to— however, she is happy to assist at this trying time."

"Her sister-in-law? The same woman who worked for your stepmother?" Gwinnie asked.

"Yes, she was the housekeeper at Soothcoor Mansion. Now that we are selling that property, she is available for other work."

"Father said you were selling the mansion."

"It was Miss Southerland who encouraged Mrs. Southerland to approach me with her idea. She assured her I was a much nicer person than my ugly phiz would suggest."

Gwinnie laughed. "You have never been ugly, my lord, just a might frightening with your dour expression all the time," she teased him.

"I know. I don't know how society put up with me. I'm sure all of society is thanking Lilias for taking me to task."

They smiled at each other.

Soothcoor turned away to look over the assemblage of people. "Dr. Brogan, can we begin yet? Is everyone here?"

"I believe we are just waiting on Mr. Jeffrey Simmons."

"I'm here," called out a paunchy gentleman wearing a bright-blue great coat. He stood at the far end of the bar nursing an ale. "Though I don't know why I am."

"And you are?..."

"A neighbor," Lewis told him.

"Ah, you must be the gentleman who does not wish Mrs. Southerland's establishment to be on Green Street," Gwinnie said austerely.

"That's right," he said pugnaciously. "Doesn't belong here."

"We will discuss all this at the inquest. Shall we all go downstairs for the proceedings?" Soothcoor politely asked.

"I suppose that means I'm to come, too, as Mr. Gedney wanted me here for my testimony and he hasn't taken it yet."

Mr. Gedney cleared his throat. "That won't be necessary, my lady. I understand you were with Mr. Martin last evening. He can speak for both of you."

"I beg your pardon," Gwinnie said, drawing herself up to her full height, "are you inferring he and I..."

"No, no!" Mr. Gedney turned red. "Of course, not, Mr. Martin's much too short—"

"What?" Lewis asked, slouching against the wall, playing into Gwinnie's giantess attire.

Fire leaped in Gwinnie's eyes. She planted her hands on her hips.

"Mr. Gedney," Dr. Brogan broke in. "Stop before you

go any further. I suggested Lady Guinevere join us at the inquest. After my statement of findings, she can provide her deposition and leave, and then we can continue."

"But— but— ladies, society ladies, don't attend inquests," he protested.

"Is that recorded anywhere?"

"No, but everyone knows—"

"Tradition. These are modern times, Mr. Gedney. Sometimes circumstances change and we must accommodate," Dr. Brogan told him.

"After all, the fault is yours," said the duke. "You did not take her statement when she arrived."

"And you would allow her?"

"Lady Guinevere is not recently out of the schoolroom, Mr. Gedney," the duke said.

"Oh, thank you, Father, now I'm an anecdote," Gwinnie complained, but with a glint of humor in her eyes.

Lewis stood away from the wall. "Gentlemen, I suggest you drop the discussion. Lady Guinevere will continue to find a way to hoist you on your own petard." On a sharp intake of breath, he quickly looked at her. "Don't say it, don't even think it," he said, compressing his lips against a laugh.

Gwinnie had opened her mouth with another suggestive retort, but instead, she compressed her lips against another laugh. "Very well, Mr. Martin— this time."

The duke shook his head. "I need to get her married off," he muttered.

"As I was attempting to say, let's begin the inquest," Dr. Brogan said.

CHAPTER 9

THE INQUEST

Gwinnie followed her father down the narrow, worn wood stairs to a cool, stone-walled room. Barrels lined the walls, and on the far wall, a rack held bottles. It was markedly colder and damp down in this room. Lanterns hung on two walls and from the posts at the end of the stairs.

The light flickered. Gwinnie saw a makeshift table had been made of boards set over more barrels. A stained white tablecloth, not as long as the table, had been placed over the boards to provide a touch of respect for the deceased. A body lay under a shroud on the makeshift table.

Dr. Brogan carefully drew back the shroud to Mrs. Southerland's shoulders. Gwinnie could tell she had been disrobed except for her shift. She looked at her, trying to remain calm. She appeared to be sleeping, her gray hair, free of its cap and pins, swirled about her head. Gwinnie took a deep breath.

"First, we will discuss the neck wound, the cause of death. Note how the right side is lower on her neck than the left side, and the cut is clean, while the left side is higher and jagged. This indicates to me the action of the blade was right to left, suggesting the person who sliced Mrs. Southerland's throat did it with their left hand."

Gwinnie raised a gloved hand to her neck as she

breathed deeply. Next to her, Mr. Martin lightly touched her elbow, silently asking if she was alright. She looked at his concerned face and nodded, then turned back to listen to Dr. Brogan.

"So, you are saying we are looking for a left-handed person?" one of the other coroner's men asked.

"Most likely, but not necessarily. This brings me to the second observation. Note the bruising around her mouth. Someone grabbed her from the right, placing a hand over her mouth so she could not cry out. I do not believe Mrs. Southerland gave up without a fight. Under the fingernails of her right hand is skin and blood. On her left hand is blood, most likely her own as she tried to pull the attacker's hand away. There are no other marks on her body," Dr. Brogan finished. He pulled the shroud over her.

"Mr. Gedney?"

"Thank you, Dr. Brogan. Mrs. Southerland was discovered by the back door to her establishment, Mrs. Southerland's House for Unfortunate Women, on Green Street. The discovery was made by two young women: a Miss Marke and a Miss Warden. They were returning from a shopping expedition. I'm told all the residents of the house have Friday afternoon free and often go shopping. There is no curfew on Fridays."

"That is not entirely correct," Gwinnie said. "The doors are locked at 9:00 p.m. Failure to return by that time is grounds for expulsion."

"Expulsion!" another man exclaimed.

"Yes," Gwinnie said simply. "Please continue, Mr. Gedney."

"When I spoke to them, they were still distraught, but said they did not see anyone in the alley or in the small backyard of the townhouse. This is where I would continue, with questioning Lady Guinevere..."

Gwinnie bowed her head slightly, then looked at the men who encircled Mrs. Southerland.

"I arrive at Mrs. Southerland's at 1 p.m. dressed as Miss Sarah Knolls to provide some private, one-on-one training to Miss Petrie. It was her day to serve as housemaid, and I was shadowing her and teaching her what she should know as a housemaid in a great house. Miss Petrie is enthusiastic, but lamentably slow to put activities in a proper sequence," she said.

"Excuse me, Lady Guinevere," one man said. "Why do you go there in the guise of another?"

"For acceptance. These women are intimidated by persons of rank. This is my way of getting them to relax and hear what I am saying, and not worrying so much if they are going to cause an insult."

"I see. Clever," the man said.

"Thank you. It was getting close to teatime, so I joined Mrs. Southerland in the parlor. Serving us tea would be another lesson for Miss Petrie. It was also getting close to the time I knew my father would send someone to escort me home. I was surprised when Mr. Martin arrived. He told me the footman who typically escorted me home had sprained his ankle and the duke, my father, requested Mr. Martin to fetch me instead."

"Mrs. Southerland and I invited him to share tea with us before I had to leave. He agreed and sat down. When Miss Petrie brought up the tea, she had a note for Mrs. Southerland. Mrs. Southerland begged our pardon that she might read it.

"Quite suddenly, she seemed overjoyed with happiness. Giddy as a schoolgirl. Her writing desk was next to her chair in the parlor. She quickly wrote a note, then said she had to go out for a few minutes. Not long, she said, and would Mr. Martin and I remain at the house until she returned. She implied she might have some exciting news on her return. We agreed."

"She never gave you any hint as to what that exciting news might be?" Mr. Gedney asked.

"No, not at all. Mrs. Southerland then asked to borrow my short cape— she didn't want to take the time to go upstairs to get her coat. I agreed, knowing on her it would serve as a long cape. After she left, Mr. Martin and I chatted for the next thirty minutes or so until we heard screaming, and that is when we ran out of the room and down the stairs just as the women managed to get the back door unlocked. Mr. Martin went outside to check on Mrs. Southerland. I escorted the girls and Miss Petrie down to the kitchen, and I requested Miss Petrie to make another pot of tea for the ladies to calm their shock.

"Shortly thereafter, Mr. Martin returned and confirmed she was dead, and advised he needed to fetch the coroner if he was available. I asked him to stop at The Thirsty Pig first. Miss Wooler, the cook, and Mrs. Albert, the housekeeper, liked to go to the pub on Friday afternoons. I was certain he could find them there and send them back to the house. He agreed. I stayed with the women in the house until Mrs. Albert and Miss Wooler arrived. I left the returning women in their care and then went to the parlor to try to write a letter to Lord Soothcoor and to my father. Unfortunately, I couldn't think straight. All I could think about was Mrs. Southerland. I don't know how much time passed before Mr. Martin returned with Dr. and Mrs. Brogan. They decided— over my protests— that I should return to my home. Mr. Martin escorted me in Dr. and Mrs. Brogan's carriage. He dropped me off and I went into Malmsby House and presented my father, the Duke of Malmsby, with the horrible news."

Gwinnie crossed her hands together in front of her as she surveyed the jury. There were excited whispered comments among them.

"If you have finished interrogating my daughter, Mr. Gedney, I will see her home." The duke's irritation was plain in his voice.

"A moment, Your Grace, if you will," said Mr. Simmons from the other side of the table. He bowed when he saw he had the duke's attention.

"And you are?"

"Simmons, Your Grace, Jeffrey Simmons of Simmons Tobacco and Snuff on Bond Street. You might be familiar with us."

"As I neither smoke, chew, nor take snuff, I am not."

"Oh, yes well, I live on Green Street, two houses down from... from that woman's establishment," he said, nodding his head toward Mrs. Southerland's body.

"You're the one Mrs. Albert told me about," Gwinnie said hotly, stepping forward. "You're the one who wants Mrs. Southerland's House for Unfortunate Women closed down!"

"It doesn't belong in a genteel neighborhood," Mr. Simmons retorted. "With her dead, maybe now it will be closed down."

The duke pulled Gwinnie back beside him when she looked ready to explode. "Gwinnie!" he admonished.

"No, Father," Gwinnie said, looking first at him then the Earl of Soothcoor, "he has been canvasing the neighborhood, inciting the other neighbors, writing articles, shouting at the women. He is the nuisance, not the charity."

Soothcoor frowned. He looked at Mr. Simmons. "How long have you lived on Green Street, Mr. Simmons?"

"Eight months, my lord, and I certainly wouldn't have moved there if I knew about *her* presence on the street."

"Mrs. Southerland has been on Green Street for over three years," Gwinnie said hotly.

Soothcoor looked at Gwinnie from under frowning brows and raised his hand to still her words.

Gwinnie compressed her lips and relaxed back against her father's side.

The earl dropped his arms and folded his hands together. "Mr. Simmons, if you have a problem with the location of Mrs. Southerland's establishment, then your problem is with me."

Mr. Simmons's face crumpled in confusion.

"I own that house, and as Lady Guinevere has stated, the charity has been in that location for three years. In that time, it has never had a problem with the neighbors."

"Mr. Simmons, Lord Soothcoor, this is hardly the time or location to have this discussion. We are here to determine the cause of death," Dr. Brogan said.

"I'd have to disagree, Dr. Brogan," Lewis said laconically. He'd been standing more toward the back wall in a shadowy corner where he could see everyone. He stepped forward.

"How do we know Mr. Simmons didn't choose to kill Mrs. Southerland as a way to shut down the charity?" Lewis suggested.

"Such is my thought," declared Gwinnie.

"How dare you, sir! Who are you?" demanded Mr. Simmons.

"Lewis Martin, Bow Street." Lewis did a curt bow in his direction.

Mr. Simmons looked across at Mr. Gedney. "Is that why you invited me to this inquest? So you could accuse me of murder? I won't be a party to this. I'm leaving!" he declared.

"No, you will not," declared the duke. He looked toward Lewis. "Mr. Martin, if you would, please?"

Lewis gained the stairs before Mr. Simmons could get through the other men. He stretched his arms from one stairway post to the other, blocking the stairs.

"Stand aside," Mr. Simmons demanded.

Lewis smiled congenially at him as he shook his head. "Sorry, I can't do that. You heard the Duke of Malmsby, you're not to leave."

"No one is accusing you," Soothcoor said.

"Yet," Gwinnie said.

"Gwinnie," growled her father.

"Dr. Brogan, Mr. Gedney, at what time was Mrs. Southerland killed?" Soothcoor asked.

"Based on when Mr. Martin appeared at my house, and the statement we heard from Lady Guinevere, I'd say between 4:30 and 5:00 p.m.," Dr. Brogan said.

"Mr. Simmons, where were you at that time?"

"At my shop, serving my last customer, Baron Morbank."

"And the baron can vouch for being in your shop with you at this time?" Lewis asked.

"Yes, of course."

"Now, see how easy that was," Lewis said, stepping away from the stairs. "Though I imagine Mr. Gedney will want to know whom you stirred up in the neighborhood so he can question them as well. Your agitations could have caused someone else to commit murder."

"No!" Mr. Simmons protested. "That was never my intent..." He trailed off, looking stricken.

Gwinnie suddenly smiled and bounced on her toes.

"Excuse me." One of the gentlemen brought in as a juror raised his hand.

"Yes?" Dr. Brogan said.

"Mr. Simmons approached me regarding Mrs. Southerland's establishment," he said, almost apologetically.

Dr. Brogan frowned. He looked at the rest of the jurors. "Were any others of you approached by Mr. Simmons, or otherwise engaged in negative discussions about Mrs. Southerland's?"

Four gentlemen raised their hands.

"That has certainly thrown the fat into the fire," Lewis whispered.

"What do you mean?" Gwinnie whispered back.

He nodded toward the coroner.

Dr. Brogan pushed back the edges of his jacket and settled his hands on his hips as he turned to face his officer. "Mr. Gedney, what instructions did you give the parish constable when you requested he gather a jury?" he asked tightly.

Mr. Gedney flushed. "Nothing in particular, Dr. Brogan."

Dr. Brogan took in a deep breath. "Gentlemen, any of you who have had discussions with Mr. Simmons, please provide your names to my clerk. You are dismissed from the jury but expect to be recalled as witnesses. This inquest is adjourned for three hours to allow for jurors— without prior connection to either Mrs. Southerland or Mr. Simmons— to be found as your replacements,"

"Will I need to repeat my deposition for the new jurors this afternoon?" Gwinnie asked.

"No, my lady," Dr. Brogan said in a kinder tone, his hands easing from his hips. "The clerk will read your statement."

"Mr. Gedney, if you would take over now?" Lewis suggested. He attempted to repress a smile at Gedney's discomfiture. The man would actually have to do some work.

"Lady Guinevere and I are leaving," the duke said. "Thank you, Mr. Martin, for your assistance. Please carry on, I shall expect a report this afternoon."

Lewis stepped away from the stairway as the duke and Gwinnie made their way to the stairs. He had to smile when he noted Gwinnie positioning herself so she passed near Mr. Simmons and could look down on him. She whispered something to him Lewis couldn't hear. The man visibly swallowed and stepped back.

CHAPTER 10
ROSE

Gwinnie was taking the pins out of her hair when Rose entered her dressing room to assist her with changing clothes. "What are you doing? I thought you wanted that complicated coronet hairstyle this morning. I certainly worked hard enough on it."

Gwinnie laughed. "I did, then. It fit nicely in my poke bonnet. Between the hat and my shoes, I believe I was four inches taller." She pulled another pin from her hair and began to unwind the plait. She frowned as she looked in the mirror. "Unfortunately, it didn't have the effect I'd hoped it would have."

"And how is that, my lady?" Rose asked.

"I was striving for intimidation, but I don't think I achieved that. I think the only thing I achieved was the label of being an eccentric."

"Well, that's not so terrible, is it?"

"I believe that is what all unmarried women of a certain age are considered. But where I failed, Mr. Martin succeeded."

"Being intimidating?"

"No, quite the opposite, by being full of good humor! He laughed at mishaps, and he laughed at things forgotten. Interestingly, both scenarios had Mr. Gedney furious, but he couldn't say anything because no one else took his words amiss. It was comical. Mr. Gedney was like an escaped bonnet caught on a tree branch, dancing in the wind." She smiled at the inquest memory.

"You like him, don't you?"

"Who?" Gwinnie asked.

"Mr. Martin, of course."

Gwinnie looked up in the mirror to see Rose's face behind her. "Not in the manner you are suggesting," she demurred. "He is a comfortable gentleman for me to talk to. You are fully aware I find that so seldom. To other gentlemen, I am *The Duke's Daughter*," she said with sarcastic emphasis. "The only other man I've been able to talk that easily with is my brother."

"What does he do differently?" Rose asked.

Gwinnie thought for a moment. "You will be shocked if I tell you," she said.

"Does he importune you?"

"No, however, he allows his humor to be suggestive," she said with a slight smile, "and we banter back and forth as I did with Lancelot before he married Cassie and moved out of Malmsby House. I miss that repartee."

"Well, if you like him, why don't you encourage him to court you?"

"Rose, he is shorter than I am and is not of our social circle."

Rose looked at her through the mirror, a sour expression on her face.

"What?" Gwinnie asked, seeing Rose's expression

"Do you think your family would truly care?"

"Yes!"

"Why? Are you forgetting your Aunt Elizabeth?" Rose asked.

"My Aunt Elizabeth?"

"She married a potter. Did your family spurn her?"

Gwinnie looked down at her dressing table, replete with porcelain pieces for storing hair pins, face powders, hair powder, and perfumes. "No-o— but she is a clay artist herself. It made sense she would fall in love with a gentleman who shared her passion for clay."

"What about her daughter, your cousin, Helena? She was not born into society, yet she married an earl."

"But we are her family, and we are society."

Rose rolled her eyes.

Gwinnie could not help but smile at her action.

"You will contrive to find fault whatever I say, won't you?" Rose asked.

"Probably," Gwinnie admitted, her shoulders slumping. Why was she making excuses? She *was* drawn to Lewis, as she thought of him now. She'd never met a man who wasn't in her family who made her laugh like Lewis did. And those blue eyes— sometimes, when they looked at her, she felt her insides trembling. She wanted to reach out and touch him. In her bed at night, with the bed curtains pulled, her thoughts turned carnal. She imagined him in ways she had never imagined any man— real or fantasy. She bit her lower lip to stop her wayward thoughts. They would never suit. Would they?

There was a knock on her dressing room door. Rose answered it.

"Excuse me, Lady Gwinnie," said the maid, Mercy. "The duke says as how the Earl of Norwalk's party shall be here in forty minutes. He asks that you join them all in the first-floor gold parlor."

"Thank you, Mercy. I will," Gwinnie said. "Rose, please fetch my forest-green gown."

Rose nodded. "That is a lovely gown on you." She went to the cupboard.

"You don't think it is too fancy for a meeting? Or do you think I should wear black for Mrs. Southerland?"

"I think a mourning dress would not be appropriate, as you are not family; however, if you wish to show some regard for the deceased, you could carry your black shawl and wear your late mother's black onyx parure."

"Hmmm," Gwinnie said thoughtfully. "I like your idea. Let's do that. But just the earbobs and bracelet. The necklace would be too much."

"As you wish," Rose said, as she helped her into the green dress. Afterward, Rose brushed her long, dark-red hair. "Do you wish me to put it back up in the coronet style?"

"No, that made my head ache," Gwinnie told her,

which, while true, was not her real reason. She did not want to tower over Mr. Martin as she had earlier in the day. "Just do the bun-roll you often do at the base of my neck."

"Of course. We'll secure it with pins and your black hair comb."

"Yes, perfect. I don't know what I would do without you," Gwinnie said, smiling at her long-time lady's maid.

Gwinnie saw Rose's expression fall. Something was wrong.

"Rose?"

"Yes, miss?" Rose said, forcing a smile and brightness to her face.

"What is it?"

Rose shook her head vigorously. "Nothing, miss." She began picking up clothes about the room, her face averted from Gwinnie's.

Gwinnie stood up and went over to Rose, laying a hand on her arm to stop her. "I messed it up, didn't I?"

"I don't know what you mean," Rose said with forced lightness. "Excuse me, I want to get the room straightened."

"The room can wait."

"And you need to go downstairs to the company."

"Company can wait. We've been together a long time. When I said I don't know what I would do without you, you crumbled. Rose, that is only an expression to show my appreciation. I would never stand in your way. What is it you want to do? Away from me?"

Rose stood straight and held her head high, though she worried her hands before her. "I know I am only a lady's maid, but I thought— I thought I would ask Lord Soothcoor if he might consider me for a position with one of his charities... I've come to enjoy the work we've done and would like to do more."

Gwinnie looked at her, stunned for a moment, then smiled, her eyes shining. "Yes!" she said. "A glorious *yes*! I support you, though you have to help me find your replacement."

An Artful Decision

"Yes, miss. Of course, miss, but there is no saying he will accept me."

"Oh, he will," Gwinnie said.

She stepped forward to hug her maid, startling Rose. Such intimacy was not done between mistress and maid. Rose tentatively hugged her back.

"Now I'd best get downstairs. I'm already late as it is. We'll discuss how you can approach him tomorrow."

"Thank you, Lady Gwinnie," Rose said. "Thank you."

Gwinnie grabbed the shawl from the back of the dressing-table chair where Rose had draped it, threw it around her shoulders, and went out of the room and downstairs to the parlor.

~

GWINNIE WALKED into the gold parlor while Mercy was organizing the tea and mini-sandwiches on the table between the two front windows.

"Ah, I am not late," she said, as she entered the room.

Her cousin rose from her seat next to their grandmother, the dowager duchess. "Come sit by us!" Helena invited.

"I should be delighted," Gwinnie said, coming up to her to give her a kiss on the cheek. "I apologize for my behavior Friday evening. I had hardly even noted you were here, and I truly am happy to see you."

"You were distraught. Understandable with that awful murder. You know we were with the Galboroughs on Saturday. They couldn't decide if the charity Mrs. Southerland led was a good institution or not."

"I am not surprised," drawled her grandmother. "They are a sanctimonious pair. Thankfully their children are not."

"Mother, that is enough," Gwinnie's father said.

The dowager duchess shrugged nonchalantly. "You take away an old woman's fun. So, please introduce us to the gentleman standing at attention behind you."

The duke nodded and turned to look behind him. "This is Tom Cott, veteran of the 88th Regiment Foot, pugilist, and associate of Mr. Martin. He has agreed to provide escort and guard services for my family and yours, Norwalk, while you remain in London."

"Arthur, you are being ridiculous again," dismissed the Dowager Countess of Norwalk.

"Charlotte, you did not see the body of Mrs. Southerland with her slit throat. Gwinnie and I did this morning at the inquest."

"You poor thing," exclaimed Helena, grabbing Gwinnie's hand.

"Yes, what happened at the inquest?" Norwalk asked.

"Nothing. Gwinnie gave her statement, then the inquest was adjourned," the duke said disgustedly.

"Adjourned? Why?"

"Four jurors had information relevant to the inquest so they could not serve on the jury."

"Arthur, when will the inquest reconvene?" his mother asked.

"Hopefully, this afternoon, if the coroner can get the jurors replaced," the duke said.

"Do you need to be at the continuation of the inquest?" Helena asked.

"I gave my statement this morning, so they said they would read my statement to the new jurors," Gwinnie said.

"Soothcoor and Mr. Martin will be in attendance," the duke explained.

"What do you think will be the outcome of the inquest?" asked Helena.

"Nothing."

"Death by persons unknown," Gwinnie said lugubriously.

"That is so sad," Helena said.

"And not acceptable," growled the duke. "Until I am comfortable in the knowledge that the woman wasn't killed in a case of mistaken identity, we can't rule out the validity of the threats Charlotte and I have received."

"Agreed," said Norwalk.

"Ridiculous," said the Dowager Countess.

"No, Mother, it is not. I think we should leave London tomorrow."

"But my club!" protested his mother.

"Will be safer without you there. You have a general manager to manage the club," Norwalk said.

"But I'd planned some seminars for the members," she protested.

"Write a pamphlet," her son said curtly.

The Dowager Countess frowned at him. "You and Helena can return. I will stay here."

"No."

"Norwalk!" protested his mother.

"Charlotte," Helena said softly. She placed her hand over her womb. "I should feel better if I had your company."

Lady Norwalk looked at her daughter-in-law. Her expression softened. "All right. If you all insist— though I still disagree on the need."

"Thank you," Helena said, looking down.

The earl and his mother began making plans with input from the duke. The dowager duchess grasped the hand of Helena. "Well played!" she whispered.

Helena grinned. "But Grandmother, I learned from you."

Gwinnie fell backward against the sofa cushions, laughing softly.

CHAPTER 11
WHITE'S CLUB

Lewis handed the footman at White's his card. "I am meeting Lord Soothcoor here for dinner," he said softly, with his winningest smile. He knew the footman was staring at his card, wondering if he should be let in as the card identified him as a Bow Street agent. He looked Lewis up and down, then back at the card. He handed the card to the club's butler.

Lewis knew his attire was fitting for the club. After the inquest, he'd gone back to his house to check on Daniel and write his reports for the Duke of Malmsby and Lord Soothcoor. He hadn't been there long when he received a note from the Earl of Soothcoor, asking him to meet him at White's for dinner and a discussion of a direction for the investigation.

He dressed in gray trousers and a dark blue cut-away jacket. His waistcoat was a blue, gray, black, and white jacquard print. His cravat was tied elegantly, but not too high. He wore one fob which connected to his pocket watch tucked into the left front pocket of his waistcoat. What they couldn't see, and would get him expelled, was the small arms pistol tucked at the small of his back. A muff pistol typically carried by a lady, but a size he'd found handy when wearing the fashionable cut-away jacket.

"Certainly, Mr. Martin, Lord Soothcoor is expecting you," the butler said.

Lewis nodded and handed the footman his greatcoat, hat, and gloves, then followed the butler through the main gathering room.

"Lord Soothcoor has reserved a private dining room; it is over this way," the butler said, as they walked among various pieces of furniture.

Suddenly a young man stood up, stepping out of the circle of his friends seated near the fireplace. "Lewis, what are you doing here?" the man asked, his tone belligerent.

Lewis stopped and turned in his direction. Why now, and why here, he thought. Jack Rockwell, Earl of Harleigh— and his half-brother. "Lord Harleigh," he said, bowing in his direction.

"You don't belong here," Harleigh said.

"Not as a member, no. Lord Soothcoor requested I meet him here. The butler is conducting me to him now." Lewis started to turn away.

"Oh God, now I'll have to see your ugly phiz at dinner. Quite ruin my appetite."

Lewis stopped, turned back, and laughed. "Not to worry, Brother, the butler has informed me Lord Soothcoor has secured a private dining room."

"Brother!" another man said. "Didn't know you had a brother, Jack— Has kind of the look of you though, through the chin and lips and that blond hair of yours, of course."

"He does not!" Harleigh denied.

"Why haven't we seen you about, before?" another man asked.

"Mr. Martin, is there a problem?" the Earl of Soothcoor said from the door to the private parlor.

"My brother has taken exception to seeing me here in his club."

"Half-brother!" Jack insisted. "Half."

"Ah," the first man who spoke said. "By-blow," he said sagely.

Lewis grinned at them all, raised a hand in farewell, and walked toward Soothcoor.

"I am sorry about that scene, my lord."

"Nonsense. I've sensed the connection since I met you. You resemble your father more than he does."

"Thank you, my lord. I take that as a compliment. The earl was a good father despite circumstances. Jack and I were raised together, and everything was fine until Father died."

"I take it the countess always resented you and turned her son against you?"

"Yes, especially as my father left me a competence. Not done, you know, leaving a competence to a by-blow," Lewis said with a smile.

"I had nearly the same situation happen to me, only my father was married to my mother. There was a time when my stepmother would have been happy if I and my next brother would have died so her prodigy could inherit. Thankfully, circumstances have occurred for her to learn the error of her ways," he said drily.

Lewis laughed. "No chance of that happening with the Dowager Countess of Harleigh and her son."

"Their loss. I am honored to know you, Mr. Martin."

"Thank you, my lord," Lewis said, bowing to the earl.

"Let's have dinner before we get down to murder discussions. Better for our digestion," Soothcoor wryly observed, as he sat down at the table and waved for Lewis to join him.

Their dinner conversation was surprisingly lively. Lewis found himself admiring the earl for his charitable interests, which seemed to be far-reaching and varied.

"How do you support so many charitable causes?" he finally asked, as the servants cleared away their dinner and left them with a bottle of brandy on the table.

Soothcoor smiled slightly as he leaned back in his chair. One strand of his straight, black-and-silver hair fell over his eyes. He pushed it away. "Guilt," he said.

"Guilt? What have you to be guilty of?" Lewis asked.

Soothcoor laughed. "Not me, my dear fellow, my peers

in the House of Lords, primarily. If I can't get them to provide the government money needed to help people struggling to live, I get it from their own pockets," he said. "I'm sure I would have more to work with if I had government funds; however, I will take from their personal coffers just as readily— And once a year I publish the accomplishments and challenges of the charities and list the benefactors. No one wants their name missing from my list."

Lewis laughed. "Well done. But I suppose we must finally get down to business, as distasteful as it is. What was your opinion of how the inquest went today after Mr. Gedney supplied new jurors?" Lewis asked.

Soothcoor compressed his lips as he shook his head. "I was extremely disappointed in Dr. Brogan. He does not manage Mr. Gedney appropriately."

Lewis nodded. "I agree. However, I believe the problem is he doesn't know how to. I don't think Dr. Brogan wanted to be the coroner; he was more or less forced into the position. He is a doctor, not a legal professional, and doesn't understand the legal profession and what should be done in the case of a murder such as Mrs. Southerland's. He is not a bad man, just without knowledge."

Soothcoor nodded. "And, as he inherited Gedney with his position, he has used— without question— Gedney to tell him how things need to go on."

"Truth from the mouth of Mr. Reginal Gedney," Lewis said, raising his glass.

Soothcoor snorted. He took a sip of brandy. "Is there a coroner in London from whom Dr. Brogan could learn?"

Lewis rubbed his chin as he thought. "I don't deal with coroners throughout London, but maybe Mr. Vincenze in the City."

"I'll make the suggestion to Dr. Brogan," Soothcoor said. "I am not satisfied with the inquest closing on the verdict: Death by Misadventure by person or persons unknown."

Lewis agreed. "But now that the inquest is over, a real investigation can begin."

"Without Mr. Gedney," the earl said.

"Yes." Lewis took his notebook and a pencil out of his jacket pocket, opened it, and laid it on the table in front of him. "What can you tell me about Mrs. Southerland's past?" Lewis asked.

"You think the murderer could be someone from her past?" the earl asked.

"That is one of several areas that should be explored — to some degree or another."

Soothcoor frowned. "Explain, please, the areas to explore."

"Mrs. Southerland was wearing Lady Guinevere's short cape. It was made in Austria and has distinctive embroidery along the edge."

"Are you suggesting Lady Guinevere was the intended victim? What about the height difference between them?"

"No, I'm not suggesting that; I'm saying it is one of the areas that must be investigated, as Malmsby has received threatening letters from individuals afraid of the new inventions he champions."

"Luddites?"

Lewis shook his head. "No, but probably those who would follow in the footsteps of the Luddites. And, what was not mentioned at the inquest is that Mrs. Southerland had been standing on the first step when she was attacked. It wouldn't have made her as tall as Lady Guinevere, but taller than she is."

"Ah, now I comprehend why this area of possibility can't just be dismissed."

"Then, there is the possibility Mr. Simmons did cause someone to take such a dislike to Mrs. Southerland and her house that they took the matter in their own hands to dispatch her, and the last possibility is— of course— a footpad. Of all the scenarios I have put forward, the last is the least likely, to my mind; however, it must be examined, and based on the witness testimony this afternoon, Mrs. Southerland's neighbors did not take exception to what she did."

"Two gentlemen came over to me privately afterward

to let me know they each had a servant at their house that came from Mrs. Southerland's, and they thought them excellent help," Soothcoor said.

"I believe that, after talking to Lady Guinevere. They took seriously their calling to educate these women for success— whether that be in service or in a shop."

Soothcoor nodded. "If you wish to know more about Mrs. Southerland's past, the best person for you to talk to is my stepmother's former housekeeper at Soothcoor Mansion. She contacted me yesterday and offered she take charge of Mrs. Southerland's House for Unfortunate Women until I can find a replacement. Under the circumstances, you can imagine my delight in the offer."

Lewis's brow's furrowed and his frown deepened. "Someone has already approached you to step in to help? Did this person know Mrs. Southerland well?"

Soothcoor laughed. "Fairly well! She is her sister-in-law! Her brother was Mr. Southerland. As Mrs. Southerland was her sister-in-law, she said she knew how things worked at the charity house. She is also the person who recommended Mrs. Southerland to me."

Lewis straightened, pleased. "That is excellent news. And she may well be just the person to help us decipher the note Mrs. Southerland wrote before she left."

"What do you mean 'decipher the note'?" Soothcoor asked.

"After Mrs. Southerland received the note mentioned at the inquest, she hurried to leave. First, however, she wrote a note using a pencil. She was so excited, she pressed hard on the under paper. Lady Guinevere was able to shave pencil graphite over it to pull out some of what was written."

"You did not mention this at the inquest."

"No," Lewis replied.

Soothcoor looked at him silently.

Lewis explained, "Neither Lady Guinevere nor I believe Mr. Gedney would act upon this information as it is incomplete. However, once it was presented at the inquest, it would become a matter of record, and we might lose any advantage we might gain from having this partial note."

"May I see it?" asked the earl.

"Certainly, my lord." Lewis removed the paper which he had protected between blank pieces of paper, from an inner jacket pocket. He handed it to Soothcoor.

My darling, yes! I have p ayed for his. I don't know wheth r t lau or cry. Take this note to butler at venor Squa . He'll s th t e. Foll i n ucti

"When she first started writing she pressed harder than when she continued. This is all that came through with the graphite," Lewis explained.

"The Grosvenor Square address could be the Soothcoor Mansion," Soothcoor said slowly. "However, the house is vacant. No servants are there. That is where my stepmother primarily resided until last spring. Now she makes her Appleton Estate her primary residence, though it is seven miles outside of London. I have decided to sell the Grosvenor property. Lilias and I are looking to purchase a smaller house on Berkley Square."

"Would Mrs. Southerland have known this?" Lewis asked.

"I don't know. She did know that Lady Soothcoor and I have been living in Lilias's townhouse that she had before our marriage."

"Can you think of anyone else whose house is in Grosvenor Square that might be where Mrs. Southerland would send someone?"

"No. This might also be a question for the sister-in-law who has temporarily taken over the charity."

"Yes, you mentioned her before. What is her full name?" Lewis asked, pulling his notebook toward him.

"Miss Millie Southerland."

Lewis looked up. "She never married?"

"No." Soothcoor held up the paper Lewis had handed him to the candlelight. "A few more letters can be seen that could not be captured by the graphite."

My darling, yes! I have prayed for this. I don't know wheth r t laug or cry. Take this note to butler at Gro venor Squa e. He'll see th t e. Follow his instructi ns

"That does fill in a few places but not enough to know the intention. I am curious by the salutation," Lewis said.

"As am I," agreed the earl.

"I will call upon Mrs. Southerland's house tomorrow to speak with Miss Southerland."

"I suggest you take Lady Guinevere with you, or she is liable to sneak out to go there on her own. I don't envy Malmsby trying to keep track of her," Soothcoor said drily.

Lewis nodded. "I will do so. Thank you for dinner this evening." He rose from his chair. Soothcoor followed him to the door. "I know you will be expecting regular updates. So will Malmsby. Will it concern you if I copy one letter for the two of you?"

"Nonsense," Soothcoor said as he opened the door. "Do what is more expeditious; however, I will expect to hear from you tomorrow."

"And so you shall, my lord," Lewis said, bowing to the earl.

In the main room, his half-brother, Jack, still sat at his table, his cronies gone to other activities. It was obvious to Lewis that Jack was well into his cups.

"Come, Jack. Let me see you home."

"I don't need your help."

"Maybe not. At least let me be your escort."

"Escort? I don't need an escort," he protested.

"Yes, you might, from footpads who take advantage of drunk members of the peerage."

"I'm not drunk," his brother protested, as Lewis helped him to his feet. He hiccupped then stumbled, trying to get his feet underneath himself. "You don't have it all, you know," he said slyly.

"Come on, easygoing," said Lewis. He signaled to a hovering waiter to assist him. Together they got Jack to the entrance hall where a footman took over from the waiter and helped Lewis get Jack's coat on him.

"Hail a hack, please."

"Immediately, sir," said the footman. He left the door open as he ran down the steps to hail the hack, then came back to help Lewis get him downstairs, out the door, and up into the carriage.

"I can walk," Harleigh protested, trying to pull away from Lewis. "Never talked to old Scruthers, did you?" Harleigh laughed. "Mother saw to that." He started to slide off the carriage seat. Lewis pulled him up and sat next to him, holding him in place.

"Does Lady Harleigh still live with you?" Lewis asked.

Harleigh snorted, his head lolling around. "As if I could get rid of her. Doesn't like my wife. Too bad. I love Cornelia!" Jack exclaimed loudly, he hiccupped, then his head dropped to his chest, and he began to snore.

Lewis wondered what Jack had been talking about, saying he didn't have it all, then mentioning Mr. Scruthers, his father's solicitor, and saying his mother prevented Mr. Scruthers from speaking to him. Mr. Scruthers wrote to ask how and where he wanted the funds invested from his inheritance, but Lewis had not been invited to the reading of the will, nor had he visited Mr. Scruthers.

He leaned his head back against the seat cushions. A mistake? And why had Jack been so antagonistic at White's? Typically, if they ran into each other, head bows were exchanged, but no words, which had suited Lewis. Lewis rubbed his forehead. He was tired this night after staying up late in Daniel's room, watching over the boy. He needed sleep.

When they reached the Earl of Harleigh's London house, the coachman helped Lewis get Jack out of the carriage and up the front steps.

Lewis rang the bell several times before it was answered.

"Your master enjoyed himself a bit much this evening," he said with a grunt, as he guided Jack's nearly limp form into the house as the coachman ran back to his carriage.

An older woman came down the stairs holding a candle. "You! What did you do to my son?"

"I brought him home."

"How dare you ply him with drinks." Her eyes narrowed as she stared at him. "What was your intent you hateful, devious creature?"

"What's going on?" said a pretty, younger woman coming down the stairs.

"Nothing," the older woman said. "Go back to bed, Cornelia."

The younger woman in a pink dressing gown ran lightly down the stairs, ignoring the older woman. "Jack! Jack!" She cupped his face in her hands. She looked at Lewis. "Is he hurt," she asked, worriedly.

Lewis shook his head. "Not at the moment, but no doubt he will have a devil of a head in the morning."

"Oh, drunk," she said, stepping back. She looked at him sadly.

"If I step away from him, he will fall to the floor. Do you have footmen or grooms to carry him upstairs?" Lewis said, as he maneuvered Jack against the wall.

"I shall get Gurney and Ross," said the butler. He disappeared into a back hallway.

"Was he at a... a..." the woman tried to ask, blushing.

"He was at White's with some of his friends," Lewis said. This woman must be his wife. She was a pretty little thing. He hadn't realized his half-brother had married; however, since their father had died, they had not been close. Looked like Jack had done well.

The woman's brow furrowed, looking at him as if seeing him for the first time since he'd arrived with Jack. "You look like Jack," she said, confusion evident in her blue eyes and on her porcelain complexion.

"Yes," Lewis said. He didn't want to say more. He didn't know what, if anything, Jack would want to say about their relationship.

"He is just another blond guttersnipe," the dowager Ccountess said, sneering. She locked her arms across her chest. "What is it you want, Mr. Martin. Whatever it is, you will get nothing!"

"I wanted to ensure Jack got home safely, my lady, whether you choose to believe that or not. Ah, here are your servants to carry Jack to bed."

The two burly manservants went under Jack's arms to half carry him, half lead him upstairs.

"Thank you," Lewis said as he stepped away. "Now that you have him, safe at home, I shall take my leave."

He opened the front door. Behind him, he heard his stepmother mutter, "Good riddance."

"Mama, why?" he heard Jack's wife ask as the door closed behind him.

He looked up and down the street. The carriage was gone, and this was not a street hacks traveled for fares. "No good deed goes unpunished." He pulled his scarf up higher on his neck and pulled his hat down. Tucking his gloved hands in his pockets, he began to walk the two blocks to a busier thoroughfare and hopefully an empty carriage.

CHAPTER 12

MISS MILLIE SOUTHERLAND

The next morning, Gwinnie and Rose climbed into the ducal carriage, followed by Mr. Martin sitting in the rear-facing seat. They were all going to Mrs. Southerland's House.

Nerves had Gwinnie plucking at a fold in her coat, scratching at an imaginary bit of fluff.

She'd never been to Mrs. Southerland's as the daughter of a duke. She'd always gone as Sarah Knolls, the daughter of a solicitor. It was a deceit, and she couldn't carry on the deceit now that she had been a witness at the inquest as Lady Guinevere and not Sarah Knolls. Mrs. Southerland had stressed honesty to the women. How would the women take the knowledge of her deceit? And Mrs. Southerland's admonitions? How would they take her being a duke's daughter?

She bit the corner of her lip. She loved them all dearly and wanted the best for every one of the women who lived there. Would they believe her or think her just another wealthy lady out doing charity for a lark?

She looked out the window. No one could understand the burden of being a duke's daughter. It was certainly unique to the position. Yes, others might laugh at the idea that being a duke's daughter was hard. It wasn't difficult, not like so many lives were. It was bound up with so many rules, so many expectations— not just from within her family, but from society!

Gwinnie wryly acknowledged she had managed to thwart most of those rules. But her grandmother had once warned her there was a danger in flaunting her ability to ignore the rules too much. And if she did that too often, others in the Ton, in high society, who had once admired her would turn to ridiculing her. She might be able to handle that, she mused with a bit of false bravado; however, her quartet would likely lose engagements, and the others in her group needed the money a concert paid to support their families. She wouldn't do anything to hurt them.

And she could not forget the role her height and large-boned stature had in her society image.

But it wasn't society she worried about today. It was the reactions of ten women who had made the hard decision to leave their lives in the brothels, the stews, the pubs, and the theater background players to carve new lives for themselves. Would they feel betrayed?

"You look solemn, Lady Guinevere," said Lewis, seated across from her.

She nodded. "I am. I'm a little frightened."

He tilted his head. "Frightened?" he queried.

Rose turned to look at her as well.

"I had an easy camaraderie with the women in the house. How will they treat me today?"

"Do you intend to be different as the daughter of a duke compared to the daughter of a solicitor?" Lewis asked

"Gracious, no. I am who I am."

"Precisely," Lewis said, nodding.

"He is right, mi lady," said Rose. "I've always seen Sarah as you, just in different clothes. Don't get haughty-like because you think they expect you to be haughty. That's not who you are."

"I know. But it is so much easier to say than to do. Haughty is an easy defense from fear."

"No 'tis not. Not for you." Rose said forcefully, from the position of trusted servant. "Relax. Smile. Laugh.

That is what Sarah Knolls did. That is what you do most of the time— unless you get to harassing your brother."

"Does she harass Lord Lakehurst?" Lewis asked.

Rose laughed. "Every chance she gets— and he does the same. Now that her brother has his own home, she must find a new target for her wit."

Gwinnie passed Rose a sour look.

"If it would make you feel better, Lady Guinevere, you may target me," offered Lewis, with a droll smile.

That drew a laugh from Gwinnie. "I thank you for your offer, Mr. Martin, but I don't know you well enough, and it would be looked down upon for me to twit an agent of the law."

"Looked down upon by whom?" he countered.

She thought a moment. "I don't know, it just strikes me as unseemly," she said uncomfortably.

He shrugged. "I have a thick skin, my lady. Let us leave it as an open possibility should you see an occasion to use me as the butt of your wit. You can do so, and I shall not take it amiss. And you might feel better for doing it."

Gwinnie laughed again. "You are a strange man, Mr. Martin."

He shrugged, then grinned at her with the cheeky grin she'd grown to love seeing. It made his blue eyes sparkle with his good humor, and she often found herself smiling with good humor back at him.

She loved this man's attitude. And he did laugh a lot, which she thought delightful. Too many men took themselves far too seriously. It was quite off-putting. She often did not take herself that seriously. How could she, being a woman over six feet tall?

At least he put her in better humor for meeting Miss Southerland, she thought, as the carriage drew up before Mrs. Southerland's House for Unfortunate Women.

~

"Hello, Mrs. Albert," Gwinnie said softly when Mrs. Albert opened the door. Rose knocked her arm. When

Gwinnie looked at her, she saw her frown and knew she was reminding her to act naturally.

"Sarah?" the housekeeper asked uncertainly.

"Yes," Gwinnie said, louder and with more confidence, "— and Lady Guinevere Nowlton," she said.

"Well, I'll be!" the woman said. "Oh, excuse me, my lady," she said, curtsying.

"No, no, no! None of that," Gwinnie requested. "I'm still Sarah, too. May we come in? We— Mr. Martin and I — would like to meet with Miss Southerland, if we may?"

"Oh, gracious, yes. Come in, come in," the flustered Mrs. Albert said. "Let me go see if Miss Southerland can see you."

"Thank you," Gwinnie said.

Mrs. Albert hurried up the stairs.

She came down a moment later. "Miss Southerland would be delighted to see you," she said. "If you'll follow me..."

"No need to show us up, we well know the way," Gwinnie said, going up before her.

"I'll have tea brought up, then," Mrs. Albert said, her tone a bit confused.

"That would be splendid," Gwinnie smiled, looking back at her as she continued up the stairs.

"Miss Southerland?" Gwinnie said from the open doorway.

"Please come in, Lady Guinevere," Miss Southerland said, rising from what had been Mrs. Southerland's favorite chair to greet them. A momentary pang stabbed Gwinnie's chest.

Gwinnie was surprised to see Miss Southerland was at least ten years younger than Mrs. Southerland had been. Only slight gray winged her temples, her hair otherwise a rich, dark chestnut brown. She did not wear a cap, as she had never been married, but wore her hair in a severe chignon that strangely suited her features. She stood of medium height and was on the thin side, which caused her cheeks to draw in. She'd donned mourning black for her deceased sister-in-law. As she approached them, she displayed a studied, pleasant— if reserved— expression.

"The Earl of Soothcoor sent me a note this morning saying you would be coming by. He had instructed me to be wary of visitors until we can understand more about Hilda's death," she said.

"That was wise of the earl. I'm Lewis Martin, from Bow Street. Lord Soothcoor and Lady Guinevere's father, the Duke of Malmsby, have charged me with investigating her death and keeping you ladies safe."

Miss Southerland blinked at him. "That is a large expectation for one man, Mr. Martin."

He smiled at her. "Yes ma'am. You are astute. I have assistance, Lord Soothcoor insisted. You have watchers and your young women will have escorts when they go out, for the time being."

She frowned. "You work closely with Lord Soothcoor, then?" she asked.

"Yes. With Lord Soothcoor, and with His Grace, the Duke of Malmsby. They are adamant about the safety of those who come in and out of this house, in light of what happened to Mrs. Southerland."

"That is reassuring," Miss Southerland said with a strained smile. "Please won't you come in and sit down?"

"I should also introduce you to my maid, Rose. She instructs the young women on what it means to be a lady's maid."

"I am pleased to meet you, Rose. I'd wager what you tell them as the role of a lady's maid is more than they suppose," she said archly.

"Yes, miss. They assume it is the job with the least responsibilities and claim an interest in that role— at least until they get a good understanding and realize it may be more arduous, depending on the mistress one works for," Rose said drily.

They all laughed.

"Would you allow me to go downstairs to the kitchen? I wouldn't want the women to see me drinking tea with you and think they will do that as a lady's maid."

Miss Southerland looked at Rose with a different expression. One leaning toward respect. Gwinnie was happy to see that.

"Yes, Rose. That would be fine," Miss Southerland said.

Rose looked at Gwinnie.

Gwinnie nodded.

After Rose left, Gwinnie and Mr. Martin took the same seats they'd had four nights ago, the night Mrs. Southerland died.

"I assume you came to meet me, as I am taking over for Hilda," Miss Southerland said primly, folding her hands in her lap. "Do you have any particular questions you'd like to ask?"

"Yes, I do," spoke up Lewis before Gwinnie could respond. "I'd like to know some of Mrs. Southerland's past."

"Why would you need to know about her past?"

"The night she died, I'd come here to escort Lady Guinevere home. While I was here, Mrs. Southerland received a letter that made her quite happy. She said she had to go out for a short time, and would Lady Guinevere and I stay here until she returned. We agreed. We— Lady Guinevere and I— believe the letter might have been from someone in her past."

"Based on her reaction to the contents of the letter?" Miss Southerland asked.

Lewis nodded.

"What did she say about it?" Miss Southerland asked, almost anxiously.

"Only that it was wonderful news, and she had to go out for a short while and would I and Lady Guinevere stay here until she returned," Lewis told her.

Miss Southerland tapped a fingertip against her lips, frowning. "Interesting. Happy, you say?"

"Exceedingly," Gwinnie said. "She quickly grabbed a pencil and paper and dashed off a note which she took with her."

"Happy," Miss Southerland repeated softly. Then she shook her head, as if shaking off her thoughts, and looked back at Mr. Martin, smiling again. "Well, what can

I tell you?" she began, sitting straighter in her chair. She folded her hands neatly in her lap.

There was a knock on the parlor door.

"Come in," Miss Southerland called out in a syrupy, singsong voice.

"Can someone open it for me," came a plaintive voice from the other side.

"Oh, no, Polly Petrie," Gwinnie said, laughing with Lewis. She stood up.

"What?" Miss Southerland protested.

"Polly has been slow to learn the proper way to do things," Gwinnie said over her shoulder to Miss Southerland as she went to open the door.

With the door open, Polly just stood there staring at Gwinnie. "You're so beautiful, Miss Knolls."

"Thank you, Polly, but don't stand there holding the tea tray; come in and set the tea service down on the table," Gwinnie instructed.

"Oh, oh, yes!" Polly stammered.

She set the tray down with more rattling of the dishes. "Would you like me to pour, Miss Southerland?" she asked on a squeaky voice, looking up at Gwinnie for confirmation if she said that right.

"No, Polly. I will pour. You may go," Miss Southerland said severely.

"Th-Thank you," Polly stuttered. She curtsied to them, then turned and scurried out of the room.

"Decorum, Polly," Gwinnie called after her.

"Oh, oh, yes," Polly said, slowing her pace and standing ramrod straight until she'd closed the parlor door behind her, then they could hear her running down the stairs.

Gwinnie laughed. "Poor Polly. She still has a lot to learn." She turned to Miss Southerland. "I promise you, Polly is not indicative of the other young women we train here."

"Perhaps a maid's job is not the proper profession for her," Miss Southerland observed frowning.

"Agreed."

Miss Southerland queried them on how they liked

their tea, then leaned back in her chair, her teacup in her hand, and looked quizzically at Gwinnie and Mr. Martin.

"What can you tell us about Mrs. Southerland?" Lewis asked.

Miss Southerland tilted her head and looked off across the room as if looking at memories. "Hilda's maiden name was Milward, Hilda Milward. She met my brother Derek when he was a groom, and she was a maid at some duke's country estate. I don't remember the duke, and they weren't there long after they married. The duke didn't want married staff, so they found another position. They were at the next great house until Hilda became pregnant with their daughter, Alice."

"She has a daughter?" Gwinnie enthused.

"Y-yes," Miss Southerland said slowly, "But let me proceed. At that position, their employers didn't want pregnant servants, as the lady of the house was having difficulty conceiving and carrying the babes she did conceive to term. Seeing another pregnant woman depressed her, so she left that position."

"But not Mr. Southerland?"

"No. She got permission from the estate steward who felt sorry for her and Derek. He let them claim a run-down building, little more than a hut, on the estate. It had been used by gamekeepers at one time. They fixed it up and Hilda earned extra money for them by making lace that she sold to a linen draper in London. I don't know how she made that connection. Hilda referred to it as her heaven-sent connection."

"She was making lace that night before the letter arrived for her."

"Frankly, I think every moment she had to herself, she made lace. She said she found it relaxing. I don't know how anyone could find it relaxing as complex as it is. It takes concentration to do some of those lace patterns," Miss Southerland declared, shaking her head. She finished her tea and set her cup and saucer back on the tea tray.

"But to continue, when their daughter, Alice, was

about six years old, they fostered her to a tenant farmer on the Earl of Galborough's estate."

"Galborough," Gwinnie mused.

"You know them?" Miss Southerland asked.

Gwinnie made a face. "Yes, we are related by marriage," she said. "But please continue, Miss Southerland."

"Hilda and Derek got positions in London. They worked hard. Soon, Hilda became a housekeeper. She was thrilled— but Alice was not happy being fostered to the farmer's family. She claimed they worked her hard from sunup to sundown except for the time she had to attend reading and writing classes at the vicarage. The vicar insisted all the village children should know their letters and be able to read the Bible."

"That was fortunate for her," Lewis said.

"Perhaps," Miss Southerland said with pursed lips. "It did allow her to write to her parents to ask them to come get her, as the farmer family wanted to marry her to one of their boys. Alice did not want to be a farmer's wife. She had other ambitions," Miss Southerland said.

"My dear brother brought her to London, and Hilda got her a position as a scullery maid. Unfortunately, it was in the house where Hilda was the housekeeper, and Alice did not want to do anything if her mother had the ordering of any of it. They argued and argued. Soon, Alice left to work somewhere else. This is when the real trouble began," Miss Southerland said. She sat straighter in her chair, her hands clasped together in her lap. A frown creased twin lines between her brows.

"Real trouble?" Lewis asked.

Miss Southerland's lips pursed tightly together for a moment. "Mr. Martin, as a member of Bow Street, you may remember a spate of robberies that occurred during society parties about five years ago?"

"Yes. Extra servants were brought in to help during events— society lending their servants to each other, and agencies hiring out servants. There was a ring of thieves working among the extra help. They stole items from the houses they were assigned to work in and turned them over to the ringleader who paid them for their efforts and then took the items to pawnbrokers to sell. Generally, to pawnbrokers outside of the city."

"Yes. Alice had become one of the servant-thieves, only she was caught. She wouldn't give up the names of the ringleaders, no matter how much Hilda begged her to. She told Hilda the friends she'd made in the ring cared more for her than Hilda ever did. Ultimately, as you might suppose, she was found guilty."

"And the sentence?" Gwinnie asked. She couldn't help but feel distraught on Mrs. Southerland's behalf.

Miss Southerland looked from her to Mr. Martin. "Transportation," she said heavily.

Lewis frowned. "Transportation seems rather severe for the offense."

"Yes. We all thought— including Alice— that at maximum she would get two to three years in prison. The magistrate decided to make an example of her and sentenced her to transportation. That surprised us all. Hilda wept and became so ill she couldn't rise from her bed. Derek determined he would discover who had talked his daughter into crime and make them pay. Unfortunately, he died shortly thereafter in a stable accident."

"Poor Mrs. Southerland," Gwinnie said. "How did she overcome her melancholy?"

"She had to, or she would lose her position. She told me she needed to look deep inside herself. She couldn't dwell in her sorrows. What she wanted to do with her life was to help others out of their bad situations, to help as many unfortunate women as she could, so they did not turn to thievery as her daughter had."

"And so, she went to Soothcoor with her idea," Lewis said.

"Not straightaway. She worked and saved money and wrote down her plan. Two years later, when she thought she was ready, she asked me to introduce her to him, as I worked for his stepmother. I did not know her intention. I thought she merely wanted a job as a matron in one of his charities. I was as surprised as anyone, I suppose, when he set her up here." She looked about the room, indicating the entire structure.

"What was your feeling when Lord Soothcoor asked you to take over the charity for a time?" Gwinnie asked.

Lewis looked up suddenly from his notetaking and stared at Gwinnie. She felt like he was trying to communicate some message to her.

"Surprised and flattered," Miss Southerland said. "I had been the housekeeper for several years at Soothcoor Mansion for his stepmother. Now that the earl is selling that property, I'm not sure what I will do. Lord Soothcoor has asked me to be the housekeeper for the new home he and Lady Soothcoor will purchase, but I don't know. I am accustomed to more activity, more parties and balls. I think they will live quietly as that is Lord Soothcoor's manner— except for when Lady Soothcoor's youngest daughter makes her debut."

"You like an active household."

"I confess I do. I may look for a new position that offers those opportunities."

"Harder work," Gwinnie observed.

"Yes, but rewarding."

"Thank you for the information you have shared regarding Mrs. Southerland. That helps me to understand her better and should inform my investigation. Unfortunately, it does not help us identify whom she might have been hurried out of the house to see," Lewis said.

"No. I'm sorry."

"No need to be sorry, Miss Southerland. It is the nature of my business," Lewis returned. He turned to Gwinnie. "It is looking more and more that the culprit is someone Mr. Simmons stirred with his protests and complaints about the charity," he said seriously, his tone of voice different than ever Gwinnie could recall. She looked at him inquisitively, but he held his expression. Something wasn't right. Something she failed to note. She decided it was time to change the subject.

"If we are done discussing Mrs. Southerland, I'd like to see the women who are here, to explain about Sarah Knolls and me," Gwinnie said.

"The persona Lady Guinevere adopts when she is out doing her charity work is for her protection. As you might imagine, Miss Southerland, dukes, and their families, may be targets for those with grudges against the aristocracy. Just recently, the duke received a missive threatening his family," Lewis said.

"You are serious, Mr. Martin," Miss Southerland said.

Gwinnie quickly looked down at her hands lest her face betray her surprise and confusion at Mr. Martin's words. Her safety was not the reason she presented as Sarah Knolls, yet for some reason, that is what Mr. Martin wanted Miss Southerland to believe. Why?

Miss Southerland nodded and pulled the bellpull. "Mrs. Albert, can you have our young women who are here come to the parlor, please?" she asked.

"Yes, Miss Southerland." She backed out of the room, and they heard her going to the second floor.

In a few minutes, there were timid knocks on the door and the women came in.

The women slunk into the parlor, acting more timid than Gwinnie was accustomed to seeing them. In her memory, they gathered together, laughing and joking, with bright smiles on their faces. Today, they were solemn and looked down, scarcely venturing to look up through veiled lashes.

Gwinnie sighed. The death of Mrs. Southerland had taken a large toll on them. Her heart ached that she hadn't been able to stay here that first night, especially since the trouble they'd gone to to preserve Sarah Knolls's persona had been for naught because of her disposition at the inquest.

"Miss Marke and Miss Warden, how are you doing today?" Gwinnie asked kindly, calling out to the two young women who found Mrs. Southerland on the back doorstep.

They tentatively looked up at her. Georgia Marke tilted her head, her expression confused. "Miss Knolls?" she ventured.

Gwinnie smiled. "Yes."

"You look so different," she said, her voice resonating awe.

The other women looked up at her.

"What happened?" Georgia asked.

"I have not been truthful with you in my visits here, for reasons Mr. Martin can explain better than I," she said, turning her head to look at him. Since he changed the story with Miss Southerland, he would also tell it to the women here. "My name is Guinevere Nowlton."

"Lady Guinevere Nowlton," Miss Southerland said crisply, sending a glare of some meaning Gwinnie did not understand at the women.?

"Yes, I have an honorary title," Gwinnie admitted, rolling her eyes. "But my friends call me Gwinnie, and I hope you will, too."

"Lady Guinevere, if we are to teach these girls how to go on in society, we must be circumspect at all times," Miss Southerland reminded her.

Gwinnie made a face. A few of the women giggled. Miss Southerland frowned in their direction.

"I would prefer," Lewis interrupted, "for them to continue to refer to Lady Guinevere as Miss Knolls. In the future, when Lady Guinevere comes here, she will be wearing the attire of Miss Knolls." He turned to the women who stood clumped together, looking confused and fearful.

"Lady Guinevere Nowlton is the daughter of the Duke of Malmsby," Miss Southerland explained.

"A duke!" "What?" "A duke's daughter!" the words coming in all tones of voice and exclamation from the women. One woman elbowed another and curtsied. Soon, they all curtsied.

"Please! Don't!" implored Gwinnie.

"Yes, that is true," said Lewis. "The duke has received some threats against his family that the duke takes quite seriously."

"But why?" one woman asked.

"Because the duke has an avid interest in new inventions, and there are people who fear the inventions will take away jobs, just as the Luddites had fears and riots in past years about new machines in factories."

"But they do," one woman said timidly.

Gwinnie sighed. "Sometimes they do. My father is

concerned about that aspect of new inventions and works with inventors and business owners to minimize the impact. Workers trained in one craft can be retrained. Unfortunately, some people have been working one way for so long they can't imagine changing. Those are the people I care the most about. What can we do for them?" Gwinnie asked.

"You're serious?" the woman asked, surprised.

"Yes. It is how I've been raised. My mother was Scottish from the Highlands. They have a culture of independence. She passed that along to her children. We, in turn, want that for everyone we interact with."

"That's not feasible," declared Miss Marke sharply.

Gwinnie sighed. "Perhaps not; however, it is worth striving for, don't you agree? And that is what I do."

The women looked from one to another as if silently communicating with each other. Gwinnie thought maybe they were.

"All right," Miss Marke said. "And are we to keep your real identity a secret?"

"It would be beneficial if you would," Lewis said.

"For whom?"

He grinned and it reached his eyes. "That's an astute question. For me, I'll admit, as I hold responsibility for her protection."

Miss Marke smiled back at him. "Thank you for your honesty. I think we can do that, what do you think?" she asked the rest of the women.

They assented.

Gwinnie smiled thankfully. "You have made me happy. I love spending time with you, teaching you about society."

"And we love your lessons. You always have such interesting stories to go with each lesson. That helps to create memories."

"Oh, good, that is what I was hoping for." Gwinnie smiled, her eyes watering. "You have made me very happy with your acceptance. I was sore afraid," she said.

Gwinnie would have walked toward them to exchange hugs, but Miss Southerland intervened.

An Artful Decision

"You may return to your studies now." Miss Southerland's voice was surprisingly harsh.

Gwinnie turned to stare at her as she noted the women immediately lowered their heads and murmured agreement. They silently filed out of the parlor.

Miss Southerland had been on the premises forty-eight hours, and she had the women acting as scared church mice. How was that possible? Maybe it was just the shock of Mrs. Southerland's passing. She liked to hope so. She would ask Rose when they left if she had learned anything from below stairs that would inform her knowledge of their strange behavior. Or maybe it wasn't them. Maybe it was her and her expectations.

Oh, her mind was in turmoil. How to settle matters between herself and the women. That was her concern. How Miss Southerland did so was not.

"You seem to have come to terms with them quickly," Gwinnie observed.

The woman raised her chin and smiled, showing more teeth than warmth. "I like to think so. It appears my sister-in-law did not suffer any fools."

So it would seem; however, that was not how she knew Mrs. Southerland. What was the truth?

"Are you aware different women come to provide lessons one or two times a month? I think Sarah Knolls is the only one who comes every week."

Miss Southerland frowned. "I heard something to that effect. Are these visits worthwhile?"

"I believe so. I know Mrs. Brogan, the doctor's wife, provides lessons on hygiene, and a friend of hers gives lessons on managing and saving money."

"These are not high society ladies come to gawk at those less fortunate?"

Gwinnie tilted her head as she looked quizzically at Miss Southerland. "Why do you suggest that?"

"Lady Guinevere," Miss Southerland said in a condescending tone, "I have served in high society longer than you've been alive. I know how society is. You may be unique. and I commend you for it."

"But—"

"Lady Guinevere, excuse me for interrupting, but we need to be going if you are to meet with the Earl and Countess of Norwalk today," Lewis interrupted.

Gwinnie turned to look at him, not understanding what he was saying. She had no appointment with Helena and Adam. By agreement yesterday, the Norwalks were leaving London today, and probably already had. By his banal expression, she realized he was telling her they should leave, most likely before she got into an argument with Miss Southerland, which she was close to doing!

"I completely forgot, Mr. Martin. My thanks." She turned toward Miss Southerland. "Please excuse me, I do have other engagements. I shall return near the end of the week as Sarah Knolls when I can stay longer and spend time with the women in lessons."

Miss Southerland bowed her head. "The women will look forward to that, I'm sure. Please be sure to notify me ahead of time."

"Thank you for stepping in for your sister-in-law," Gwinnie said, as she rose from the settee, Mr. Martin following her.

Gwinnie was surprised to find Rose waiting for her downstairs in the entrance hall. She tilted her head quizzically.

"Let me help you on with your coat, Lady Guinevere," Rose said in a deeply deferential manner.

Gwinnie knew she had things to tell her, and by her demeanor, Gwinnie judged them to be not good things. She thanked her absently, in keeping with this unknown game she seemed to be in, and went out the door; Miss Southerland watched them from the top of the stairs.

What was going on?

When she was seated in the carriage, Lewis leaned in. "I've told the coachman to take you straight home. There are to be no side trips, he said quellingly.

Gwinnie laughed but agreed.

"I'm going to check out the alley, then go to see Lord Soothcoor," Lewis continued.

"Please ask him to come by Malmsby House, I would like to speak with him."

He laughed harshly. "I'm sure you would. So would I. The story Miss Southerland told of how she came to fill Mrs. Southerland's position does not match the story Soothcoor provided to me."

"What?" Gwinnie exclaimed.

Lewis didn't answer. He closed the carriage door and then tapped the side to signal to the coachman to proceed.

∞

WHEN LEWIS STEPPED AWAY from the carriage, he looked up at the townhouse. A curtain moved, settling back into its swagged form.

Miss Southerland had watched them leave.

She was not what he expected as one of Lord Soothcoor's servants. There was something about her he could not like— And it was obvious she did not think much of the aristocracy.

He walked up the block toward The Thirsty Pig. When he came to the top of the block, he turned the corner, then turned again down the narrow alley that ran behind the houses on Green Street. There were no mews in this area, residents leaving horses, and— if they were lucky enough to afford a carriage— their equipage at a local stable for boarding.

The alley was dim, though it was nearly midday on an otherwise sunny day. The height and closeness of the buildings kept the alley in deep shadows. He noted a surprising cleanliness of the alley— compared to most alleys. The houses all had small backyards protected with gates; however, most gates were not locked, if closed, and others stood open. The gate leading to Mrs. Southerland's property was no longer locked. It would have been unlocked when they carried Mrs. Southerland to The Thirsty Pig. No one had bothered to re-lock it. He touched the gate. It swung open easily. No one had latched the gate, either. He did not like that. He went into the back courtyard, to look around in the light of day— such as it was.

It didn't look like anyone had come out the back door in the last few days. He walked over to where Mrs. Southerland had fallen. There remained traces of blood. He wondered why it hadn't been cleaned yet? He walked the perimeter of the area, not seeing anything out of the ordinary. A straggly tabby cat jumped on the wall between the properties. The creature looked down on Lewis and emitted a strident meow.

"Did you witness anything the night Mrs. Southerland was killed?" he asked the cat. He laughed when the cat turned his head and jumped down off the fence. No help there.

Lewis let himself out of the back gate and continued down the alley. This end of the alley was more cluttered with trash and household castoffs. He wondered caustically if this end of the alley was where Mr. Simmons lived. He saw the cat weaving in and out among the trash in the alley, looking for scraps the rats hadn't found yet. The cat stopped and sniffed. He clawed a white cloth out of his way to sniff further, then abandoned the area and walked on.

The cloth had dark, rusty-brown stains. Blood? Lewis bent down and picked up the crumpled, stained cloth. It was a handkerchief. He gently opened up the handkerchief. It looked to be a woman's article. The stain started as a blob, then streaked across the material as would happen if an object containing the stain was dragged across the material to clean it. Blood from a knife swiped across a handkerchief. There was a slight white-on-white pattern woven into the edges of the handkerchief, not as evident as a jacquard pattern might be, but there.

He was glad Gwinnie came to Mrs. Southerland's as Lady Guinevere, else if she'd been in Sarah Knolls' clothes she would have wanted to walk down the alley with him. The blood-stained handkerchief would have had her wanting to search every inch of the alley and speculating wildly as to the source of the handkerchief.

He partially unbuttoned his heavy greatcoat to reach into a jacket pocket to pull out his handkerchief. He unfolded it, placed the found handkerchief against it, and refolded his handkerchief. He wanted to ensure he did not inadvertently add more stains to the fabric. He tucked the pad of fabric in his greatcoat pocket just as a delivery boy with a basket of produce from a grocer turned into the alley. They nodded to each other as they passed. At the other end of the alley from where he'd started, he stopped to watch where the boy went. Two doors beyond Mrs. Southerland's.

Lewis stepped out of the deeply shaded alley to the perpendicular street and into the afternoon sunlight. In the west, gray clouds gathered, coming to strip away the welcome winter sun in an hour or so, he thought. He walked toward Covent Garden. He bought an orange from the orange girl standing outside the theater and casually looked around him to ensure he hadn't been followed. In the next street, he hailed a hackney and had the jarvey take him to White's.

He tipped the jarvey to wait while he inquired if Lord Soothcoor was still staying at his club. The doorman said he was but was not in at the moment.

"Are you Mr. Martin?" the doorman asked as Lewis started to turn away.

"Yes," he said, as a club member brushed past him.

The man nodded. "Lord Soothcoor said if you were to come by to tell you to join him at Malmsby House."

"Thank you." Lewis turned to go back to the hackney only to see it pull away. He laughed. There went the money he'd tipped the jarvey to wait. At least he wasn't in a hurry.

He hailed another hackney and gave the Malmsby House direction.

CHAPTER 13
GWINNIE TAKES A HIT

"Rose, I received an odd feeling from Miss Southerland," Gwinnie said, as the coach left Green Street. "I don't think she likes how Mrs. Southerland ran the charity. I'm not even sure they were friends. What did you learn in the kitchen from Miss Wooler and any of the women about?"

"I would agree with you. She didn't know how Mrs. Southerland ran the charity. She came in assuming she needed to be all formal and strict. Miss Wooler told me she and Mrs. Albert have been trying to educate her on how things were run, but it's like she don't believe 'em. Miss Wooler confessed to me she may have to find another position if Miss Southerland continues down the path she took when she first came. She has frightened the women."

"I noticed she calls them *girls* like they were 16 or 17."

"Yes. But since she hasn't been there even two full days yet, Mrs. Albert and Miss Wooler are willing to give her time to learn more about the house. They have told the women to have patience, too," Rose said.

"I told Miss Southerland I would return near the end of the week; however, we will return tomorrow, or should I say Sarah Knolls will return tomorrow. Sarah is not inclined to wait until the end of the week. Nor will she send advance notice, as Miss Southerland requested, for I'm certain advanced notice is something I will forget before now and tomorrow," Gwinnie said airily.

Rose laughed. "That sounds like a Dowager Duchess of Malmsby decision."

"One should always learn from the best," Gwinnie told her gravely, then the two women burst into laughter.

"I jest hope she learns before any of the women run away, back to the former lives they fled," Rose said, shaking her head.

"Can you share any details of what you learned is going on?"

Rose compressed her lips a moment. "Miss Wooler said this morning she made 'em come single file into the dining room. There was to be no talking, no laughing, no smiling, and no one was to leave the table until all were ready to leave."

"Why?"

Rose shrugged. "I asked Miss Wooler the same thing and she didn't know. But isn't that how some women's institutions are run?" she offered.

Gwinnie thought about that. "I believe the Magdalen Hospital is strict. They offer tours; however, I have never been there. Maybe Miss Southerland has."

"She might have gone there to find new maids."

"Yes, that's possible," Gwinnie agreed. She stared out the carriage window as she thought about their meeting with Miss Southerland. "I shall have to speak to Lord Soothcoor," she said. "Oh, look, we've lost our sunshine today. The clouds are coming in again. It was so nice this morning, I hope it doesn't bring more rain— or worse, snow again."

Rose looked out the other window. "I was hopin' for a more pleasant winter and spring than we had last year."

"I'll take the sun whenever I can get it," Gwinnie said, as their coach drew up before Malmsby House.

Stephen came down the front steps to open the carriage door for them, lower the step, and hand her out.

Gwinnie smiled, thanked him, and then stepped away while he handed Rose out of the carriage. "Thank—"

An Artful Decision

Something hard and sharp hit her. Pain exploded in her head. She heard Rose screaming. She felt herself falling...

The next thing she knew, someone was carrying her by her legs and someone else carried her under her arms up the stairs before the house.

"Why wasn't Mr. Martin with her?" she heard her father's voice say from her feet.

"As we was coming straight home, he went investigating the neighborhood," she heard Rose say, her voice quivering.

"We'll carry her to the Lady Margaret Parlor," her father said.

"Put me down," she complained, her words garbled and slurred. Her head ached, and she couldn't seem to open her eyes, but she wasn't lost to all sensibility, with her dress hiked up so her father could carry her legs, her dress dragged on the ground. Who carried her with their arms under her breasts? She weakly tried to kick her legs out of her father's hold.

"Stop it, Gwinnie," he ordered.

"I can walk," she complained, disgusted with how weak the words sounded to her own ears.

"Stephen, get the parlor door then fetch a doctor."

If it wasn't Stephen carrying her, who—? She couldn't think. Her head hurt too much. She felt she might pass out again, and that, she did not want.

Finally, she felt the cushioning of her grandmother's sofa as they laid her down. It amused her that her father thought to pull her skirts back down to cover her legs and tuck them around her after the way he carried her.

"Lord Soothcoor," she heard Rose say. *Soothcoor!*

"Please hold her shoulders up so I might remove her coat and bonnet," Rose requested.

Gwinnie couldn't help the whimper that escaped her lips as Rose made quick work of her hat and coat. Finally, Soothcoor laid her down against the pillows. Someone threw a heavy wool shawl across her legs.

Gwinnie felt embarrassed that it had been her father and Lord Soothcoor who had to carry her in. None of the other male servants in the house were tall enough to get the proper leverage to get her off the ground. Drat her size! Oh! Where was Lancelot— that idiot twin of hers— when she needed him? He could have brought her in easily— Lucky him. He was at his Viscount Lakehurst property in the Cotswolds with his new bride.

She wanted to cry, and she didn't know if it was from the pain or the continued reminder she was too tall—or from both.

"I'll fetch Mrs. Hunnicutt," she heard Rose say. *"We'll get a cool compress for your head, mi lady. Don't worry, there is no blood."*

Blood! Gwinnie hadn't even thought about blood. She forced her eyes open, squinting against the light. She wished Merlin were here, but after the Christmas holidays, he'd escorted Grandmother back to Versely Park and then he'd also gone on to the Cotswolds to administer to the people in the villages near Lancelot's estate that did not have a physician.

Her father and Lord Soothcoor drew up chairs near the sofa.

"What happened?" her father asked. He grabbed her hand, his eyes glistened. "Did you see anyone?"

Gwinnie's heart twisted to see the tears of fear and love in her father's eyes. She tried to shake her head, but it hurt too much. "No, no one. It happened so fast! I don't even know what hit me."

"A brick!" her father said angrily. "Stephen tried to run after the bounder, but he got away. Soothcoor and I were in the front library and heard Rose screaming and came running."

"Need to... hire... taller servants." Gwinnie managed to say with a slight smile.

"Taller servants?" her father asked.

"To carry... me."

Her father shook his head. He looked up at Soothcoor. "Even in pain she makes jokes."

Rose returned with Mrs. Hunnicutt. "I chipped a piece of ice off the block in the cellar," Rose said. "The water should be very cold to help take the swelling down."

"Thank you," His Grace said as Mrs. Hunnicutt wrung out the cloth and laid it across Gwinnie's head.

"Oh, that does feel good. Thank you," she sighed for the blissful numbing cold.

~

"LADY GUINEVERE, YOU MUST WAKE UP," a kindly male voice said. "Wake up, Lady Guinevere," the voice repeated.

Gwinnie wrinkled her brow. "No, sleep..."

"Lady Guinevere, I need to examine you. Wake up, my dear," said the voice.

Reluctantly, Gwinnie squinted her eyes open.

"That's good, now open them more... Mrs. Hunnicutt, would you close the drapes please. Sometimes with head injuries, any light can be painful."

The housekeeper hurried to close the drapes across the terrace door and on the long window next to the door.

"Thank you. Can you open your eyes more now?" the voice asked.

Gwinnie opened her eyes wider. "Oh, it's you, Dr. Walcott," she said.

"Yes. You have quite a knot on your head. You are beginning to show the bruising from that brick that hit you," he told her. "You are lucky it did not cut the skin and necessitate stitches. Now, I'm going to check your head. I know your entire head hurts, but let's see if we can ensure no bone is broken. I'm going to press lightly. You tell me if it suddenly hurts worse."

Gwinnie felt his fingers lightly push on her cheeks, her nose, her brows, her forehead, and all around where the brick hit.

"You are lucky, I do not detect any cracked or broken head bone."

"And the bruising?"

"It appears to be settling on the side of your face and under your eye. There is also a bit of skin scraping as well. You were lucky the brick did not hit your eye. You will display mottled shades of purple, blue, yellow, and red for a few days. Keep a cold compress against it to relieve the swelling. I shall leave some laudanum for you."

Gwinnie made a face. "I detest that stuff."

"Be that as it may, it does a wonder to get you to relax so your body can heal. Without it, you may be too tense to relax, and that is not good for healing. You only need to take a full dose at night, unless you suffer excruciating pain. I trust you to judge what is the pain severity. However, I do expect you to take the medicine to help you sleep. Sleep is what you need the most. I suggest you take a teaspoon in a glass of water now for the pain. If you fall asleep, know it is not the laudanum that sent you to sleep, but your worn-out body. Do you understand?"

"Yes, Dr. Walcott," she said softly. "I will take a little now. Hopefully, between it and a refreshed cold compress, the pounding in my head will ease."

"Lord Soothcoor and I will be in the library should you need us," the duke said to Rose.

"Yes, Your Grace," Rose returned.

"I will stay a bit longer to ensure she only falls asleep and not unconscious," Mr. Walcott said.

"Thank you, doctor," the duke said. He led Soothcoor out of the room.

~

"MR. MARTIN! It is good you are here!" said Stephen as he opened the door to let Lewis in.

The footman looked shaken. "What's occurred?" Lewis demanded.

"'Tis Lady Gwinnie," the young man said. He gulped. "She's been hurt."

Lewis's blood ran cold. "How?" He grabbed the man's forearms.

"Someone threw a brick. I helped her out of the carriage and then someone threw a brick at her!"

Lewis gripped the man's arm tighter. "How bad?"

"I don't know. The doctor is with her. In the Lady Margaret Parlor."

"Bloody Hell!"

The door to the parlor burst open, banging against the wall. Lewis rushed over to Gwinnie, ignoring everyone in the room.

"Stephen told me of the attack on you when I came in." He kneeled beside the sofa, his breathing harsh. "I should have been here as your guard. I would have been on the watch." He started to reach out his left hand to touch her, then drew the hand back.

Gwinnie grabbed for his hand, drawing it toward her. She laughed slightly. "You can't be everywhere at once, Mr. Martin. And you need to be investigating Mrs. Southerland's death."

"You are right. I can't do both." He ran his right hand through his blond waves, content to let Gwinnie hold his other. "It appears the living need more care than the deceased. I need to talk to your father and Lord Soothcoor," Lewis said, gently sliding his hand free of hers and rising to his feet.

"Don't go!" Gwinnie implored him, reaching out. Then she stopped, her hand falling to her side. "My apologies, I am just so confused and hurting. I don't understand what happened or why. Just seeing you relaxes me and sends the pain away, for I know you will make it all right."

She smiled up at him, a smile that ripped at his heart. "I think that is what makes me feel better. My apologies," she finished softly.

"Do not apologize, Lady Guinevere. What you speak of is my job, and I am grateful that you trust me to do my job." He raised her hand to kiss her knuckles. "Rest now. Know that those who care for you are taking all precautions they can to see to your safety. Where are His Grace and Lord Soothcoor?"

Gwinnie frowned. "They were here a while ago."

"They are in the library," Rose said.

"Thank you," he said. He looked down at Gwinnie a moment longer, then he nodded toward the doctor and left the room.

Lewis closed the door gently behind him. He stood

still for a moment. His heart was racing. He took in a deep breath and slowly let it out.

When Stephen had told him Lady Guinevere had been hurt by a brick thrown at her, a panic gripped him. He'd never felt anything like it before. He'd run ahead of Stephen and flung open the door of the Lady Margaret Parlor, not waiting for Stephen to announce him. When he'd gone down on his knees by her side, it had been all he could do not to grab her to his chest.

What was going on with him? He liked and admired Lady Guinevere, yes. He saw her as the type of woman he would choose to marry. But the feelings rioting through him were beyond friendship. They nearly overwhelmed him. They had to stop. He would be useless to his investigations if these emotions could shake his steady manner.

He gritted his teeth. *I am a bastard*, he reminded himself. *I am not worthy of Lady Guinevere.*

Besides, he told himself with cruel humor as his heart rate slowed and his normal manner returned, she did not like men shorter than she stood, even if only by a few inches.

"Mr. Martin, are you all right?" asked Stephen, approaching him from his position by the door.

Lewis turned to him, his natural wry smile gracing his lips again. "Yes, thank you, Stephen. I was taking a moment to sift through my thoughts before I speak with His Grace. Did you see who threw the brick at Lady Guinevere?" he asked, his Bow Street manner returning, pushing emotions aside.

"No sir, I was helping Rose descend from the carriage. Lady Guinevere stood on the walkway waiting for her maid."

"How far away from you would you say Lady Guinevere stood?"

Stephen thought for a moment. "I'd say six to seven feet?" he offered, his tone uncertain.

"What happened when she was hit?"

"I saw her go down. Rose screamed and rushed to her as I looked to see where the brick had come from. I saw a man running down the walk, then cross the street at an angle. I started to run after him, but Lady Guinevere needed me more."

"Was there anyone else on the street? Any street vendors, pedestrians, carriages? Anyone who might have seen the man? Might have seen what happened?"

Color drained from Stephen's face, his expression stricken. "The street-cleaning boy! He started to come to see what had happened to Lady Guinevere, but I waved him away and told him to go about his business."

Lewis reached into his jacket pocket to pull out a sixpence coin. It was the smallest he had. Regardless, if the boy could identify the man, Lewis would give him a crown. "Ask the lad to come here to tell us what he saw, and give him this to cover any tips he might miss."

"I'll announce myself to the duke and Lord Soothcoor," Lewis told him. "Please take my greatcoat and hat before you get the boy." He took off his greatcoat, remembering to get the pad of handkerchiefs from the pocket, and handed the coat, his hat, and gloves to Stephen.

"Right away, Mr. Martin. I wish I'd known— I didn't think—" Stephen sputtered.

"There is no reason you should have thought of the street sweeper," Lewis assured him. "Do not worry, just get the lad, now."

"Yes, sir."

Lewis approached the library door and knocked.

"Come in," he heard the duke say.

"Excuse me, Your Grace," Lewis said, opening the door.

"Come in, come in," said the Duke of Malmsby, waving him forward. "Did Stephen tell you what happened to Gwinnie?"

"He did, Your Grace. I went to see her before I came here. I also spoke to Stephen about the incident."

"Excellent."

"I hope you do not mind, but I have sent him out to fetch the street cleaner boy. That leaves you without a footman by the door."

"Street cleaner?"

"Yes, Your Grace, he was up the street nearer the brick thrower. He might be able to tell us more."

The duke looked at Lord Soothcoor who sat opposite him. "I saw him, too, and didn't even think—"

Soothcoor shook his head. "I didn't either, I was too caught up in picking up my end of Lady Guinevere without causing her too much embarrassment."

"She is a tall woman," her father said with a laugh.

"Yes, but she isn't nearly as heavy as one might assume her to be," Soothcoor said.

"You carried her in?" Lewis asked, surprised, then wondered why he should be surprised. The duke was her father and Soothcoor, his friend. He knew the footman Jimmie was laid up with a sprained ankle.

"Malmsby and I did."

"What about the footman, Stephen?"

"I sent him to fetch the doctor," the duke said. "But come in and take a seat," he said, indicating the other chair in front of his desk.

Lewis sat down but stood up again immediately when they heard the front door open. He crossed to the library door to open it again. Stephen and a scruffy young boy about Daniel's age came into the house. He recognized the street cleaner.

"Robbie Gilgorn! When have you taken up street cleaning?" Lewis asked. He removed the cap from the boy's head and handed it back to him.

Robbie stuffed the cap in his jacket pocket. "Johnny's sick. 'e arsked if'n I'd take 'is spot whilst 'e be sick."

"That was nice of him."

"Naw, jest pertect'n 'is turf."

Lewis laughed. "Smart lad. Robbie, this is His Grace, the Duke of Malmsby, and this is his lordship, the Earl of Soothcoor."

Robbie bowed to each man solemnly.

"So, Master Gilgorn, tell us what you saw," Malmsby said, leaning forward, his hands folded on the desk. "Did you see the man who threw the brick?"

"Cor, yes. 'e were walk'n the street fer more than an 'our like," the boy said disgustedly.

"An hour!" exclaimed Malmsby.

Robbie nodded. "We jawed a bit. Said 'e were wait'n fer sum one."

Lewis led him over to the chair he'd been sitting in and urged him to sit. He thought the boy might feel more comfortable if he felt he were having a more equal level conversation and would offer more information."

"In talking to him, did you get his name?" Lewis asked?

"Naw— 'e started to tell me, but stopped, says I don't need to know 'is name— but ta begin'n 'ad that same sound as Frankie Egan."

"An 'F' sound," said Lord Soothcoor.

Robbie shrugged. "I ain't lettered, I don't knowed ta letters, but it 'ad a sound close, like *fff*, like Frankie, like I says."

"Did you tell him your name?"

The boy looked at Lewis with disgust. "Naw, I knowed better. Says I were Sam."

Lewis grinned. "Good lad. Can you describe him? For a good description I'll give you a crown."

Robbie sat up straighter. "I ken do better. I ken draws him," he said proudly.

Malmsby, Soothcoor, and Lewis exchanged glances, then Malmsby leaned back and opened his desk drawer to pull out paper and a pencil. "Can you draw him now?" he asked as he pushed the items to the boy. "I'll see if my staff can get us refreshments while you work."

"Any sweets?" the boy asked, as he pulled the paper and pencil toward himself.

"Of course," assured Malmsby with a smile. He rang for Stephen and gave him instructions while the boy started sketching.

Lewis looked over at the drawing emerging on the paper. The boy had raw talent. Lewis had known the boy for a couple of years, hanging on the fringes of Daniel's former mudlark gang, but he would never have guessed the boy was a natural artist. He needed a teacher.

Maybe Soothcoor could get him into one of his schools.

A few minutes later a maid entered, walking carefully, carrying a loaded tea tray."

"Place the tea things on the table by the window," the duke directed. "Thank you, Mercy, we will serve ourselves."

"Yes, Your Grace. The doctor is about ready to leave. Said he's satisfied Lady Guinevere won't go unconscious."

Malmsby rose to his feet. "Thank you, Mercy. I will speak to the doctor before he leaves. Gentlemen, please serve yourselves.

Lewis looked over Robbie's shoulder. "I think I've seen this man before." He frowned, his mind whirling as it went through the scenarios that might bring the man's identity to mind.

Lewis turned to walk to the tea things as he thought. He poured himself and Robbie a cup of tea, putting plenty of sugar and milk in the boy's cup. He put an apple tart by the boy's cup and carried everything to the desk.

"Thankee, Mr. Martin. An' I'm done wit ta sketch as best as I ken 'member 'im," Robbie said.

Lewis clapped him on the shoulder. "You did a good job. We can use this to spread the word at Bow Street. I think I've seen him before, but I can't think where."

"When we was jaw'n, 'e says sumpth'n 'bout never should 'ave agreed. Says 'e never wants to be a Brown Bear guest agin. Does that 'elp any?"

Lewis grinned. He patted Robbie on the shoulder, then reached into his jacket pocket. "Here's the crown I promised you."

"Cor! I thought that were just jaw'n!"

"Your Da's a stone mason, correct?"

"Aye."

"This should help your family get through the winter until your Da's work picks up again."

"Aye, Mr. Martin! Thankee! Ken I go now? Johnny's depend'n on me to keep 'is street clean."

"What do you think, Lord Soothcoor? Can he leave?" Lewis asked.

"Do you know where he lives?" Soothcoor asked.

"Yes."

"Then yes, but I think he needs another tart for his help," the earl suggested.

Lewis laughed and fetched one, handing it to the boy. "Thank you, Robbie, for your help."

"Will her ladyship be all right?" the boy asked anxiously.

"We think so."

He dramatically wiped the back of his hand against his forehead. "Phew. That's good ta know. She's a right one."

"That she is," agreed Lewis.

Robbie rose from the chair and followed Lewis to the door. "Ya need anythin' else drawed, I can do it for ya—fer a price a'course."

"Naturally. And I may take you up on that," Lewis said, as he saw him out the front door.

The duke came out of the Lady Margaret Parlor just then. "We need to get Gwinnie up to her bed chamber. Dr. Walcott doesn't want to give her any additional laudanum until she is in bed, and she vehemently agrees."

"We can carry her up like the Duke of Ellinbourne and I carried Miss Anne up the stairs when she injured her ankle at Versely Park."

"How was that?" the duke asked.

Lewis held his arms out before him crossed. "We crossed our arms and held each other's forearms, had her sit on our arms while she had her arms around our necks. We also had someone walk behind us to ensure she did not fall backward."

"I can help you to do that, unless you have a groom you'd prefer to do it with me?"

He glared again at Lewis. "I'm a father before I'm a duke. Let's do this. Soothcoor can follow behind."

They collected Soothcoor from the library and then helped Gwinnie to her feet.

"Oh, my head is spinning," she said.

"Just stay standing for a moment, that should fade," Lewis said. He told her how they intended to get her upstairs.

"And you carried Ann upstairs this way?"

"Yes."

"I'm willing to try," she said.

The duke and Lewis crossed arms and grabbed each other's forearms. Gwinnie reached around to twine her arms about their necks, then sat on their arms.

"Ready, Your Grace?" Lewis said. "Lift."

"Oh!" Gwinnie exclaimed.

"Anything wrong?" her father asked.

"No, just surprised."

The men walked, carrying Gwinnie between them, Soothcoor following. Rose ran ahead to clear their way. They made their way slowly down the hall to the stairway and then slowly climbed each stair together.

"It's a little unnerving not to touch the handrail," the duke said.

Lewis laughed. "Yes, but we're doing fine. How are your wrists holding out?"

"Better than I imagined, but not as good as I might hope," admitted His Grace.

Rose opened the door directly into Gwinnie's bed chamber, bypassing the dressing room. She pulled down the bedding before they turned to let her lie back. Her father helped her get her legs up on the bed.

Lewis took in the bed chamber décor. He thought it suited Gwinnie. It was done in a pale blue-green. It wasn't overly frilly, more elegant than full of frills. He could imagine her with her red hair down, spread across the pillows—

He pulled his thoughts up sharply and backed away from the bed. "That should make you more comfortable." He turned toward the duke. "I need to take the sketch to Bow Street. I'll return tomorrow, Your Grace," he said stiffly. He turned and left the room before he was tempted to linger and allow more visions of Gwinnie to come into his mind.

CHAPTER 14

THE DOWAGER DUCHESS TELLS
A TALE

The Dowager Duchess of Malmsby felt horrified that she had been gone from the house when Gwinnie was injured. She and Mrs. Morrison— with Mr. Cott as their guard— had visited her dear friend Lady Oakley to discuss recent events and to learn the latest city gossip.

On learning the news from Stephen, the Dowager Duchess rushed up the stairs to check on Gwinnie. Coming out of the room was one of the maids carrying a tray.

"Is she awake," the duchess asked the maid.

The maid curtsied. "Yes, Your Grace, and fretful. She wanted nothing to do with the healing tisane Cook sent up to her. She's asked for a good cuppa tea."

"Good," said the duchess.

She pushed the door open slowly. The room was dim, the curtains drawn against bright daylight.

"Gwinnie," the duchess called out softly.

"It is all right, Grandmother. Come in," Gwinnie said.

"I wanted to see how you are," she said, as she came into the room.

"My head hurts, but not like earlier, and light bothers my eyes, otherwise I am awake and conscious, and there was no blood to require stitches so I would say that makes me all right."

Her grandmother sat on the edge of the bed. "Have you had some laudanum?"

"Earlier, when Dr. Walcott was here, but no more until tonight, when I want to go to sleep. He said with a head injury it is better that I stay awake for now. You can help keep me awake. I think Rose is nearly hoarse from constantly talking to me."

Rose, seated by the window, laughed. "Not yet, mi lady."

"Can you tell me what happened?"

"What I can remember, which isn't much. One moment I was waiting for Rose to leave the carriage, and the next moment, my head exploded in pain, and I was on the ground. I don't know more than that."

The duchess frowned. "Those aren't exciting details. You need to work on your story, Gwinnie," her grandmother fussed.

Gwinnie laughed a little, then grimaced. "That hurts my head— Rose, the compress is not cold enough anymore."

Rose removed the compress from Gwinnie's forehead. "I will get a fresh compress for you." She left the room quietly.

"I visited Mrs. Southerland's this morning." She plucked at her blanket and stared up at the canopy.

"You visited her? Not alone, I hope."

"No— Rose and Mr. Martin went with me."

"What did you think of her?"

"I have not decided what I think of her," Gwinnie told her grandmother. "Let's just say I'm glad she is not Mrs. Southerland's permanent replacement. But we did manage to learn more about Mrs. Southerland that will help the investigation."

"Like what?"

"She has a daughter named Alice."

"No, she doesn't," countered her grandmother as she brushed hair away from Gwinnie's face.

Gwinnie's brow furrowed. "That is what Miss Southerland told Mr. Martin and me, and that her daughter was involved in those robberies of society houses during the season festivities five years ago. Remember those?"

"Yes, I do. Lady Oakley was one of the hostesses whose house was burgled during a party. She had a beautiful brass Chinese bowl disappear and some female guests reported missing jewelry they had been wearing. But Mrs. Southerland didn't have a daughter."

"That is not what Miss Southerland told us. How can you be so sure she didn't have a daughter?"

"Because she told me she never could have children."

"Told you? I didn't know you knew Mrs. Southerland," Gwinnie said.

"Remember when I found out about your charity work and was annoyed that your father knew and I didn't?"

Gwinnie laughed slightly, "You gave me quite a lecture about not telling you about all of my activities."

"Yes, and quite right. I have a reputation to maintain!"

"So you told me. Repeatedly."

"*Hmph*. I went to visit her."

"You did! She never told me."

"I asked her not to. We discussed how she became interested in helping unfortunate women. She said it was because of her niece."

"Niece!"

"Yes." The dowager duchess nodded slowly. "Her niece, Alice Southerland, the base-born child of her sister-in-law."

"The woman who is now leading Mrs. Southerland's House for Unfortunate Women?"

"I would assume so," her grandmother said.

"Why would she lie?"

Her grandmother shrugged. "As much as you admired Mrs. Southerland, you need to consider she might have been the one to lie."

Gwinnie's expression fell. That was not something she wanted to consider as truth. But she must clear her mind of her affection for Mrs. Southerland.

For now.

"We have to let Mr. Martin know!" Gwinnie said. "—And Lord Soothcoor."

Her grandmother nodded and stood up. "I'll have Malmsby send notes to them."

Rose returned with the cold compress. "I'm sorry I took so long, I—"

"No matter," Gwinnie said tiredly. "I need it to numb my thoughts as well as my injury."

Her grandmother grabbed her hand and squeezed it gently. "This will get sorted out. Trust Mr. Martin."

Gwinnie's eyes watered. "I do." She turned her head away as the duchess left the room.

~

LEWIS ENTERED Daniel's room to find him playing solitaire on the counterpane with an old deck of cards Lewis had had in the house. Lindsay must have found them for him.

"I'm bored," Daniel said with an exaggeratedly long expression.

Lewis laughed. "I'll bet you are, but cracked ribs are nothing to ignore. How is the wrist?"

"It's healed, see?" He moved his left wrist in all directions.

"Yes. You are lucky it wasn't broken."

"I know. You're not going to start the lecture again, are you?" Daniel asked sourly.

"The one about sliding on ice? No, I will let that one go for now. Being confined to this bed is punishment enough. Mrs. Fullerton told me the doctor is pleased with your progress. He told her you may get out of bed—"

"He did!" exclaimed Daniel. He tossed his blankets aside.

Lewis put his hand on Daniel's shoulder, holding him on the bed. "*TOMORROW*," he continued, "for meals and quiet activities like reading." He felt Daniel's shoulder slump under his hand.

"Better than lyin' in this bed, I suppose," he said glumly, pulling the blanket back over himself.

Lewis nodded, then let his hand drop. He walked to the chair by Daniel's desk and sat down. "I saw Robbie Gilgorn today."

"You did? What was he doin'?"

"Street sweeping for Johnny, who he said was sick."

"That sounds like somethin' Robbie would do."

"I didn't know Robbie was an artist," Lewis said.

"Yeah, He's good ain't he? What did he draw?"

"He drew a picture of the man who threw a brick at Lady Guinevere."

"No! Is she hurt?"

Lewis nodded. "Unfortunately, yes. He hit her in the head."

Daniel threw off his blankets again. "I gots to get up. I gots to get my gang together." He jumped out of bed.

"Whoa! Stop!" ordered Lewis. "You are not going anywhere." He pushed Daniel back onto the bed.

"But they can find him. You know they can!" Daniel protested. "No one gets away from hurtin' Lady Guinevere," he said fiercely

"And he won't get away," Lewis assured him. "I took the sketch to Bow Street. He's been identified as Freddie Suthers, a carter. Works out of the Wild Hare Inn. Mr. Trolley is bringing him in."

"Good." Daniel settled back in bed. His brows drew together in a pensive look. "Why would a carter throw a brick at Lady Guinevere?"

"I don't know. From what Robbie said, it seemed like he might have been paid to do it."

Daniel's lips quirked sideways. "I cain't see someone protestin' them new machines payin' fer their dirty work."

"Very good," Lewis said, nodding. "I happen to be in agreement with you. I need to write a note to Lady Guinevere's father and Lord Soothcoor. I think my writing supplies are still up here unless Mrs. Fullerton, in her efficiency, took them back downstairs."

"Not that I saw, but I did sleep late this mornin'.

Stayed up late readin' that book you lent me. Cor' it were good!"

Lewis laughed. "I'll tell him you liked it when next I see him."

He sat down at the desk again and opened the drawer to find his writing supplies. He wrote quick notes to the duke and the earl. Then he stood up and turned toward Daniel. "I have to go out again this afternoon and will probably not return until late; however, we will have breakfast together tomorrow morning."

"Downstairs?" Daniel asked.

"Downstairs," agreed Lewis.

~

Since they knew Miss Southerland had told differing stories of how she came to replace Mrs. Southerland, Lewis wondered how much else of the story of Mrs. Southerland's past was true. He'd decided to see if Alice Southerland had been transported to Australia.

Lewis thanked the clerk in the Old Bailey records office for his assistance and left the building. He walked slowly, considering what he'd learned and thinking about what he should do next.

Miss Southerland told Lady Guinevere and himself that Mrs. Southerland's daughter had been transported to Australia for her part in the theft ring that hit during society parties. Yes, she had been charged, according to the records, but charges against her had been dismissed. Interestingly, three other names showed up in the records that he recognized, people who were questioned but did not have charges against them: Millie Southerland, Derek Southerland, and Freddie Suthers.

Millie had worked the same party Alice had and was questioned regarding the thefts. Derek Southerland and Freddie Suthers were questioned regarding receiving stolen goods.

Alice had been charged because a silver spoon had been found in the pocket of the apron she'd worn during a party that suffered thefts. She claimed she found it on

An Artful Decision

the floor, picked it up, and dropped it in her pocket intending to return it to the butler later. She said she forgot about it and hung the apron up before she left. Ultimately, her room was searched, and nothing was found, and since she had not removed the silver from the house, charges were dropped.

The two names in the records that intrigued him were that of Derek Southerland and Freddie Suthers. Why was Derek Southerland suspected of participation? According to his sister, he'd been a groom at that time. Was that true?

And why should Freddie Suthers' name show up among the Southerlands? That he was associated with the ring of thefts five years ago convinced him Suthers was not part of the threats against the Duke of Malmsby for his invention support.

Was Suthers a corruption of the Southerland name? Were they all involved together, though no proof was found? He'd copied down the list of items stolen. He wondered if any had been found. The newspapers might have more information about the thefts and the stolen goods. He didn't have time to search for those today. But he was curious about Derek Southerland's death. He thought he served in the Mayfair area so Dr. Brogan could have the records. He had time to pay him a visit today.

He hailed a hack and directed him to Dr. Brogan's surgery.

～

"Is Dr. Brogan available?" Lewis asked the young man talking with a woman seated in a waiting room of Dr. Brogan's surgery.

"He is with a patient at the moment, and this lady here is ahead of you," he said gesturing to the woman seated in the plain wood chair thrust up against a wall.

"I do not wish to see him as a patient. I am Mr. Lewis Martin from Bow Street."

"Bow Street!"

"I need to see the coroner's records from five years ago. Does he have them here?"

"Oh, death records. Yes, he had the last ten years of records brought here. If that is all you need, I can show them to you," the young man said.

"That would be appreciated," Lewis said with his winningest smile.

"Certainly, right this way," the man said, leading Lewis across the room to another door.

"And you are...?" queried Lewis.

"Beg your pardon. I am David Asher, Dr. Brogan's assistant." He pushed open a door to an office. "We haven't had the chance to get them organized yet. When did you say this death was?"

"I believe it was four years ago, certainly not more than five."

"Then you need these books over here," Mr. Asher said.

"Do they record all the information that is also on the death certificate?"

"Yes, and sometimes more. Would you mind going through these? I am supposed to stay with the patients in the waiting room and take a summary of their complaint before the doctor sees them."

"I can do that," Lewis said, stripping off his gloves and removing his hat.

The man smiled thankfully and hurried back to his station.

Lewis took off his coat and laid it across a chair, then selected a book and started reading. It was forty minutes later before he found what he was looking for. He looked again at the date. Four months after the Old Bailey proceedings where Alice Southerland was absolved of guilt.

Lewis yawned and ran a hand along the back of his neck and stretched his head from side to side. If he'd had to read many more entries, he might have fallen asleep before finding it.

Derek Southerland had been impaled by a pitchfork in his neck. That didn't sound like a stable accident. The verdict was murder by person or persons unknown.

An Artful Decision

What caught his attention was the angle of the pitchfork. He stood up to envision being attacked with that angle against his neck. For a normal person to pierce him that high and upward thrust angle, wouldn't they have to hold the pitchfork low and pointed up? But the description of the wounds did not match a horizontal entry. They were almost vertical. Did that imply a short person? Or just someone carrying it low and thrusting upward?

He wondered how tall Freddie Suthers stood?

The door to the office opened behind him. "Mr. Martin!" said Dr. Brogan. "Mr. Asher told me you were going through old death records."

"Yes, and I think I found what I was looking for. Come here and take a look at this," he invited, moving his chair aside. "See the entry here for Derek Southerland?"

"The deceased Mrs. Southerland's husband?"

"Yes."

The doctor leaned over and read the entry. "Interesting. The entry wound wasn't deep, but it caught the carotid artery on the right side."

"He bled out."

"Precisely."

"Could he have been saved with prompt medical attention?"

"I can't say for certain, but based on what is written here, I would think so."

"Thank you, Dr. Brogan."

"Why are you looking into this man's death?"

"I think five years ago he was part of a band of robbers."

"You think his death might have been a falling-out among thieves?"

"I don't know; however, it is possible. Well, I got what I needed. I will get out of your office and let you get on with your day."

"It is near the end of the day, Mr. Martin. I am closing up and going home to my wife."

Lewis looked at his pocket watch. "I didn't realize it was that late. Thank you for the information."

"Are you continuing to investigate Mrs. Southerland's death?"

"Yes. The Duke of Malmsby and Lord Soothcoor are not satisfied."

Dr. Brogan looked down. "I understand. I don't know what to do about Mr. Gedney."

Lewis started to put on his coat. "I think Lord Soothcoor might have some ideas for you. If he doesn't reach out to you soon, you might consider contacting him."

Dr. Brogan nodded. "Thank you, I will."

Lewis picked up his gloves and settled his hat on his head. "Good night to you, then." He left the doctor to his musings. Lewis had enough musings of his own to consider.

CHAPTER 15
DANIEL AND HIS GANG

The note from Mr. Trolley came while he was getting dressed the next morning. Lewis smiled as he accepted the note from Lindsay. His letter opener was in Daniel's room. He didn't bother to retrieve it but slid his finger under the thick seal.

He scanned it quickly, then as anger surged through him, he scrunched the paper in his hand and then threw it across the room.

"Bloody Hell!" he ground out from between clenched teeth.

Mr. Suthers did not take his load to Cambridge yesterday. He was nowhere to be found.

"Did you say something, Mr. Martin?" Lindsay asked.

Lewis shook his head to clear it. "My apologies, Lindsay. The man who injured Lady Guinevere has eluded capture," he said grimly.

"Oh, no, Mr. Martin! What will you do now?"

"Find him!" he vowed. Then he remembered his promise to Daniel. "— after I have breakfast with Daniel."

~

LEWIS RATTLED down the stairs to the house's small

dining room on the ground floor. Daniel was before him, digging into a hearty plate of eggs and ham.

"Now that you are up, dressed, and moving around, how are the ribs?" Lewis asked, as he sat down and shook out his napkin.

"Wrapped too tight," Daniel complained. "I can't breathe."

"Next time you see the doctor, ask him if they can be loosened."

"But I can't breathe now!" he complained.

"They won't hurt if you sit or lie quietly. You need more breath to move."

"I had to move to come downstairs," he said.

"Yes," Lewis said. He took a sip of coffee. "But you're not supposed to do much more moving than that."

"What are you doing today?" Daniel asked.

"I'm going to Malmsby House to discuss with the duke everything I learned yesterday."

"And court Lady Guinevere a bit," Daniel said slyly.

"Daniel. I can't court Lady Guinevere, so stop the teasing," Lewis said severely.

"Why not? You're a man and she's a woman."

"It isn't that simple in our society," Lewis said.

"Well, it should be," Daniel declared.

"Besides, she doesn't like men shorter than she."

Daniel made a rude noise. "That's just her way to keep the rakes and rogues away. It's easy to say."

"What makes you think you are an expert on women?"

"Livin' and watchin'," he said sagely.

"Well, get your ideas of Lady Guinevere and myself out of your head. It is not going to happen. Right now I have a responsibility to her protection, and that I will take seriously. Nothing else."

"*Hmph.* Well, I'm done. Can I go to the library and spend time there today?"

"Yes. That is a perfect place for you to relax."

"'Bye," Daniel said crisply, then stood straight and walked slowly out of the room.

An Artful Decision

WEDNESDAY MORNING, snow flurries swirled through the misty, pale-gray air, melting when they touched the ground. Lewis pulled his gloves on when he stepped out of his house. He wondered how hard it would be to find a hack this morning. It seemed like the least change in the weather and all hacks disappeared. He walked down the street to the next block. Luckily, a hack was discharging a passenger two houses down. Lewis hailed the jarvey.

"Where to?" the man asked over his shoulder as Lewis opened the carriage door.

"Malmsby House," Lewis said shortly, his mind full of thoughts of Freddie Suthers and where he might be. But the closer the carriage came to Malmsby House, the more Lewis's thoughts shifted to Lady Guinevere.

Yesterday he'd allowed his emotions to surface. That was not typical for him. He could not afford to lay himself bare in that way, not when he knew he was not a viable suitor for Lady Guinevere— despite Daniel's assertions to the contrary.

He'd been caught by a pretty face with a sense of humor. A rare combination, and he had allowed the novelty to overtake him.

He breathed in deeply, his exhale a white cloud.

He could admire her— and should! Everyone who met her should admire her, admire her for her intelligence, her talent, her daring, and her giving heart. But admiration drew the line.

He needed to do a better job of keeping an emotional distance from her. If he did not, he could embarrass her and that could drive a wedge into their friendship, splitting it apart. Yesterday, news of the attack on her caught him off-guard. He needed to be sure he wouldn't react in that way again.

By the time the carriage stopped in front of Malmsby House, Lewis thought he had himself well in hand and his thoughts had returned to the mysteries before him. Stephen opened the grand front door. "They're in the gold parlor, Mr. Martin," the footman said as he took his winter outerwear.

"They?"

"The family, and Lord Soothcoor. Follow me, please."

Stephen led Lewis up the stairs to the first-floor parlor. Lady Guinevere must be feeling better, Lewis thought. He was relieved to hear she was not confined to her bed.

The footman opened the white double doors and stentoriously announced: "Mr. Martin."

Lewis's lips quirked sideways at Stephen's loud, formal announcement. But it did cause everyone to look toward the door.

"Mr. Martin! Good, you are here," declared the duke.

Lewis bowed. "Your Grace." He turned to the dowager duchess and bowed to her and then Lord Soothcoor.

"We were just discussing the different stories heard from Miss and Mrs. Southerland."

"You have discovered discrepancies? I have more to tell you," Lewis said, as he walked further into the room. Lady Guinevere was reclining on a blue-and-gold sofa with a gold shawl draped over her. "Lady Guinevere, may I say you are looking better today," Lewis said formally, bowing in her direction.

"Thank you, Mr. Martin. I feel better," she said with a radiant smile.

Lewis nodded curtly, his expression a studied neutrality, and deliberately took a seat far from her. He turned his attention to Lord Soothcoor. "My lord, the account of how Miss Southerland came to be the matron of Mrs. Southerland's House for Unfortunate Women that you related to me on Monday evening does not match the account she related to Lady Guinevere and me."

"So Lady Guinevere told to us."

"And the story of Mrs. Southerland's daughter, Alice, does not match the story Mrs. Southerland related to me, last summer when I went to the charity house to meet her," stated the dowager duchess.

"In what way," Lewis asked.

"She said Alice was her niece, not her daughter. Said she is the base-born child of Miss Southerland."

Gwinnie held her hands to her head. "Even if I didn't have a headache still, this would be enough to give me a headache. Why all the conflicting stories?" she asked.

Lewis laughed harshly. "There is more to add to the pile of lies and mystery. I went to the Old Bailey yesterday to look up the records from those robberies and when Miss Alice Southerland was charged. The record shows others providing testimony at that time were Miss Southerland, Derek Southerland, and Freddie Suthers—Lady Guinevere's attacker. The charges against Miss Alice Southerland were dismissed. She was neither transported nor sent to prison."

"What?" said Lady Guinevere.

"Why all the lies?" the Duchess asked.

Lewis shook his head. "I also looked up the death record for Derek Southerland. He didn't die in a stable accident. He was murdered. With a pitchfork to his neck, by the angle, probably by someone shorter than him."

"Do we know how tall he was?"

"No. But you haven't heard the worst yet," Lewis said. He took in a deep breath and let it out forcefully. "I'm sorry, but Trolley didn't capture Suthers. He is somewhere at large, most likely in London." He hung his head, looking at the floor, then raised it.

The duke leaned back in his armchair, crossing one leg over the other. "Somehow, I am not surprised," he said, his dark brows pulling together.

"Trolley said in his note to me that several agents are out looking for him. They had a printing plate made from Robbie Gilgorn's drawing and are passing out flyers."

"And when does that ever work?" the duke asked.

Lewis shrugged. "You are correct, Your Grace. It is a dubious road to take; however, at the moment it is the only one we have."

"What do we do about Miss Southerland?" Gwinnie asked. "I don't feel comfortable leaving her in charge of the charity."

Soothcoor turned toward her. "Why? Granted we have determined she is a liar, but it appears Mrs. Southerland may have been one as well and she ran the charity."

"When we were there, the women looked frightened and Mrs. Alberts and Miss Wooler said she was a bit of a martinet, tending to want to run the house like Magdalen Hospital, very rigid."

"Couldn't that be from lack of knowledge?"

"Yes, but if she was as close to Mrs. Southerland as she led you to believe, wouldn't she have known how the house was conducted?"

Soothcoor nodded. "You are right. I fear I am still looking for easy answers."

"I think Sarah Knolls should visit her today," Gwinnie suggested.

"No," said the duke. "You are still recovering from a head injury."

Gwinnie glared at her father. "I have a headache no worse than any other headache. You are overreacting to the bruise on my face."

"No, I am a father looking to protect his daughter from any more harm!" refuted the duke.

Gwinnie looked like she wanted to rebut his caring. However, she was lucky to have a father who cared when so many women did not.

"Mr. Martin! Mr. Martin!" they heard a man yelling from downstairs.

"Sir, please!" Stephen responded.

"I've got to speak with Mr. Martin!"

"That's my man's voice," Lewis said. He rose from his chair and quickly went to the door and opened it. He looked down the stairs.

He saw Mr. Lindsay shake off Stephen's hold. But Mr. Cott was coming to aid Stephen, his typically pleasant expression one of a man set to pummel someone out of existence.

"Mr. Lindsay, stop!" called out Lewis. "Stay where you are a moment— Mr. Cott, Stephen, it is all right. Mr. Lindsay works for me," he said in a calming voice.

Mr. Cott trembled as he physically shook off the intruder alert.

"Mr. Lindsay, what's the emergency?" Lewis asked.

Mr. Lindsay ran up the stairs to Lewis. "It's young Daniel, sir. He's cut off the rib wrapping, dressed, and nipped out of the house. I tried to stop him, but he was too fast. He said to tell you he'd send word when his gang found Mr. Suthers."

Gwinnie and the duke appeared at the open parlor door. "What happened?" boomed the duke's voice.

Lewis turned to look up at them. "Daniel has removed his rib bandages and has taken it upon himself to find Mr. Suthers. I must go," he said harshly.

Gwinnie ran down the steps. "If he does find Mr. Suthers, what shall we do if he comes here looking for you?"

"Lock him up, tie him up, or give him enough laudanum to put a horse to sleep, just see he doesn't leave!" he said grimly. He started to go down the stairs with Mr. Lindsay.

"Do you know where he would go?" the duke asked.

"Stephen, my coat, please— I believe so," he said, turning back to the duke. "He's gone to rally the mudlarks."

"But they wouldn't be down by the Thames in this weather, would they?" Gwinnie asked.

"No, but they've made friends with some of the longshoremen, and at this time of year can gather in one of the warehouses, generally one of the Partridge's warehouses. Excuse me, I must go," Lewis said. He thanked Stephen for his coat and hat. He went out the door while still putting his coat on.

∽

DANIEL and his mudlark gang had been useful eyes and ears in the city. They helped Lewis on numerous occasions track down stolen goods, and even find Lord Soothcoor's nephew after he'd been kidnapped and sold to a chimney sweep.

Daniel, as the leader of the gang, was uncannily smart. His intelligence and leadership skills were two reasons why Lewis decided to foster Daniel. Daniel's mother had been grateful, for that meant she had one less mouth to feed. She was a proud woman and would not let Lewis pay her what Daniel brought in from his street activities; however, Lewis found ways to gift her the items she needed without coins changing hands.

But his young foster— for all his intelligence— was also impetuous. Lewis felt he should have anticipated this behavior from Daniel and done something more to warn him against removing his chest wrappings and warn Mr. Lindsay and Mrs. Fullerton against Daniel's impetuousness. But it might not have mattered. Once Daniel learned Lady Guinevere had been injured by this man, he would move heaven and hell to see him arrested. He adored Lady Guinevere.

As he rode in the hackney carriage toward the docks, Lewis admitted he did, too. He had to sit across the parlor from her and work to keep his expression neutral. When Mr. Suthers was captured, he would have to tell the duke he could no longer look out for Lady Guinevere. Hopefully, he would keep Mr. Cott employed and that man could take the chore. Lewis didn't feel he could do so any longer without revealing his feelings for Guinevere, to the embarrassment of himself and the lady.

He had the jarvey set him down at the East India docks. He thought the gang might be at the Partridge Warehouses, purchased last year from Waddley Spice and Tea Company. The former owners of the warehouses had negotiated an agreement with the Partridge family; they would provide a safe corner of their dock warehouses to the mudlarks for their help in finding Lord Soothcoor's nephew.

He opened the side door to the warehouse and climbed the stairs to the storage floor. Five boys jumped up when they heard him, their expressions anxious. When they saw who was there, they relaxed again. Lewis did not see Daniel among them.

"Have any of you seen Dan Wright, today?" he asked, using the name he used among his friends.

"No, sar," one boy said.

"Hain't he away at that fancy skool?" another said.

"Not at the moment." Lewis admitted. He took off his hat and ran a gloved hand through his hair. He thought for sure this would be where Daniel would come.

"Listen, if you see him, tell him to come to Malmsby House. It is urgent that he do so," Lucas said. "Do you know of any other place he might go? He's looking for a man who hurt Lady Guinevere. I thought he might come for your assistance."

"He hain't been 'ere an' hain't arsked fer 'elp. But I'd 'elp."

The other boys nodded and murmured agreement.

"Thank you," Lewis said. He put his hat back on his head. Where could Daniel be? Lewis decided to head for the rookeries, as that was the type of place Mr. Suthers would likely hide out. Easy to get lost and forgotten there. Lewis had some resources in the area as well that might help him for a few coins.

A little over an hour later, Lewis circled back to the warehouses to see if Daniel had showed up. He'd had no luck in the rookeries with any of his informants. This time there was only one boy upstairs in the warehouse, the youngest of the gang, a dark-haired child with soulful eyes. And he was waiting for him.

"Mr. Martin!" he cried out, surging to his feet. "Dan said as 'ow you'd return. Said I was ta say—" His expression grew serious. He held up his hand and pushed up one finger. "Soothcoor 'ouse." Second finger. "'Round back." Third finger up. "Servant's door," he finished, then grinned, flashing missing teeth, obviously proud to remember what he was to say.

"Soothcoor Mansion!"

"Aye sar. That's wot he say."

"Thank you, lad. Here—" he pulled a coin out of his pocket and handed it to the boy, then ran down the stairs.

CHAPTER 16

SOOTHCOOR MANSION

There was a hard knock on the Malmsby front door a little more than thirty minutes after Lewis had left. Hearing it, Gwinnie came out of the music room and watched Stephen open the door.

"Are you Daniel?" Stephen asked, pulling the door wide open.

"No, I'm Billy and I needs to see Lady Guinevere," the lad said with arrogant bravado, his fists squarely resting at his waist.

"I'm here," said Gwinnie from the doorway of the music room.

The lad brushed past Stephen and marched down the hall to Gwinnie. "I has a message from Dan fer Mr. Martin. Is he here?" Billy asked.

"No, he is out searching for Daniel now."

The boy nodded. "Dan said if he weren't here I'ze to leave a message with you. Tell 'em that man he's search'n for is in Soothcoor Mansion, and to come quick."

"I understand. Where is Daniel now?" Gwinnie asked.

"Fillin' in fer me. I clean that street. Dan said as how someone here would most likely try to capture him so he couldn't come here hisself."

Gwinnie laughed. "You had best get back then. Tell

Daniel I request he only watch the house. Someone will come soon."

The boy nodded then marched back to the door, looked up at Stephen, waiting for him to open the door again, and then marched out.

"He's a different one," observed Stephen.

Gwinnie absently agreed, contemplating what she should do with Billy's information. "Stephen, where is Mr. Cott?"

"He accompanied His Grace to the bank."

"Blast!" She ran upstairs to her room. "Rose! Help me out of this dress and into my Sarah Knolls clothing."

"Are we going to the charity house?" Rose asked as she helped Gwinnie out of her dress.

"No. You are going to take a note to Bow Street while I go to Soothcoor Mansion."

"Soothcoor Mansion!"

"That is where I believe Mr. Suthers is hiding out."

"Lady Gwinnie, that be too dangerous."

"I'm just going to join Daniel in the street watching the house, making sure he doesn't leave. I'm not going to do anything to get myself in danger. That is why you are taking the note to Bow Street."

Rose frowned. "But—"

"I'm not like the heroines in my brother's stories. I am not going to do something to put myself in danger. I'm going to be an observer. The way my head still aches, I couldn't do anything else. Now put this dress away and get my other clothes while I write a note for Bow Street," Gwinnie said.

She pulled paper and a pencil from a small desk by the window. She had no time for ink and quill. By the time she was finished with her note, Rose was waiting with her Sarah clothes. Gwinnie donned them quickly, then took the hairpins out of her hair.

"Rose, can you tie this mass back with a hair ribbon?" Gwinnie asked as she shook her head loose from its confining pins.

"Why did you take your hair down?"

An Artful Decision

"I'm not wearing a bonnet, I'm just wrapping a shawl over my head. I'll draw less attention to myself."

"Yes, my lady," Rose said primly, obviously not in favor of Gwinnie's plan.

"Thank you. Here's the note for you to take to Bow Street. We'll leave together. I'll wait here for you to get your coat from your room."

They went down the servants' stairs and out the tradesmen's entrance to the house. They walked swiftly two blocks before Rose had to turn off toward Bow Street.

"I don't feel right about this," Rose complained. "Especially with your head injury yesterday."

"I'm fine. My headache actually feels better out in the cold," Gwinnie assured her, not admitting the occasional dizziness that struck her. Hopefully, that had all passed. "Now hurry along."

"Yes, my lady."

Gwinnie continued walking. She supposed she should have hailed a hackney, but she didn't. The mudlarks roamed all over the city on foot. She could as well, she thought with a smile. And the cold did help her aching head.

~

A FIFTEEN-MINUTE WALK brought her to a corner of Grosvenor Square. She saw Billy at the other end but not Daniel. Most of the houses she passed still had the door knockers removed. Their owners had not yet returned to the city after the holidays. She walked toward Billy. When he looked in her direction, she lifted an arm to wave at him, then she immediately felt a hard poke in her back.

"No, don't turn around," said a woman's harsh voice behind her. "Just keep walking toward the corner and mews entrance on the right."

Gwinnie did as she was told. She could do little else as the sudden poke in her back had set off a wave of dizziness. Through her coat, she could not tell if what the woman held at her back was a knife, a pistol, or a stick.

Given her aching head, Gwinnie did not feel confident she could overpower the woman. In any other circumstance, it would be the work of a moment. However, perhaps that was just as well. Gwinnie wanted information.

"Miss Southerland?" Gwinnie guessed.

"Shut up!"

"You *are* Miss Southerland. What is going on?" Gwinnie asked, slowly walking forward.

Keeping her hands low, in front of her waist, Gwinnie motioned to Billy to stay where he was and wait as she questioned Miss Southerland.

"I said shut up!" She poked her weapon harder into Gwinnie's back. Gwinnie thought it now felt like a pistol barrel.

"This way," Miss Southerland said, pushing her into the mews.

Gwinnie did not fight her. She didn't feel she could. She must reserve her strength. The pistol eased away from her back a little. "See the lantern hanging up ahead?"

Gwinnie nodded.

"That's the back of Soothcoor Mansion. I had such a sweet little business operating out of that house."

"Business?" Gwinnie asked meekly.

"Yes, a business fencing stolen goods," Miss Southerland said with a delighted laugh and another poke in her back.

"I don't understand," Gwinnie said. Though she did, all too well, and that Miss Southerland did not intend for her to leave Soothcoor Mansion alive. She had to keep her talking. She knew Lewis would come if she had sufficient time. "I thought you were the housekeeper for Lady Soothcoor."

"I was. Easy job, she had more staff than she needed, not that she knew."

"Why?"

"So they could be leased out to big parties to steal for me," she said proudly.

"You were behind the thefts five years ago where your daughter was arrested?"

"That was all neatly planned to turn attention elsewhere," Miss Southerland said with a self-satisfied tone to her voice. She opened a gate, then pushed Gwinnie through into the back kitchen garden and storage building area behind the house. She shoved Gwinnie toward the house.

Gwinnie noticed she didn't contradict Alice's relationship to her.

"See that storage building? I told Lady Soothcoor we needed it, so she had it built for me. It used to be full of stolen goods, but when she moved to Appleton, I had to move that stuff, too. Good thing my son is a carter, eh?"

"Freddie Suthers is your son?"

"Fine boy, does whatever his mama says."

"Including throwing a brick at my head," Gwinnie said sourly.

"Yes, but not hard enough," she groused. "You were supposed to either be dead or laid up for a while. Here it is a day later, and you are up and about. All you got is a big ugly bruise on your face."

"Why? What have I done to you?" Gwinnie asked.

"Go down those stairs," Miss Southerland ordered. "What have you done? You've taught those girls to be good! I can tell now I'll not be able to undo that training. I'll need a new bunch of girls to train up to be my greathouse thieves."

Gwinnie felt a glow of warmth in her heart that she'd had that effect on the women. She slowly went down the dim stairs to the servants' area of the great house, placing her hand against the wall to keep herself steady. "Mrs. Albert and Miss Wooler wouldn't let you get away with that."

"They turned in their notices this morning, which suits my needs just fine. What I didn't count on was Soothcoor's interest in his charity. My sister told me he was interested. Didn't believe her. I thought he just let her run it however she wished. That's a bit of a problem. Not sure if that house is going to work out for my plan, now. Guess I didn't need to off my sister-in-law."

"You killed Mrs. Southerland! Why?"

"I told you; I wanted her house for my school."

"A school for thieves."

"Smiling, obedient, ghosts, walking unnoticed amongst the wealthy, stealing from them and bringing their stolen goods to me for a remittance," she said playfully.

At the bottom of the staircase was a worn oak door. Miss Southerland reached around Gwinnie to knock three times. The door was opened by the man in the young street cleaner's picture!

Gwinnie drew in a sharp breath.

"Lady Gwinnie! What are you doing here!" she heard Daniel say. Her heart sank at the sound of his voice.

She looked around the man to see Daniel tied to an armless wood chair before a scarred table.

"I could ask the same of you," she returned. She suddenly felt lost.

"Yeah, I guess so. Mr. Martin is gonna be so mad at us," he said gloomily.

Gwinnie allowed Miss Southerland to push her into the room. She landed on her knees.

"Lady Gwinnie!" Daniel exclaimed.

Gwinnie looked up at him and winked, then slowly rose to her feet. As voluble as she'd been, Gwinnie didn't think Miss Southerland could allow them to live, but it also seemed she couldn't decide if they might have a use or not.

Someone would get a message to Lewis— Mr. Martin — she corrected herself. He'd come, she knew, and that feeling of being lost faded away.

"What are you going to do with us?" she asked, adding a tremor to her voice. She stood hunched, though she watched them both carefully. Headache or not, she was a strong woman; however, there was no need for them to know that— and she didn't know how badly her injured head might betray her. Her head pounded.

"I don't know yet." Miss Southerland's eyes narrowed. "I want to know how you both ended up at this house."

"I doubt we would be here if you hadn't had this man

—" Gwinnie pointed at Mr. Suthers, "— throw a brick at me."

Miss Southerland rounded on the man. "You were followed! Didn't I tell you to make sure no one followed you?"

"No one. I swear Mama, an' I went a twisty ways here. I on'y stopped to buys a meat pie. I was so hungry."

"You're Freddie Suthers's mother?" Gwinnie asked.

"His name is Frederick Southerland. He's a loyal, good boy, not like his twin, Alice, the bitch. Freddie dear, pull a chair behind the boy's and tie her to it, and tie the two chairs together."

"Alice Southerland?" Gwinnie asked, as Freddie maneuvered her into the chair and put her hands behind her back. "The one who was originally arrested in one of your thievery schemes?"

She looked back over her shoulder at Miss Southerland as she spoke, while interlacing her fingers together and pushing her arms as hard apart as she could. Though Freddie pulled the rope as tight together as he thought it would go, he couldn't fully see her tied hands, for Daniel's hands and ropes were in the way.

"She wouldn't have been arrested if she'd brought that spoon to me, like she was supposed to. And none of us would have been called to testify, neither. They called us in because we were all seen together and come from the same agency."

"But all charges were dropped."

"Can you believe that stupid cow left the spoon in her apron pocket? That's what got her and us pulled in."

"But since she didn't remove it from the house, the homeowner believed her story that she'd picked it up to turn in later and forgot it was there," Gwinnie said, continuing the story for her as she unlinked her fingers. Her ropes instantly sagged slightly, as she'd hoped, giving her a bit more space to move her fingers. She felt for the knots in Daniel's ropes. String musicians possessed strong fingers, she thought, repressing a satisfied smile. She used her finger strength to her advantage.

"That was the only smart thing she did," Miss Southerland said, still pointing her pistol at her.

Gwinnie recognized the firearm as like the small pistol used at Ann and Ellinbourne's engagement ball last June. The one used to wound Lord Candelstone.

"What happened after that?" Gwinnie asked to keep her talking.

"The chit fled town! Left a note saying she didn't want to be in the family business, as she called it. Weren't no family business, were my business. Then she wrote to my brother and tried to get him to leave, too. I wasn't haven' non'a that."

"You killed Derek Southerland? Your brother?"

"Nah." She walked around her and Daniel, tied to their chairs to stand in front of Gwinnie. "My Freddie done that." She put her arm around her son's shoulders and hugged him to her.

Gwinnie took advantage of Miss Southerland's new position to work harder on the knots. When Daniel's ropes loosened, she held on to them to prevent them from falling to the floor and giving her game away. She tapped Daniel's hands to signal him to loosen her bonds. It took a bit of tapping with her fingers and presenting her knots to him before he understood and started to eagerly work on the rope around her hands.

Miss Southerland's eyes narrowed. "But you evaded ma question. Just how'd ya come ta this house?"

The more she talked, the more Miss Southerland's language degenerated to the accent of the stews. Gwinnie found herself fascinated by the change. How did she acquire a refined accent to begin with? An accent that allowed her to become an upper servant in a great house?

"My gang found ya!" Daniel said proudly.

"You," corrected Gwinnie, automatically.

"You sound like Lewis," Daniel grumbled.

"What gang?"

"Us mudlarks! Can't do much mudlarking in winter so we wander the city. One of the gang was on this street, showed the picture to someone else on the street, who saw Freddie coming in and out of the house."

"I told you not to let anyone see you."

"I did, Mama. There were never anybody about."

"Well, obviously, someone saw you. We were going to have to give up this location anyway, seein' as how the earl is selling the building. Do you have everything packed up?"

"Yes, Mama."

"Even the pantry?"

Gwinnie saw a stricken look cross his face. "I gots most out," he said slowly.

"Most is not all, get busy getting everything out of there. Now!" she yelled when he hesitated.

"But, Mama—"

"I said *now*. I'll watch these two, then we'll set fire to the house."

Freddie tromped down the hall toward the kitchen. They could hear him making noise moving things around.

Gwinnie felt Daniel's ropes give way. She grabbed his hand to warn against movement as Miss Southerland came closer to her. The woman transferred the pistol to her left hand, then grabbed her chin in her hand. "You're not even that pretty," she said.

"Yes she is!" yelled Daniel, leaping out of his chair.

Surprised, Miss Southerland turned toward him.

Gwinnie took advantage of her inattention to push the hand carrying the gun up. The gun went off, exactly as Gwinnie hoped. She wrestled Miss Southerland to the floor. The woman thrashed and kicked until Gwinnie sat on her.

"The ropes, Daniel!"

But Daniel was ahead of her and pushed one immediately into her hand, then went over to the door leading to the hall Freddie walked down and closed and locked the door. Then he turned toward the door that led up to the tradesman's entrance and locked that too.

"Daniel, come over here to tie her legs together."

Footsteps pounded down the stairs. "Gwinnie! Gwinnie," they heard.

"We're here. We're all right!" Gwinnie yelled back, grinning. "Daniel, go unlock that door again."

Daniel scrambled up off the floor.

"No!" screamed Miss Southerland, bucking again to get Gwinnie off her.

Though Miss Southerland's actions brought on a new wave of dizziness, Gwinnie stayed where she was.

Lewis pushed the door open and started to rush in, but stopped. Behind him was Mr. Cott. Lewis started to laugh and leaned against the door frame.

"I'd say you have things managed."

Gwinnie looked down at her position and started to laugh, too, though her heart pounded in her chest. She'd perched atop the woman's back, one hand holding down her neck, the other pressing down on the woman's arse, and Gwinnie's skirts were in a froth about her knees.

Lewis rushed to Gwinnie's side, a hand outstretched to lift her up, his eyes filled with relief and tenderness. She came up swiftly and easily into his arms. She sagged against him. Mr. Cott trundled into the room, lifted Miss Southerland, and tossed her over his shoulder.

"Wait!" Gwinnie said. "Her son is around here too!"

"You mean Freddie Suthers? He's trussed up and tossed in his cart," Lewis said.

"I knew you would come," she said. "I just needed to keep her talking." She leaned her head against his.

Lewis pulled her head down to kiss her.

Gwinnie closed her eyes, a tingling in her chest descended to her lady's privates. Heat surged back up. Her breathing grew heavy, and she felt like she was sinking into him.

He drew back, his hand reaching up to cup the back of her head. His brilliant blue eyes searched her face, full of hope and uncertainty. "I've wanted to do that for the longest time. You have no idea," he whispered.

A whimpered escaped her lips as she bowed her head, seeking solace in the shelter of his shoulder, the weight of their new-found desires filling her with warmth and happiness. "I knew you'd come," she re-

An Artful Decision

peated with a watery smile. "I knew you would save us. I never doubted you for a moment, Lewis."

He drew back his head to look at her. "Seems you did a good job of saving yourself," he observed.

"Only because I knew you were coming and would back me up," she said.

He drew her against him again.

Gwinnie sighed, then remembered his promise that she could tease him at any time. "If only you were a few inches taller," she breathed, smiling, wanting to see his cheeky smile in return.

He stilled, then slowly released her, his expression solemn, almost angry. "We need to get you home, and Daniel back in his bed," he said curtly.

At his expression and the curious tone of his voice, Gwinnie's heart plummeted like a stone.

He led her outside, his manner slowly withdrawing from her. Gwinnie felt confused. A moment ago, he was kissing her in the most outrageously wonderful manner, smiling and caressing her, sending the pounding in her head away. Now he was all business. Bow Street Runner business.

Why? Here was the man she tried to put all manner of barriers against, telling herself she could not possibly be attracted to him. Yet she was. Had been for months.

Outside, he hailed a hackney for her, giving the jarvey instructions to take her directly to Malmsby house, and giving her a bow as the carriage drove off. She looked out the window at him until the carriage turned the corner.

Their discourse went through her mind. She remembered briefly thinking she wanted to tease him and wished he were a few inches taller. Her brow furrowed. Had she said that aloud? Had it not come out as a tease?

Her cheeks flamed with embarrassment. She must have. It was a thought that had plagued her for months. Why? Why had she been so caught up in a gentleman's height and her demand that he be taller than her? — It had become her protection, her armor to keep men away. A habit to say.

Was height something to be concerned about? What

an idiotic creature she was. She would be sure the next time she saw him to apologize and beg his forgiveness. Would he grant it? Had she hurt him too much for reconciliation when they had scarcely come to terms with their feelings? Would he ever forgive her for the walls she'd built around her heart? Could she ever convince him she was ready to let him in?

A pang of self-disgust washed over Gwinnie as she berated herself for clinging to such trivial notions as height as a measure of worthiness. Tears rolled down her cheeks. The rocking in the carriage brought back the dizziness. She held her head in her hands.

Were second chances granted for eight-and-twenty, silly widgeons? Maybe Grandmother would know.

CHAPTER 17

HIS GRACE REMEMBERS

Gwinnie stumbled into Malmsby House, her head hurting almost as badly as it had the previous day. Stephen caught her before she could fall, all her strength drained from her body.

"Your Grace!" yelled Stephen, as he eased her into sitting on the chair in the porter's alcove.

Gwinnie closed her eyes until she heard heavy footsteps coming down the stairs. It was her father and Lord Soothcoor.

"You fool girl!" cried out her father.

"I know, I know," she said. "Please help me to the Lady Margaret Parlor."

"You should be in your bed."

"I know and I will when I recover a bit. Please, if you just give me your arm, I can walk," she said, as she struggled to her feet.

"Stephen, have tea and brandy brought to the parlor," the duke said. as he supported Gwinnie to stand up.

"Let me get on your other side," Lord Soothcoor said.

With her father and Lord Soothcoor on either side of her, she made it to the ground-floor parlor, despite the pounding in her head, and lay back against the sofa pillows.

"Where is Mr. Martin?" her father asked gruffly. "I expected him to see you home, or at least Mr. Cott."

Gwinnie licked her lips. "Taking care of Daniel and his prisoners, I imagine," she said, trying not to let her feelings rush out.

"Prisoners?" asked Lord Soothcoor.

"I will tell you, but can I get a cold compress for my head?"

The duke rang for the maid, giving her further instructions. By the time Stephen came back with the refreshments, Mrs. Hunnicutt followed behind him with the cold compress.

Her father poured her a small glass of brandy and insisted she drink it first, while Mrs. Hunnicutt poured her tea and prepared it as she liked it.

"Thank you," Gwinnie said softly. The cold on her head did a wonderful job easing the pain. She sighed her relief. "Where is Grandmother?"

"She'll be here in a moment," Mrs. Hunnicutt said, as she pulled off Gwinnie's boots and swung her feet onto the sofa. "She said she wanted to bring down the laudanum from your room."

Gwinnie made a sour face at the word laudanum, refusing to admit it had helped her yesterday.

"Tell us what happened," her father said, he and Soothcoor sitting in the chairs they'd pulled up close to the sofa the other day.

"Not without me here, Arthur," said the Dowager Duchess of Malmsby, coming into the room, clutching the laudanum bottle in one hand. She placed it on the table near Gwinnie's head and then sat at the other end of the sofa, pulling Gwinnie's feet into her lap and covering them with the shawl.

"Daniel had learned through his contacts that Mr. Suthers was seen going in and out of Soothcoor Mansion through the tradesmen entrance. He sent the street cleaner to us to tell Mr. Martin where Mr. Suthers was. Daniel stayed behind to keep watch."

"Why didn't he come here as Mr. Martin had instructed him to?" asked her father.

"Because he knew we would try to detain him, and he did not want to be detained. Unfortunately, Suthers saw him watching and captured him. He brought him into Soothcoor Mansion and tied him up in the servant's hall."

"And him with his broken ribs," said her grandmother, shaking her head.

"Daniel was confident his gang could find Mr. Suthers, he just had to get them looking, and he was correct."

"Why did you go to Soothcoor Mansion?" her grandmother asked.

"I wanted to keep Daniel company and be another set of eyes in case Mr. Suthers left the house. But I didn't see Daniel anywhere. I saw the street cleaner down the block and was about to hail him when I felt the end of a pistol in my back held by Miss Southerland.

"I was surprised. I did think her a liar and wondered why; however, I never considered her a killer. She killed Mrs. Southerland, and she had her son, Fredrick Southerland, murder her brother."

"Freddie Suthers is Freddie Southerland?"

"Yes. He is at his mother's beck and call, doing anything she wishes."

"Why did she want to take over the charity? Was it just someplace to live until she could find another position from where she could run her theft ring?" Soothcoor asked.

Gwinnie started to laugh but stopped when another pain shot through her head. "No. She thought she could have a school for thieves!"

"A school for thieves!" repeated her grandmother, incredulous.

Gwinnie nodded. "She thought it would be easy to turn these women to theft in exchange for them getting better living and paying positions."

"I take it she found out that would not be easy," drawled Soothcoor.

"No, especially since she treated them like a military regiment ordering no talking, laughing, or any camaraderie. I don't know if you have received it yet; however,

Miss Southerland said Mrs. Albert and Miss Wooler have turned in their notice."

Soothcoor sat up straighter. "No!"

"That is what she told me, I don't know if that is true or not," Gwinnie admitted.

"I wouldn't doubt that it is. Excuse me, I need to go to Mrs. Southerland's House for Unfortunate Women now. Hopefully, I can stop Mrs. Albert and Miss Wooler from leaving."

"I'll go with you," the duchess said. "I might be able to bring some peace to the women."

~

AFTER HER GRANDMOTHER and Soothcoor left, her father stayed behind with her, staring at her with troubled eyes.

"What is it?" she asked.

"I owe you an apology, my dear. I have failed to give you the proper attention."

"I don't know what you mean, Father, you have always been a caring father."

"But I didn't take an interest in what you did, nor did I see that you had the proper suitors. You should have been married by now."

Gwinnie snorted. "I have never 'taken' in society, that you know. I have been happier playing my violin."

"Your grandmother told me you are thinking you get more enjoyment now out of teaching these unfortunate women, such as are at Mrs. Southerland's, how to make better lives for themselves."

"Well, that is true, but I considered that a confidence I told her; I am not happy she shared it. But what does it matter? Neither are considered the appropriate activities for a duke's daughter," she said, laughing.

The compress shifted down the side of her head. Gwinnie raised an arm to resettle it on her head. Her father grabbed her hand. "What's this?" he asked, looking at the red, angry rope scrapes on her wrist.

"That's from when my wrists were bound." She

looked at both her wrists. "I hadn't realized I'd rubbed against the rope so hard. They do burn a little."

"You need Mrs. Hunnicutt's arnica salve for your wrists," he said. He rang the servants' bell.

Stephen came to the door.

"Ask Mrs. Hunnicutt for some of the salve she uses for burns and scrapes," the duke said.

"And a new cold compress, please," Gwinnie called out.

"I should give you some of this laudanum," her father said.

"Not yet," Gwinnie said. "I'll take more when I get upstairs. I'd rather have another small glass of brandy, if I might?"

Her father frowned but poured her a finger-full. "Do you think you will be able to walk upstairs?"

"I think so. I can lean on the balustrade on one side and on you on the other. Together, we can get me upstairs," she said with a slight grin. "Despite my large size."

Her father shook his head. "You have forever talked of your large size. I don't see you as large and don't see where you get that from."

"Father," Gwinnie began patiently, for she knew her father would not see her flaws, "I am taller than any other woman in society. And most of the men. That makes people uncomfortable."

Her father shook his head. "Balderdash. You are like your mother in size and shape."

"No, I'm not. I am taller than she was and so were you."

"Where do you come up with that notion?" he asked, frowning at her now.

"I just know it."

Her father leaned back in his chair and crossed his legs. He looked at her consideringly. "When was the last time you looked at the painting of your mother and me that hangs over the fireplace in my library?"

"I see it every time I go in." She frowned, not understanding his question.

"You may look in its direction; however, you do not

see it. Your mother and I are standing together in the gardens of Versely Park. She is wearing a flat-brimmed straw hat, and I am wearing my beaver, and she is taller than me."

"She is not standing on a hillock?"

"Is that what you thought all these years?" he asked her.

"I don't know. I never really thought about it," she said slowly, thinking back on her life.

"Your mother was four full inches taller than me—and I am not a short man."

Gwinnie remembered her mother, and remembered her as being tall, but didn't remember her taller than her father. In her memories, they stood the same height. "She was really that tall?"

"Yes."

"And that didn't bother you or her?" she asked.

"She didn't like being that tall; however, I never let her use that as a reason to push me aside. I fell in love with her when I saw her galloping across the hills of her grandfather's Scotland property, no hat on, her hair flying out behind her, and moving as one with her horse." He smiled. "I didn't know who she was then, though I had my suspicions, and I convinced your Uncle Hamish to introduce me. That was the best decision of my life."

Gwinnie stared at his glistening eyes. "You miss her."

"Every day. But after a couple of couple of years, I began to feel her presence, pushing me to get on with life."

"Is that why you turned your attention to inventions?"

"Yes. And would you think worse of me if I confess, I feel the desire to wed again?"

"Wed again?" Gwinnie repeated. A multitude of thoughts and memories raced one after the other through Gwinnie's mind, more happy than sad. She tilted her head to the side. "No-o," she said slowly. She smiled at her father. "I think Mother would want you to."

"Such is my thought as well. It's been over ten years since we lost her."

Gwinnie laughed lightly. "If she were one of Lakehurst's ghosts from his novels, she'd be likely to kick your arse."

Her father laughed with Gwinnie. "Yes, she would," he said softly, his lips quirking sideways as he thought of his late wife.

"Would you like me to help you upstairs now?" her father asked.

Gwinnie bit her lower lip, then shook her head. "No. I think I would like to stay here. I expect Mr. Martin, or at least Mr. Cott will come here, and I would speak with them if I might. Also Rose, when she returns— I'm surprised she has not returned yet."

"I'll let Stephen know. Another letter came in the post today from my stalker. I haven't read it yet. I'll be in my library studying this new note if you should need me— And Gwinnie, please send for me if you need me."

"I will, Father."

~

GWINNIE DOZED ON THE SOFA. It felt like at least an hour had passed before she heard the front door open and voices come from the entry hall. She blinked a few times, then pushed herself up straighter on the sofa. The compress on her head now felt warm. She pulled it off and laid it on the tea tray that still sat on the table beside her. The room had chilled. She felt a slight draft from the terrace doors, and she noted the coals in the iron stove heater were more embers.

She laughed to herself. "*Forgotten*," she mused. The household assumed she'd gone to her room. She reached over the cold tea service to pull the bell. She needed the room warmed, a new compress, and hot tea. But more importantly, she wanted to know who had arrived!

Mercy soon opened the door.

"Gracious, my lady, we all thought you'd gone to bed!"

"No, I decided to stay downstairs for a while longer.

Would you close the curtains over the terrace doors? There seems to be a draft coming from them."

"Immediately, my lady! And I'll add coals to the heating stove."

"Lady Gwinnie?" It was Rose's voice.

"Yes! Come in please. I was worried about you."

Rose hurried to her side. "Stephen said you'd gone to bed; I was about to go upstairs to check on you."

Gwinnie laughed. "No, I wanted to wait for you and hoped Mr. Martin would come as well."

"He's here," she said, looking over her shoulder at the door where Mr. Martin stood just outside.

"Mr. Martin. Come here, please," Gwinnie said, her mind working furiously to devise a way to ease the hurt she'd caused him. She didn't mean it seriously. But he frowned as he entered the parlor, his posture stiff.

"Mr. Martin," Gwinnie said. "Sit here, please," she said, indicating the chair her father had sat in earlier.

"My lady, I should go straight away to speak to the duke."

"No, you should come straight away to sit here. I have a few things to say— Rose, please fetch me a new compress for my head. Mercy, my tea is cold, could you please get a fresh pot before you finish with the coals?" she told the two servants, shooing them away with her hands.

"Now, Mr. Martin," she said severely when the women left the room. She smiled at the sight of the parlor door left open after they left. "I remember, quite clearly, a conversation we had yesterday— Hard to believe it was only yesterday, but so it was. In this discussion you informed me that I should feel free to use you as the butt of my wit."

"Yes, I did, my lady."

"Then why today have you taken offense to my wit? You told me you had thick skin, and should I see an opportunity for wit I should take it, and you would not take it amiss. But you did take it amiss. To my great sorrow, you did!"

"I do not understand, my lady," Lewis said, frowning.

"Go away with you then to my father's library for your

meeting with him, and while you are there, take a careful look at the painting over the fireplace of my father and mother. Maybe that will open your mind," Gwinnie declared. She waved him away.

"Go! Go!" she said, "and don't come back until you figure it out," she ordered when he didn't immediately get up, trying to frown at him, though a smile fought the frown for prominence.

Lewis's brows drew together, but he rose from the chair and left the room as Rose returned with the cold compress.

CHAPTER 18

MR. MARTIN LEARNS A LESSON

"Come in, Mr. Martin, come in," the duke said, when Lewis appeared at his door. "As you might imagine, I should like to know how the events of this afternoon went down."

"Yes, Your Grace. As you heard my man say, my ward removed his bandages binding his ribs, got dressed, and went to his contacts to discover the whereabouts of Mr. Suthers. I do not know whether to punish or praise the boy." He shook his head as he ran a hand through his wavy blond hair.

The duke laughed. "It is often that way with children. Especially when they think they are doing good. I remember when my son as a child rescued a puppy from a swiftly flowing stream." The duke shook his head. "He tossed the puppy onto the shore, then grabbed hold of a fallen tree before he was swept down to the river. My heart was in my throat as I saw all this from a distance. I didn't know if I would reach him in time. He thought it a jolly fun heroic adventure!"

Lewis laughed with him. "Rather goes with the stories he writes," he said, though his eyes darted to the fireplace and the painting above. It was at an odd angle for him to see properly from where he sat.

"Yes, it does," the duke agreed. "I see you looking up

at the painting of Gwinnie's mother and me." The duke rose from behind his desk and walked toward it.

Lewis rose as well and followed the duke.

"Lady Guinevere said there was something I should see in this painting."

The duke laughed lightly. "Yes, I believe I know what it was." He turned toward Lewis. "I hope you understand what a fortunate man you are, Lewis," the duke said, patting Lewis on the back.

Lewis started at the duke calling him by his given name, but kept his face blank. He looked closer at the painting. He believed he recognized the location where the painting was done as in the Versely Park gardens. He smiled as he remembered the area. Then his eyes caught something else. At first, he thought it a painter's trick of light atop the duke's hat, then he realized what Gwinnie referred to. A smile spread across his face. "Thank you, Your Grace," he said. "If you will excuse me?"

"Yes, but do come back at sometime today, I have another letter for you to review," the duke said with a laugh.

Lewis only half heard the last of what the duke said. He ran out of the room, down the stairs and pushed open the Lady Margaret Parlor doors without knocking.

The dowager duchess sat in the room with Gwinnie.

"Are you sure?" he asked from the doorway, ignoring the duchess.

Gwinnie rolled her eyes, then clapped a hand on her head to prevent the fresh compress Rose provided from falling off. Her grandmother looked down into her fresh cup of tea and compressed her lips in a pursed smile.

"Yes. And I've decided I want a courtship as your debt for not following my humor after your promise."

"A courtship," he said, coming into the room, walking like a stalking beast toward her.

"How exciting," the duchess said.

Lewis pulled a confused and delighted Gwinnie to her feet.

"Oh? What are you about?" she asked, thrilled, until he bent forward and hefted her over his shoulder, the compress falling to the floor. His arms wrapped around the backs of her thighs. "Lewis! What are you doing? Stop!"

The duchess giggled as she pulled the shawl free from Gwinnie and tossed it back on the sofa. "Be careful, Mr. Martin," the duchess trilled.

"Lewis," he corrected her.

"Thank you, Lewis!" The duchess beamed at him as she made sure the door was open wide and nothing was in Lewis's path.

"Lewis, you are going to hurt yourself!" protested Gwinnie. "I'm too tall! I'm too heavy!"

Lewis ignored her. He climbed the grand staircase with his precious treasure over his shoulder. He only nodded at the duke when His Grace opened his library door to see what was going on. The duke's lips quirked into a smile. He crossed his arms and leaned against the door frame, and Lewis began to climb the second flight of stairs.

"Father! Make him put me down," Gwinnie called out to her father. "This is the most embarrassing situation. Not fit for a duke's daughter."

Her father shrugged as Lewis continued up the stairs.

"Lewis," Gwinnie pleaded in a softer voice. "You will hurt yourself. You have nothing to prove to me, I swear it," she said, as he achieved the second-floor landing.

He turned toward her room and opened the door to her sitting room. "Lewis, please, I love you!" she said.

He eased her down until she stood before him, then grabbed her face between his two hands. "As I love you and have done so since the day after Ann's and Ellinbourne's betrothal ball. It tears at my soul that you were hurt and are still hurting. You cannot fathom the agony that I let you down."

"But you d—" she started to protest, but he laid a finger against her lips.

"You will never convince me otherwise," he said, as he leaned in to kiss her.

Gwinnie wrapped her arms around him, pulling him as close to her as she might. She gathered herself up to his kiss. Any lingering thoughts she might have harbored about the effect of their difference in heights vanished. He finally pulled back and laid his forehead against hers.

"If I kiss you anymore," he said harshly, "I will want to carry you through that door' to your bedchamber, for I want more than just your lips. My body screams for all of you. I have visions of your glorious red hair spread out across the pillows as I come to you."

Gwinnie shivered and closed her eyes briefly.

"I trust this courtship you are demanding will not last long, but no matter, for I promise you for as long as the courtship will be, that is how long before I let you out of my sight, our bedroom, our bed."

Gwinnie's insides quivered and tightened in a way she had never felt before.

"Lewis," she whispered, clinging to him.

Lewis stepped away. "To bed with you now, and a nighttime draught of laudanum. I want you well and strong."

Gwinnie smiled coyly at him, but did move away from him to open the door between her bedroom and the sitting room. Rose stood in her bedroom waiting for her.

Lewis breathed in deeply, willing his heart to slow its racehorse pace, and turned to leave the sitting room and go back to the duke's library to see the latest letter threat.

~

LEWIS SAT down in front of the duke. "Am I to understand I have your approval?" he asked.

The duke smiled. "Heartily. I would say you are a perfect complement to my Gwinnie. I could only wish you could have found each other a few years ago."

"You know I was born on the wrong side of the blanket."

"Yes, and that you are Harleigh's get. He was proud of you, you know."

Lewis dipped his head. "Thank you for that."

"No need to thank me, it is the truth. We do need to get together to discuss settlements and all but not now. There are more pressing matters."

"To say nothing of the fact Gwinnie says she wants a courtship."

"A courtship!" her father barked a laugh.

"It's my penance for failing to catch one of her, ah— witticisms."

"Ock! She's playing with you," the duke said, leaning back in his chair.

Lewis's smile broadened into a grin, his eyes twinkling. "So I would assume."

The duke shook his head, then he straightened. "We do have other business to attend to. I received another letter today."

"So you said earlier."

"This one is most interesting. Either the writer is careless, or he means to incriminate someone else in the threats."

"What do you mean."

"Here's the letter. Take particular look at the outside of the letter and the various fold marks."

Lewis looked at the duke quizzically but accepted the paper from him. He read the inside quickly. It represented more of what had been received before. He turned it over. The first thing he noticed was the paper had been originally folded in half. When he turned it over, he saw the letter had been franked, but not where one would assume, at the top of the correspondence. It appeared to be at the bottom left, but someone refolded the letter forward to put the frank on the outside top right. But folded to the back from the bottom and sealed with sealing wax. To hold the front fold down to ensure the frank remained visible, a small dab of wax was applied underneath the folded part.

Lewis looked at the duke quizzically.

"I'm sure you are aware that Parliament seat holders have postage franking privileges. It is common practice— though frowned upon— to frank a few sheets of blank paper so one doesn't have to always be around when a family member wishes to send off a letter. Yes, franked letters should only be used for official mail; however, the practice of allowing friends and family to share in the privilege through pre-franked letters is common. I myself am guilty of this practice.

"And this letter bears franked postage by a Parliamentary member? A marquess, I'm guessing, by the design? Do you know whose signature this is?"

"The Marquess of Alton."

Lewis opened the letter and read it again. "The Marquess of Alton is not excited by the new inventions, but neither is he against progress, from what I've read in the papers."

The duke nodded. "I have been studying and puzzling over this letter for an hour now. The author is someone in his household."

"Someone close enough to have access to his study."

"Yes. I believe the letter author, when they grabbed a piece of paper to write upon, was unaware they grabbed a franked blank paper."

"Looking at how it was refolded, I'd venture they did not post this letter themselves but requested another do so. This other person— likely a butler or a valet— seeing the original paper had been previously franked, tried to be helpful and save a few pence by changing the folds of the letter to ensure the frank to cover postage displayed."

"My guess is my threatening letters come from Robert Alton, Earl of Wicholm, first-born and heir to Alton. He is a strong agrarian man. The only new ideas he seeks are improved crop planting and land contouring for crops. He is against new inventions, particularly those for crop planting and harvesting."

"Protecting his tenants?"

"I don't know."

"We should talk to the marquess and discover who has access to his franked stationary," Lewis said.

"As it happens, we can do that tonight. He will be at Soames Chop House near Parliament. When he is in town, he is a frequenter of the Wednesday night gathering of various members of Parliament."

"Will they let me in?"

"As you are with me and are investigating a crime against me, then no one may say against you."

"Then let's go. If I can solve two cases in one day, along with getting an agreement with Gwinnie for a courtship, this will be a most memorable day in my life!"

The duke laughed, then became serious. "I should certainly like to stop looking over my shoulder for danger to me and Gwinnie."

"As would I!"

~

THE DUKE AND Lewis passed through the white-washed front public rooms to the private chamber in the back of Soames Chop House. The hall leading to the private room was paneled, and the paneling so polished over the years, they looked more like black wood paneling than brown.

On the walls hung pictures of England's prime ministers for two hundred years without favoring Whig or Tory in placement.

The duke pointed at the pictures. "Soames is adamant his establishment will not become either a Whig or Tory bastion. He hopes to have Soames Chop House be common ground." The duke laughed slightly. "A noble wish; however, where loyalties run deep, emotions run high."

Lewis nodded as he looked around. Double doors were open at the end of the hall. A liveried footman in a white wig and black buckled shoes stood at the door, an attire harkening back to the previous century.

"Good evening, Jeffery. I have Mr. Lewis Martin with me this evening. Has Alton arrived yet?"

"No, Your Grace. But Your Grace—" the footman started to say.

The duke patted his shoulder. "Good man, Jeffery, good man," the duke said, walking past the footman into the room.

Lewis suppressed a smile at how easily the duke bypassed the footman who was no doubt ready to say Lewis would have to leave.

"Malmsby!" came cries from around the room. "Well met!"

The duke lifted his hand in acknowledgement to his friends. A couple came over to speak to him.

"Planning to attend the opening session this year?" one young buck asked him.

Malmsby made a face. "I would prefer not to; however, I have been persuaded that my attendance is important, though I'm not quite sure for whom," he ended forcefully. Those around him laughed. "Let me introduce you to my friend, Mr. Lewis Martin. Hope you don't mind me bringing him here. We have other events to also attend this evening, and it was easier to come to all together. Besides, he's soon to be my son-in-law," he proclaimed.

Lewis smiled at the men who gathered around to wish him well, though he was surprised that the duke would make that announcement here. Nothing was finalized yet. Nothing sent to the papers.

"You look familiar," one man said. "You related to the Harleighs?"

"Yes," Lewis said.

Another man turned around and called across the room. "Harleigh, there is a relative of yours here that's going to marry Lady Guinevere, if that don't beat all. You holding out on us and not sharing that news?"

Harleigh got up from where he was sitting and walked toward Lewis. "News to me, too, Ralston," he said.

Lewis had felt every muscle in his body tense when he realized Harleigh was here. He kept his face still as stone until Harleigh put his hand out. The action startled Lewis, but he felt relief flow through his body. He took his brother's hand in his.

"Thank you for what you did for me Sunday night," he said. "Cordelia told me everything."

Lewis smiled a genuine smile, one that reached his blue eyes, crinkling them at the corners. "Isn't that what relatives do?" he asked playfully.

"Demme, Harleigh," said another gentleman around

them, "if that smile don't look like the late earl's," shaking his head.

Lewis's smile dimmed. He didn't want to get Harleigh into an uncomfortable situation.

"Mr. Martin," the duke said from his side, "Alton has arrived."

Lewis nodded. "I have to go. Give my best to your wife, Harleigh."

"I will. And Lewis, go see Scruthers. Rosevale is *yours*," his half-brother said, stressing '*yours*.'

Lewis would have liked to stay and question Harleigh as to what he meant, but their quarry was present. He nodded to Harleigh and followed the duke back toward the entry to the room.

"Alton, a moment please," the duke said to the Marquess of Alton.

"What is it Malmsby? And who is this with you?"

The duke gently took the elbow of the marquess and steered him out of the room. "This is Mr. Lewis Martin. He is a Bow Street agent working with me to discover who is threatening my family."

"Bow Street!" Alton said loudly.

From in the room, several men turned to look at them. The duke led the marquess farther away from the private meeting room.

"And what do you mean, threatening a duke of the realm?"

"I've been getting threatening letters, letters that threaten harm to myself and my daughter, Lady Guinevere. The Dowager Countess of Norwalk has received similar letters."

Alton frowned. "What has this to do with me?"

The duke's lips compressed into a thin line. "The most recent letter I received— just his morning— had your frank on it."

"What? That's impossible." He pulled himself free of Malmsby's clasp.

"Here, my lord," Lewis said deferentially. "This is what the duke received. If we have misinterpreted this, please let us know."

"I most certainly will!" growled the marquess. "I thought we were friends, Malmsby."

"We are, and that is how I know you did not write this letter. But that looks like your frank to me. Are you in the habit like most of us are of franking multiple blank sheets of paper at once to save time later?"

"Yes, I do that. They are in my desk drawer," he said, "and no one goes in my study save for me, my valet, and Richard, my heir."

Lewis watched the marquess closely as he examined the letter. Read it first then turned it over to see the frank. His face drained of color.

"That is my frank," Alton said softly. He shook his head, then looked up at the duke. "You will not receive any further communications of this sort on either plain paper or my franked stationery. That I can promise you," he said, with anger rising in his voice.

"My lord, there needs to be some sort of reparations made to the duke and Lady Norwalk," Lewis said to the marquess. "Need I remind you it is a crime against the king to threaten the life of a peer of the realm. The duke has had to hire guards for protection. Lady Norwalk left town to safeguard her family."

"You are correct, Mr. Martin." Alton's lips worked back and forth as he considered what to say.

"I have a suggestion. Richard will—" Malmsby began.

"So you know who did this."

"We had our suspicions, and your younger son is a member of Lady Norwalk's Gentleman's Trade Club, so we thought that ruled him out," the duke said.

Alton's brow furrowed. "I knew he had joined some business club but not which one."

Malmsby nodded. "He often comes with me to lectures and seminars on new inventions. His particular interest has been what might help agriculture without harming tenant farmers and freeholders."

"I see. I didn't know."

"I suggest for the next two months your heir attend the lectures and seminars on farm innovation, and write a document for Lady Norwalk advising her on what innovation she might want to invest in and have the Gentlemen's Trade members learn. I am certain there will be at least one that can see its benefit. This must be a convincing document like one might write for Parliament," the duke suggested.

The Marquess of Alton looked thoughtful for a moment, then he smiled. "I like that idea. I have been against new machines because I don't have the time to investigate them and learn all of them to make an educated decision. This document you propose my technology-phobic son write is the type of documents we need, especially if written by previous naysayers."

"Such is my thought. How do you want to present this to your son? I do want Mr. Martin to be part of the discussion as he has been part of our investigation to see where the letters came from, we took them that seriously. Lord Wicholm needs to understand these letters are not larks."

"I agree. What if we come together to Malmsby House tomorrow, about 11 a.m.?"

The duke looked at Lewis.

"That will work for me," Lewis said, immediately thinking of the time he could spend with Gwinnie as he started his courtship activities.

CHAPTER 19

THE COURTSHIP BEGINS...OR
DOES IT?

When Lewis returned to his townhouse that night, he felt exhausted but satisfied with the events of the day. He picked up his mail from the table by the front door, stuffing it in his jacket pocket.

He couldn't help smiling as he walked up the stairs to his room, loosening his cravat as he trudged up each step. Gwinnie and he had come to an understanding. He breathed in deeply. That had to be the weakest description—the most timid description—for what had occurred.

Truthfully, he found it difficult to believe his Junoesque goddess could care for him as much as he'd come to care for her. It made no sense. However, he was a practical man, and not one to bypass as heavenly a gift as Lady Guinevere.

He found it hard to fathom that neither his height nor his base-born state bothered her in the slightest. If it bothered others, that was their concern, not hers. She eschewed the pomp and circumstance of her birth. *It simply was as it was.*

Gwinnie's sense of humor and love of the absurd delighted him, as did the other side of her— the side full of compassion for those for whom life dealt harsh hands.

He wondered what he should do as his first courtship

action tomorrow. Knowing Gwinnie, it should make her laugh.

He shrugged out of his jacket and laid it across the chair, then remembered the letters he'd stuffed in his pocket. He took them out and walked over to the lamplight by the bed to see what they were. The first was a note from his friend Harry Liddle, a thief-taker in the Mendip Hills. The second letter was from the Dowager Duchess of Malmsby.

> Dear Mr. Martin,
> I would like Daniel Wrightson to return to Versely Park with me for the duration of his recuperation.

Lewis snorted. He couldn't see Daniel agreeing to that!

> To this end, I will visit Mr. Wrightson tomorrow morning while you are at Malmsby House, and put the scheme to him. If he is agreeable, we shall leave Monday morning.
> I should let you know I intend to appropriate Mr. Cott from Malmsby's employment into my employment. You will have to find another guard for Arthur.

Lewis shook his head. He should have seen that coming. The move would be to Mr. Cott's benefit. He would not complain.

> I hope to have you up to Versely Park again soon, this time as my guest.
>
> Sincerely,
>
> Lady Vivian Nowlton
> Dowager Duchess of Malmsby

Lewis privately conceded it would make his courtship with Gwinnie easier if Daniel were not present. He did not trust Daniel to find another reason to leave off his rib wrappings and go amongst his gang again. He'd never heal if he didn't let himself.

What did Gwinnie want in their courtship? He hoped she did not want a long courtship; he didn't know how he would be able to keep his hands off her for an extended time. And the duke would be watching.

~

LEWIS LEFT his house early the next morning, shortly after breakfast, when he knew the London shops would be open. He caught a hackney to Bond Street where Littledean Fine Porcelain had their London showroom. He hoped they had what he wanted, and he hoped Gwinnie was enchanted and amused.

Thirty minutes later, he was on his way to Malmsby House with his purchase. The clerk had carefully wrapped the object in a Littledean Fine Porcelain box and then, at his request, in a plain wrapping to disguise the nature of the gift.

"Mr. Harold," Lewis said, when the Malmsby House door opened. "Is Lady Guinevere feeling better? Is she up yet today?"

"Yes, Mr. Martin. She is in the gold parlor. You may go on up, sir," the butler said with the indulgent smile of a long-time privileged retainer.

"Thank you, Mr. Harold." Lewis left his coat, hat, and gloves with the man and mounted the stairs two at a time. The parlor door was slightly opened. Lewis peeked inside. Gwinnie was alone in the room, reading.

Lewis knocked gently on the door, then went inside.

Gwinnie turned around, her countenance blossoming into a warm, welcoming smile. "Lewis!" She started to get up.

"No, don't get up," Lewis said, coming quickly over to her side.

"I've been waiting since daybreak to see you! I was hoping you'd come early for breakfast."

"I had an errand to run, first. Here," he said, handing Gwinnie the box. "I am starting this courtship you requested with a special present for you. No flowers or box of chocolates, I'm afraid. It is a Gwinnie-only present."

She looked at the box with surprise and delight. She pulled Lewis down to sit next to her on the sofa. She unwrapped the box, then looked quizzically at him when she saw it came from Littledean Fine Porcelain.

He nodded and smiled back at her.

She opened the box and carefully separated the silk and tissue wrappings from around his gift. It was a small trinket box, but what captured her heart was the porcelain figure of a blond man playing a pianoforte! A statue exquisitely designed and painted. And on the inside of the trinket box part, it was signed by Elizabeth Littledean, her aunt!

"Did you know they had this when you went to their showroom?"

"I *hoped* they had it," Lewis corrected. He ran a figure over the man playing the pianoforte. "I saw one in your grandmother's china collection at Versely Park when I was there last year. Since that was the first time we met, I thought you might appreciate it."

Gwinnie held the trinket box carefully in her cupped palms. Her eyes glistened. "Appreciate it? Just appreciate it? I *love* it!"

"Enough to shorten this courtship?" Lewis ventured.

Gwinnie laughed, then set the porcelain piece down on the table so she could pull her handkerchief from the cuff of her long-sleeved dress to dab at her eyes and nose. "I deserve this courtship. The answer is *no*. But it is a stunning entry in our journey," she acknowledged with a watery laugh.

"Can you tell me more about our journey so I may understand how to go on?" he asked plaintively, a suggestion of a pout on his lips.

"No," Gwinnie said simply, a teasing note in her shining eyes. "You shall have to figure it out."

He clapped a hand to his chest. "My love, you will unman me!"

"Well, I certainly hope not before our wedding night," Gwinnie said levelly.

Lewis's eyes widened, and he fought against a big laugh. "You are a vixen."

"Perhaps," she agreed tranquilly, leaning against him. "No," she corrected, sitting up again, "what I am is eight-and-twenty, not a naïve debutant miss."

He laughed. "I wouldn't want one of those!" he exclaimed with a mock shudder.

In the doorway to the gold parlor appeared Stephen. "Excuse me, Mr. Martin. The duke requests you join him now in his library. The Altons are expected momentarily."

Gwinnie slouched and pouted. "Duty calls," she sighed.

"Hopefully this will be the last of the nasty issues we must face, and we can concentrate on us and our lives moving forward."

"Yes," she agreed as she stood.

He gave her a kiss on her cheek before he left her.

It was promising to be a beautiful morning.

~

"I DID NOT WRITE THOSE LETTERS!" Robert Alton, Earl of Wicholm, protested when shown the small stack of letters the Duke of Malmsby had received. "I know I ain't the smartest of fellows like Dicky, but I wouldn't do a ham-handed thing like this." He pushed the letters back across the desk toward the duke.

He turned to look at his father. "Do you think I would or could threaten a lady? What you must think of me!"

The earl looked shattered. Lewis wondered if they'd been too hasty in their assumptions.

"But you and my valet are the only ones who go in there," the marquess said.

"Why do you think that?" the earl asked. "Grandmother is in there all the time for her correspondence."

"She has a desk in her sitting room," protested the marquess.

"But she doesn't have access to franked letter paper at her desk," his son said.

"Do you know of times she has taken advantage of franking privileges?" asked Lewis.

"Every time she sends a letter to her best friend, Lady Culbrith, in Bath," said the earl.

The marquess frowned but slowly nodded in agreement.

"... You think she might have written these letters?"

"I do," said the earl.

"Your mother was Emily Satterwaithe, correct?" Malmsby asked.

The marquess nodded.

"I believe I have heard my mother affectionately call her Emily Scatteredwits," the duke said drily.

The marquess hung his head and looked down. "I could see that," he admitted, hiding a smile.

"If the author of these letters is the dowager marchioness— and this time let us not rush to assumptions," Lewis said, "how do you wish to handle this?"

The marquess looked at the duke.

A knock at the door interrupted them.

"Excuse me, Your Grace," said Stephen, opening the door a crack.

"Yes, come in, Stephen, what is it?"

"The dowager duchess has returned from her outing, accompanied by the Earl of Harleigh. They say it is imperative they see Mr. Martin immediately. They are in the Lady Margaret Parlor."

"Harleigh!" repeated the duke. He looked at Lewis. "You had better go and find out what this is about."

Lewis nodded and begged pardon to Lord Alton and Lord Wicholm. When he came out of the study, he had an urge to turn and go to the gold parlor first to see Gwinnie, but ignored the desire as he knew he would not leave her side immediately. He went down the stairs to the ground floor and walked toward the parlor. The door was open.

"You wanted to see me?" he asked from the open doorway.

"Yes" the duchess emphatically said, waving him over

to her. "We have a small fire we must extinguish before it becomes a society firestorm!"

"And this firestorm involves me?" Lewis asked, as he walked into the room.

"Yes, and Gwinnie," the duchess said, in patent disgust.

"Then it's a good thing I overheard Stephen and followed Lewis downstairs," said Gwinnie, coming into the room.

Lewis saw her balance wobble, and quickly went to her side to steady her and lead her into the room.

"I say, Lady Guinevere, that is a nasty bruise on your face," said the earl, looking at her closely.

"Yes," Gwinnie said, smiling at the man she now knew as Lewis's half-brother. "Dr. Walcott has said it might take two weeks to heal. I hope the headache that came with it does not take as long."

Lewis led her to an armchair, and when she was seated, tossed the sofa shawl across her legs.

She grabbed his hand as he moved to sit in a chair next to hers. They smiled at each other.

"Well," said the earl, "I can see how this may be more difficult than I'd hoped."

"In what way," Lewis asked, as he rubbed his thumb across the back of Gwinnie's hand.

"The Dowager Countess has decided to make mischief," said Gwinnie's grandmother.

"The worst," said the earl, "I'm so sorry, Lewis, I don't know what to do."

"What is it?"

"I told Mother you were likely going to wed Lady Guinevere. I was and am delighted for you, as is my wife. Not Mother. I have never seen her in such a rage! She threw a vase across the parlor, then stomped back and forth. She said she won't allow it, she won't allow you to get anything within society, that you don't deserve it."

Gwinnie pushed back in her chair. Lewis, however, shrugged.

"I am not surprised at her attitude," he said.

"But this time, she is not just spouting words," the

earl said. "She says if you do not foreswear Lady Guinevere, she will ruin her reputation and the reputation of Mrs. Southerland's charity. I admit I have not heard of that charity; however, Mother said it is important to you. She will affirm to any who will listen that Lady Guinevere is a courtesan, which is why she has not married, and the women in the house are her courtesan students."

"Hmm. Does your mother indulge in snuff?" Gwinnie asked.

Lewis looked at her quizzically for a moment, then smiled in understanding.

"Yes, a vile, heavily perfumed snuff. I can't stand the scent. Why do you ask?"

"That rumor originated with Mr. Jeffery Simmons, proprietor of a tobacco and snuff shop. He moved on to the same street as Mrs. Southerland's charity. He didn't like the charity being where he lived, so he tried to start a campaign to see that the charity moved elsewhere."

"Now that is interesting," said the duchess, leaning back against the sofa pillows. She folded her hands together and smiled. "With that information I may see a way to tame Lady Harleigh—"

"It wouldn't matter to me what she said," said Gwinnie, looking up at Lewis. "It has taken me too long to find Lewis, I am not giving him up now," she said emphatically.

Lewis's face lit with a big smile that carried to his bright eyes. He raised her hand to kiss her knuckles.

"I'm sorry, Lady Guinevere, but you don't know how she can be. She is a prominent, powerful source in society," exclaimed her son, rubbing his hands together.

"Only because I have, for the most part, retired to the country," the duchess countered. "Do not concern yourself with that notion— Lewis, it is time for everyone to know you are the Earl of Harleigh's son. Sally doesn't know it yet; however, she is giving a party Saturday night for all of society that remain in the city. A Winter Soiree, I think. Gwinnie, this will be a perfect opportunity for your former music teacher to take charge of your players.

They will practice here, of course, for the first event of the season."

"Your Grace," Lewis said with a smile and twinkle in his eyes, "with your knowledge of society and penchant for devious plans, I think you might also be of assistance with a conundrum we have upstairs. Might I request you come with me to meet with the Marquess of Alton and his heir, Lord Wicholm."

"Does this concern Emily Scatteredwits?"

He looked at her with surprise. "It might," Lewis admitted.

"I do love that woman; however, she comes up with the most hairbrained schemes. She doesn't know how to scheme appropriately, and when we were younger, I did try to teach her."

Lewis laughed. You may not be in favor of this scheme either."

"Ah! Another fun problem to solve," the duchess said as she stood up. "Please wait for me, my lord," she said to Lord Harleigh. "We have more planning to do. I declare I have not had this much fun since my house party at Versely Park last spring."

CHAPTER 20
A WINTER SOIREE

Gwinnie stood with her grandmother in the ballroom of Lady Oakley's townhouse. Last year, during the dreary, cold weather, Lady Oakley redecorated her house from the Chinese décor influence to Egyptian décor influence, with pyramids and camels and sphinxes replacing snarling dragons.

"Where did Lady Oakley get her designs from?" Gwinnie asked her grandmother as she looked about the room. By the press of people in attendance, one would hardly believe that most of London society remained out of the city following the holidays. Lady Oakley and her grandmother had certainly outdone themselves to get this many people to attend on such short notice.

"Sally has relations who have traveled through Egypt, trying to find the source of the Nile River. They weren't successful; however, their stories influenced her."

Gwinnie nodded. "With so much gold in the décor, the dress I am wearing blends in. I should have worn my green ballgown."

Her grandmother looked at the gold net with the white silk undergown Gwinnie wore. It sparkled in the candlelight. Across her arms she carried a gold Chinese silk shawl worked with colorful flowers at either end. Unfortunately, not all of Gwinnie's bruise had faded away; however, Rose had arranged for one side of her hair to drape down, shadowing one eye and covering most of the bruise, then swirl up to be caught in a gold-and-diamond comb. It was not in any current style; however, it suited Gwinnie, giving her a dramatic look that her grandmother quite liked.

"You look beautiful," her grandmother said. "The white and gold makes your red hair stand out more."

"And that is a good thing?" Gwinnie teased, her eyebrows rising in doubt.

"You know it is— Ah, look, the Harleighs have arrived, late as I requested to the earl. The Dowager Countess doesn't know it yet; however, they will be going against convention when they are introduced. First the Altons shall be announced," the duchess said as she raised her hand and gave a slight wave.

Gwinnie tried to see who she was waving at. It appeared to be the Dowager Marchioness of Alton on the arm of Lord Louis Rumport. They appeared to be laughing together as they approached the receiving line.

"Lady Alton had no one to escort her to society events, particularly her youngest grandson, Richard. He was off following in your father's shadow, researching new inventions."

"Are you implying Lady Alton wrote those awful letters?"

"I'm not implying, I know she did. She admitted it to me when I paid a call on her Thursday. In that scatter-witted brain of hers, she thought if she could stop your father from researching new inventions, her grandson would as well. She assumed she would be doing both of us a favor by having more of their attention."

"That is the most ridiculous reason I have ever heard," said Gwinnie.

"I know, but that is our dear Emily," her grandmother said with a sigh. "She said she got the idea from a book she read."

"So why is she now on the arm of Lord Rumport instead of one of her grandsons?"

"The poor dear is lonely. So is Lord Rumport, so I suggested they attend society events together. They may part ways once they arrive; however, they will have company arriving and leaving, avoiding any pitying glances or whispers, and keep society wondering," her grandmother said with a knowing smile.

Following the announcement of Lady Alton and Lord Rumport came Lord Alton and his sons.

With Lady Alton's introduction setting the order of precedent for the oldest family members to be introduced despite rank, Lady Harleigh was encouraged forward for her introduction. She did not understand why she went before her son but recovered and smiled at everyone, greeting Lady Sally Oakley.

In the back of the large room, Gwinnie's quartet was setting up. She saw them and turned to walk toward them. Her grandmother stopped her. "You have to see what comes next."

Gwinnie looked at her quizzically, but stayed as she requested.

The next introduction was to be the Earl of Harleigh. He stepped forward with his wife Cornelia, on one side and suddenly— Lewis on his other side!

"What?" Gwinnie breathed. She placed a gloved hand over her mouth for fear she would squeal. Her eyes danced. She grabbed her grandmother's forearm as she bobbed on her toes excitedly.

"Lord Jack Rockwell, Earl of Harleigh, his wife Lady Cornelia Harleigh, and his brother, Mr. Lewis Martin," intoned the butler.

A roar of gasps and whispers rose in the room. Gwinnie's eyes gleamed as she looked at them, her lips compressing against tears.

Harleigh and Lewis wore nearly identical evening attire of midnight blue coats and dress trousers with gold-and-blue waistcoats. Even their neckcloths were tied the same. The only difference between them was the jeweled stud in their cravats. Standing next to each other in the candlelight at the top of the stairs, no one could argue against a relationship between the men.

The voices in the room grew louder.

The duchess pulled Gwinnie closer to where the

Dowager Countess stood. She looked about ready to yell, her eyes bulging from their sockets, her mouth opening.

The duchess grabbed the countess's arm and pulled her around to face her. "It is too late, Elizabeth. You will only look the fool."

"You, you arranged this! Well, it is not over yet," hissed Lady Harleigh. "I can still ruin your granddaughter."

"You can try, but you will find no one will believe you. I know you picked up those rumors at the snuff shop. Mr. Simmons admitted to spreading rumors about Mrs. Southerland's charity house at the inquest into her murder. It is all documented as part of the inquest proceedings."

Devastation suffused Lady Harleigh's complexion with red.

Lewis came up beside Gwinnie. He tucked her arm through his, smiling at her.

"You bastard," Lady Harleigh spat at him.

"You have made that abundantly clear over the years," Lewis said. "Now if you will excuse me, I will take Gwinnie over to the refreshments for a celebratory glass of champagne with Jack and his wife," he said with a slight bow.

Lady Malmsby grabbed Lady Harleigh's arm. "Elizabeth," Lewis and Gwinnie heard Lady Malmsby say softly as they walked away, "you don't want to cause a scene here. It would not look good for you..."

~

Gwinnie enjoyed spending time with Lady Cornelia and Lord Harleigh. With Lewis, she met many people who said they'd been to events where her quartet played and were glad to finally have an opportunity to meet her. The kind words all around her made her realize how she'd hidden behind her music. When she said as much to Lewis, he nodded.

"Personally, I confess to being glad you hid," he told her. "If you hadn't, you'd have been married long ago."

Gwinnie laughed. "I doubt that!"

"I don't," said her grandmother, coming up to them.

"Lewis is the only man who has not been intimidated by my being taller."

"There are other gentlemen in society taller than you, and I've seen you hide away from meeting them."

Gwinnie made a sour face. "I wasn't ready," she finally said.

Her grandmother laughed. "That I can believe— Lewis, I believe Lady Elizabeth Harleigh feels embarrassed and contrite for her attitude this evening."

Lewis cocked an eyebrow in disbelief.

"No, it is true," said the dowager duchess. "I and Lady Oakley have been much in conversation with her this evening. We have listened to her— which she feels no one has ever done before— and did not ridicule her. She feels more in charity with her son for accepting you, and for you not attempting to take any glory from being his brother."

Lewis laughed. "Glory? Glory in what?"

"That you do not seek favors due to your close relation to a peer of the realm."

Lewis snorted. "I have no need of favors."

"If she comes up to you tonight to apologize, please hear her out. You do not need to agree, but let her speak."

"I will do that much for my brother."

"I should think her charity will be short-lived when she discovers you met with Mr. Scruthers yesterday," Gwinnie said.

He shrugged agreement.

"Who is Mr. Scruthers?" asked the duchess.

"My father's solicitor," Lewis explained, "and keeper of all his documents, including one that signed over his Rosevale property to me the year before he died."

The duchess looked at him sharply. "Is this a property Lady Harleigh wanted?"

Lewis compressed his lips before he spoke. "Yes. Jack told me she was confused as to why it was not mentioned in the will. Then she assumed it had already been gifted to her and the old earl forgot to tell her. Evidently, he signed over or sold minor properties to others at various times if they looked like they might put demands on other resources. His only mention of the property in his will was a request that Mr. Fortingay continue to manage the property."

"And you did not know you owned this property?" the duchess asked.

He shook his head with a wry smile.

Gwinnie explained, "Lady Cornelia told me Lady Harleigh intended to make it her dower property, even though there is a small dower estate connected to the earl's acreage. Rosevale is larger, and Lady Cornelia said it is beautiful, with the most magnificent gardens she has ever seen." She looked at Lewis. "I can't wait to see it myself."

"I haven't seen it since before I went to university," Lewis said. "It was a property that was in my mother's marriage settlements, if she had married my father."

"Ah," acknowledged the duchess, nodding. "That explains why he gave it to you."

"And why Lady Harleigh wanted it. She has always been jealous of my mother," Lewis said.

"She and I did speak about her jealousy. She said it has possessed her for longer than you have been alive. I told her I understood why she would have such feelings, but it was time to put them aside. She agreed," the duchess told them.

Lewis looked at the duchess askance. "I don't believe it."

"Lewis, give the woman a chance at least."

"As I said a moment ago, for my brother's sake, I shall," he reluctantly said. He saw his brother and Cornelia joining a set on the dance floor. He turned to Gwinnie. "This dance, my lady?"

Gwinnie looked at him in delighted surprise. "Most assuredly!"

"I haven't had occasion to dance since my university days, but I think I remember how," he assured her.

Gwinnie laughed. "You've probably had more occasion to dance than I."

"If either forgets the steps, we can whisper them to the other."

"Done," affirmed Gwinnie with a grin.

After the dance, Gwinnie was surprised to find herself the recipient of multiple requests for a dance. Lewis encouraged her to the dance floor, while he, at her grandmother's urging, danced with other young misses in society. Still, he kept his eyes darting back to Gwinnie, his bright beacon.

At the end of a dance, he escorted his partner back to her mother at the side of the room where the chaperones sat, then looked up to search out Gwinnie. He finally spotted her on the other side of the room in conversation with Lady Harleigh.

Every muscle in his body tensed, even though he witnessed Gwinnie smile and laugh with the Dowager Countess. His eyes narrowed. His hands curled into fists. He did not trust Lady Harleigh. He'd lived with her too long, suffered her abuse for too long to believe she could suddenly desire forgiveness.

"I say, Mr. Martin," said Lord Wolwich coming up to him.

Lewis waved him away, murmuring his apologies, as he started to make his way through the crowded room toward Gwinnie.

～

"Lady Guinevere."

Gwinnie turned at her name. Behind her stood Lady Harleigh, smiling at her. Gwinnie smiled tentatively back at her. "Lady Harleigh," she acknowledged with a slight inclination of her head.

"I'm so glad I caught up with you," the woman said.

"Indeed?"

"Yes. I know I have been odious to Mr. Martin. It is so hard to explain," she said. "Did you know he is the image of the late earl, my husband?"

"I have heard that, yes," Gwinnie replied, relaxing a little in the woman's presence.

"You should have seen my Jack and him when they were lads, running about the estate, getting in all manner of mischief," Lady Harleigh said with a memory smile.

Gwinnie laughed, "I can imagine so. That is the way of young boys, isn't it?"

"Yes, indeed," agreed Lady Harleigh. "Would you walk with me for a bit? I need to get out of this stuffy, noisy room. We could talk about the two men as boys," the Dowager Countess said, hooking her arm with Gwinnie's.

Gwinnie was suspicious of the countess; however, there was nothing in her manner that displayed animosity. Gwinnie allowed herself to be led out of the ballroom.

"I'm not surprised Mr. Martin joined Bow Street," Lady Harleigh said in a chatty fashion. "He was a right-versus-wrong child. He liked law, and spent the most ridiculous amount of time helping villagers. The old earl tried to get him to be a solicitor, thought it a good job for him since he would need to work."

"You say *job* as if it were a dirty word," Gwinnie observed.

Lady Harleigh stopped a moment. "Well, jobs aren't bad, they are just not for us, you know."

Gwinnie frowned. "No. I don't know. Isn't being a peer a responsibility?"

"Well, yes, of course."

"And having a responsibility can be a job."

Lady Harleigh pursed her lips. "You are mistaken. I'm surprised at your notion. Someone has not provided you a proper education," she said sharply.

Gwinnie looked at her askance.

"Responsibilities are performed by granting others the tasks associated with a responsibility in exchange for coin. This is how we keep the country healthy. We don't do work, we don't have jobs, we delegate."

"Oh, I see," Gwinnie said. She supposed that was one way of thinking about responsibility, but not one that readily leapt to her mind.

"What about Parliament?" Gwinnie suddenly asked.

"What do you mean?"

"How do you consider attending Parliament?" Gwinnie asked.

"As an honor, of course."

"Not a job."

"Heavens, no!"

Gwinnie considered that, then shrugged. "All right— We've been talking, and I suddenly realize I haven't been paying attention to where we are going," she said laughing. She pulled her arm from Lady Harleigh's and looked around. The hallway was darker than she liked, though elegant with Chinese decoration, not the newer Egyptian designs.

Lady Harleigh twittered. "Oh, just to one of Lady Oakley's retiring rooms. It's right here," she said, pointing to a door a few feet away.

Gwinnie frowned as she looked up at a dragon-shaped sconce. Lady Harleigh opened the door.

Gwinnie looked back at her. "I don't think—"

Lady Harleigh shoved her through the door.

~

Lewis didn't see either Gwinnie or Lady Harleigh by the time he made it across the room to the ballroom entrance hall. Icy fingers crawled across the back of his neck and down his spine as he searched.

Something was wrong.

He hailed the footman standing at the top of the grand staircase. "Have you seen a red-haired woman in a white-and-gold gown come this way?" Lewis asked, his voice filled with urgency. "She may have been with an older woman in a mauve gown."

"No, sir, not down these stairs," the footman replied, his voice tinged with annoyance.

Lewis frowned as he looked around. His heart beat faster. "Where does that hallway lead," Lewis asked, pointing to a dimly lit hallway on his right.

"The old bedroom wing. Off limits to guests, as it has not been redecorated yet."

"How is it off limits? I don't see any rope or sign," Lewis question, raising an eyebrow.

"Lady Oakley said the dim light would discourage people from going that way."

Lewis nodded his understanding, but he kept looking in that direction. "Thank you," he said absently, nodding at the footman. Lewis put his hands behind his back, clasping his fingers together as he walked away. He did not return to the ballroom but lingered in the hall, watching guests come and go into the noise and gaiety of the ballroom, and watching the darkened hallway.

When the footman was engaged with other guests, he saw Lady Harleigh hurry out of the dark hallway. She paused to seemingly regain her composure. She lifted her chin in her imperious manner.

She was alone, and he'd seen her leave the ballroom with Gwinnie.

"Lady Harleigh," he said congenially, masking his concern. "Have you seen Lady Guinevere?"

She glared daggers at him, mouthing the word *bastard* before sweeping past him. Lewis couldn't deny the surge of anger that rose within him when Lady Harleigh insulted him. But anger wouldn't find Gwinnie. So much for the reconciliation Lady Malmsby claimed she desired.

His brow furrowed as he stared after Lady Harleigh. Where was Gwinnie? What had she done to Gwinnie? Shivers slid down his spine. He walked toward the dark hallway, ignoring the footman's calls after him.

~

Panic tore through Gwinnie as her foot found air. Her heel slipped and skidded on the edge of a steep step, throwing her balance off. This was not a room! Gwinnie's arms flailed as she fell. Panicking, she twisted sideways, trying to find something to grab. Her twist brought her up against the stair rail. She desperately grabbed the railing and hung on, though her momentum wanted her body to tumble down the stair. She wrenched her shoul-

An Artful Decision

der, hearing it pop as her body slid more. Her grip slowed her enough she got her feet pointing down the stairs.

Finally, she realized she wasn't moving any longer. She released the death grip on the handrail, finger by finger. Her shoulder screamed in pain as she moved her arm down to her side. *Dislocated*, she thought.

Her breath came in rapid gasps. She mentally checked the rest of her body. There was soreness on her hip and back, and the foot that had come down first felt like a sprain, but no pain felt as severe as the pain in her shoulder. She pulled herself up to a sitting position and sat there, resting her dangling arm across her lap. The staircase was black as pitch.

Gwinnie let her initial panic go. She inhaled deeply, and let it out, a slight smile rising above the pain. Lewis would come, as he had at Soothcoor Mansion. She catalogued her pains as she waited.

~

LEWIS OPENED unlocked doors and knocked on locked ones, calling Gwinnie's name. A faint trace of lilies in the air— Gwinnie's scent— drew him down the hall.

"Sir! Sir!" said the footman, catching up to him. "I told you this hallway is off limits."

"Two women have been down this hall and only one came out," Lewis said curtly, brushing past the footman.

"Preposterous," declared the footman. He pulled Lewis's arm. "Come sir, I must insist!"

"I am Lewis Martin, a Bow Street agent" Lewis said firmly. "I am investigating this hallway. Inform Lady Oakley— better, find the Duke of Malmsby and inform him that Lewis Martin needs him here."

"This is ridiculous, there is nothing here—"

Lewis shook his arm loose. "Go!" he yelled.

The footman jumped at Lewis's tone, then scurried back down the hall.

When Lewis came to a narrow, plain-paneled door, his gut twisted. Instinctively he knew this was the door.

The door at Soothcoor Mansion flashed in his mind. Another door separating him from Gwinnie. He pressed down on the door handle, and put his shoulder to the door, but it was locked. He rapped loudly on the door.

"Gwinnie? Gwinnie," he shouted, his voice echoing down the hallway. "Are you in here?"

"Lewis! Yes, I'm here. It's the servants' stairs." Her muffled voice sounded all right. He breathed a sigh of relief.

"Are you all right?"

"Well, at least I didn't hit my head," Gwinnie responded.

Lewis laid his forehead against the door, his eyes watering in relief. He chuckled and sniffed for a moment of respite amid chaos. Trust Gwinnie to offer sarcasm when everything was not all right, Lewis mused, a small smile tugging at his lips. "I'll reframe my question: what hurts?" he asked, his voice filled with both relief and concern.

Behind him came the Duke of Malmsby and Lady Oakley with her footman trailing behind.

"I'm fairly sure my ankle is not broken," she said with a forced chuckle. *"But I think I dislocated my shoulder, and my back and hip have been trying to claim attention, too."*

Lady Oakley laid a gentle hand on Lewis's shoulder.

"Egad! What happened?" the duke bellowed, his voice booming.

"Hello, Father! Lady Harleigh pushed me down these stairs," Gwinnie said, her voice tinged with a disquieting mix of amusement and exasperation. *"The steps are fairly steep. I think she was trying to kill me— Do you realize that's three times in one week someone has had an intention to kill me!"* Gwinnie exclaimed, striving for jovial outrage.

Then her voice broke, as fragile as glass, and they could hear tears. *"Can someone come get me, please?"*

"I'm coming, my love," Lewis said. He turned to the footman. "Do you have a key for this door?"

The man shook his head.

"Lady Oakley?" he asked.

She shook her head, then looked at her footman. "Take him to the first floor. I believe that door to this stairway is unlocked."

An Artful Decision

"Right away, my lady," the footman said, turning before she'd finished talking. He led Lewis down two floors and through a maze of halls to the stairway. The door was unlocked, but Lewis could see there was no light in the narrow stairway.

"Candles, man!" Lewis demanded, his heart pounding in his chest.

The footman found a tinderbox and a branch of candles. He handed the lit candles to Lewis.

"Go back up to the duke," Lewis urged, his voice demanding. "Tell him I will likely need assistance to get her down if she is injured as extensively as she mentioned."

Lewis started up the stairs, the candles held high. "Gwinnie! Can you hear me?" Lewis yelled up the stairs.

"Barely."

"I'm on my way. Hold that in your heart," Lewis reassured, his voice filled with determination. "I am on my way, my love."

When he reached the next floor landing, the stairs went up at a different angle, not directly over the last stairs. Lewis paused for a moment, catching his breath before continuing up the stairs towards Gwinnie.

"I see your light!" He heard Gwinnie cry out.

He took another bend in the stairs, and then he saw her.

CHAPTER 21
LEWIS'S MINISTRATIONS

Between them, Lewis and the duke slowly carried Gwinnie down the steep stairs to the first floor, the footman carrying the candleholder.

"Is there a bedroom on this floor," Lewis asked.

"Lady Oakley's," the footman responded.

"Which way," Lewis asked.

"Oh, but sir, you can't—"

"Which way, my man, which way?" demanded the duke.

The footman looked like he was about to cry, but led them to a room at the end of the hall and opened the door into a beautiful pale-green bedroom. His jaw nearly dropped to see a couple standing in the middle of the room, passionately embracing.

"Out of the way," bellowed Malmsby, not even glancing at the couple.

"Oh, oh!" the footman squealed, fairly dancing in place as the lady worked to pull the sleeve of her white gown back over her shoulders, and she and the man scurried out the door, the footman following behind them.

Gwinnie turned her head to look at Lewis. They struggled against laughing. "Would it be bad of me to admit I needed that laugh?" Gwinnie asked.

Malmsby harrumphed. His mouth turned down in

the frown he'd had since he'd joined Lewis on the stairs to carry her down.

"May I check your ankle?" Lewis asked. "You said you did not believe it was broken, but it should be checked."

"No, please do check it," Gwinnie said.

"Your grace?" Lewis asked, turning to her father.

Malmsby had begun pacing the room, but he nodded.

Lewis carefully pushed her skirts up so he could feel her ankle and leg. His breath caught in his throat, and heat coursed through him as he ran his hand over her ankle and calf. For his sanity, he quickly determined there were no broken bones. He quickly pulled her skirts back down and straightened.

"I don't detect any broken bones," he said, looking at the duke.

Malmsby thrust his lower lip out. "Good. I should go get the dowager duchess," he said grimly, walking toward the door.

"Wait, Your Grace, if you would please," Lewis said.

"What?"

"I'd like your assistance to get her shoulder back into place."

"You know how to do that?" Malmsby asked, his expression one of worry and doubt.

"Yes, I've done it many times." He looked at Gwinnie. "This will hurt, but it is best to take care of it as soon as possible. Can you trust me?"

"Of course."

"Good. Now I want you to relax as much as you can. Breathe evenly. I'm going to bring your arm along your side."

Gwinnie winced as he moved her arm. Her face contorted in pain, and she let out a sharp gasp.

"It's going to hurt a lot more in a moment," Lewis warned, his voice filled with empathy. "But I promise, it will feel better after. Just hold on, my love, my warrior woman— Your Grace, if you would stand on the other side of the bed and put a hand on that shoulder to keep it down."

An Artful Decision

"You think I won't be able to stand the pain and shall scream and thrash about?" Gwinnie asked indignantly, though her breathing remained fast.

"Sometimes movement is involuntary," Lewis said, smiling down at her. "And now I can see you tensing up in anticipation. You need to relax. I am going to turn your hand and arm, then slowly bring it up to the side, but you need to relax to let the head of your arm slip back into place. Do you understand?"

Gwinnie turned her head to look up at him. "I love you," she said.

"As I love you," Lewis said conversationally, as he moved her arm slowly. "And no one is going to try to kill you again," he promised. "I can't bear the thought of anything happening to you. I have too many plans for us."

"You do?" Gwinnie asked with a slight laugh, her eyes fixed on Lewis.

Lewis flashed her his cheeky smile that never failed to make her heart quiver.

Malmsby listened and watched Lewis and Gwinnie closely. He smiled for the first time since he saw his broken daughter sitting on the staff staircase.

"You are going to be stuck with me for years and years," Lewis continued calmly, keeping her attention on what he said over what he did.

The door to the bedroom opened with the dowager duchess and Lady Oakley rushing in. Malmsby raised a finger to his lips to tell them to be quiet. He listened and watched Lewis closely, his brows furrowed in concern.

Lewis knew the ladies were there but did not spare them a glance. His mind and soul remained entirely on Gwinnie. "I'm thinking we should leave London and move to Rosevale," he continued. "It is a beautiful property. Perhaps we can start a charity house there, what do you say?" he asked, as he gently pulled her hand toward him.

The shoulder slid back into place.

"Ah-h!" Gwinnie said, panting. "That feels so much better! And your idea has merit! Yes!" she exclaimed. She started to raise her arm to hug Lewis, but he stopped her, gently pushing her arm back down.

"No, love. Your arm is back in place, but it is not healed. In the state it is in, it could slip out again. You need to keep it in a sling for a few weeks." He sat on the edge of the bed and looked up at the women who'd entered.

"Lady Oakley, might you have a cloth we can fashion into a sling for Gwinnie?"

"I'm sure we do," Lady Oakley said, her worried expression clearing. "I'll go ask my housekeeper. She'll have just what you need, I'm sure of it."

"Gwinnie," exclaimed her grandmother. "I'm so sorry about Lady Harleigh. It's not like me to be taken in like that by someone. I'm quite aggrieved! I don't understand it. I thought her sincere! This is all my fault," she said, approaching the bed.

"In my experience with Bow Street, I have found that sometimes the craziest people are the ones who fool us the best," Lewis told her, to ease her guilt.

"She belongs in a place like Camden House," Gwinnie's father said flatly. "I *will* be speaking to the earl about this."

"Isn't that the sanitarium Soothcoor ended up owning after he was accused of murder last year?" Gwinnie's grandmother asked.

"The same. I assume the Harleighs have left?" inquired Malmsby.

"Yes, Lady Harleigh professed a headache," his mother said.

"I will deal with her later," Lewis said.

"With my accompanying you!" Malmsby insisted. "It was my daughter she tried to kill."

"We don't know that killing me was her goal," said Gwinnie. "I agree she wanted to cause me harm."

"You are too nice for your own good," stated her father.

Lewis shook his head. "Unfortunately, you are correct, Gwinnie. We don't know if this was a crime of opportunity or premeditated for death or injury."

An Artful Decision

"Leave her until tomorrow—or Monday even," Gwinnie suggested. "Give her time to think no one will accuse her of anything. I don't want to give her any of my precious time that I could spend with you, Lewis."

The housekeeper came into the room carrying a muslin sling with padding and multiple ties. "Here you go, my lady," the woman said. "Made this myself when young Mary, the scullery maid tripped and tried to catch herself with her arm. Clean break, the doctor said, but had to be held in place for quite a while to heal."

She crossed to the bed to fit the sling on her. There was padding on the outside to guard against bumps, and ties for around her neck and around her waist.

Gwinnie winced a little when it was first positioned around her arm, then she relaxed. "Why a tie around my waist?" she asked, as the woman passed the ribbon around her to tie at her side.

"So's you don't forget and try to move it. Keeps it tight against your body, it does."

Gwinnie thanked the woman, as did the others. The housekeeper blushed and waved her hand before her to tell them it was nothing, just doing her duty before she bustled out of the room.

"Can I go home, now?" Gwinnie asked plaintively, looking up at Lewis.

He grinned at her. "Yes," he said, leaning close, "I just wish it were my home," he whispered.

Gwinnie blushed as she looked at him, a small smile curving her lips.

"Let's see if you can put any weight on that foot," he said louder, encouraging her to slide to the side of the bed.

The duke came around to her side and he and Lewis helped her to her feet.

"I can put my toes down a bit, but otherwise, it's a hop."

"We'll support you," her father said.

"I'll have our carriage called," said the duchess, sweeping out of the room.

Gwinnie's father looked seriously at Lewis as they

helped Gwinnie to walk out of the room. "I know Gwinnie said she wanted a courtship; however, under the circumstances of this past week, I prefer you marry her as soon as possible."

"Father!" protested Gwinnie in surprise.

"I should be delighted to, Your Grace," Lewis said.

"Don't 'Father' me, Gwinnie, you two are in love. I'll pay for the special license," he said gruffly. "That way I'll know someone is watching out for you."

Lewis grinned. "Our thoughts are running along similar paths, Your Grace. I love Gwinnie and want to protect her body and soul. I petitioned the Archbishop on Thursday and picked up the special license yesterday."

"What?" Gwinnie exclaimed. "You haven't even proposed to me yet!" she protested.

"Good man," said her father.

Lewis stopped in the middle of the stairs, forcing the duke to stop too. "A courtship is to allow a man and woman to determine compatibility. We have more than determined compatibility. Do you agree or not," Lewis asked Gwinnie.

Gwinnie compressed her lips and gave him a side-eyed look. "Y-e-s," she said, drawing out the word. Her lips quirked up on one side. "Except for the matter of height," she said.

"Aargh!" Lewis cried out. "Excuse me, Your Grace, I need your daughter for a moment." He pulled her around to face him and kissed her soundly. He then let her go and stepped back. "Height is not an issue! — Thank you, Your Grace, for your indulgence. Shall we continue? I'm certain your coach will be here soon, if it isn't already."

The duke chuckled, the sound rumbling out of his chest. "I shall enjoy having you for my son-in-law. And don't you think it is time you started calling me Arthur?"

EPILOGUE
ROSEVALE, APRIL 1817

Lewis looked up from his ledger when he heard the strains of a violin floating in the open study window, riding the faint breeze that brought with it the scent of roses.

Gwinnie was taking a moment for herself. *Good*, he thought. He rose from his desk and walked to the open window. His beloved wife stood in the wildest, in appearance, of the gardens, the one not conforming to a type of plant or orderly planting. All colors surrounded her as she swayed with her music. She'd shunned her bonnet again and sun glinted on her rich red hair. More freckles would bloom across her cheeks. Lewis didn't care. He loved each kiss the sun bestowed on her face.

He looked back at the papers on his desk, then back at Gwinnie and made a decision. He would join Gwinnie outside. He rang a staff bell and requested tea be prepared for the garden, then he walked out of his study and to the ground-floor parlor that fronted the terrace.

The doors and windows were open to the spring air. He passed through the doors and walked across the terrace and down the rose-bordered path that would take him to the wild garden. Beyond the wild garden was a small apple orchard, the trees in full bloom.

He sat on a wood bench at the edge of the wild garden.

Rosevale was a more beautiful estate than he remembered as a young man. He could see why his father had requested Mr. Fortingay remain as the estate manager. The man had a manner that communicated with plants better than people. A couple of society peers had wanted to steal him away from Rosevale; however, the man had thankfully turned them down, saying he was content at Rosevale.

The inside of the manor was like a favored, well-worn jacket, comfortable but not elegant. Gwinnie and Lewis found it suited them. Eventually they would make changes, but they were not in a rush. There were two wings to the house that had been shut up years ago. Lewis had never been in them. When he and Gwinnie toured the closed-up rooms with the old caretaker couple, they'd become excited at the possibilities for turning part of Rosevale into a school or a charity. They didn't know yet what they wanted to do. They were in discussion with the Earl of Soothcoor for suggestions. In the meantime, they were having the wings cleaned and restored.

Supervising this effort filled Gwinnie's days.

Daniel had gone to Versely Park with the dowager duchess the Monday after the Winter Soiree. He discovered he liked the country, but had returned to school after three weeks. He wrote that he was looking forward to coming to Rosevale at the end of the school term.

Lewis spent much of his time getting acquainted with his inheritance and his investments. He and Harry Liddle were contemplating starting an inquiry agency when they discovered they only lived five miles apart. Further, to his and Gwinnie's surprise, they were only eleven miles from Gwinnie's twin brother and his wife, and less than a half-day's journey from Versely Park! Those discoveries delighted Gwinnie. And Merlin knew he wanted a medical practice in the Cotswolds, so he would likely be close as well. Only the Duke of Malmsby seemed to prefer the city, but they would coax him out for visits.

Lewis heard the clattering of china behind him. Their tea had arrived. Gwinnie had heard it too. She turned.

"Lewis! How long have you been sitting there?" she asked, nearly skipping to him. She held her violin and bow in one hand away from her and gave him a one-armed hug with the arm that had long recovered from its injury.

"I don't know. Fifteen minutes or so. I was enjoying hearing you play."

"It is a beautiful day to play outside. I'm glad that last year Bella convinced me to try it."

"I ordered tea."

"I see," Gwinnie said. "Let me put my violin away and we can indulge in some relaxing time together."

"I can think of a better way to spend relaxing time together," Lewis said, flashing his cheeky smile and brilliant blue eyes at her.

"Relaxing? I am nearly always out of breath and positively spent," Gwinnie declared. "But I do enjoy it," she said with a sly smile.

Before Lewis could say anything else, she ran into the house to put her instrument away. When she returned, she saw he had poured her tea and prepared it as she liked it. "I could get used to this." She took a sip.

He smiled at her. "I had a letter from Soothcoor today," he said.

"And?"

"He made a few suggestions. One I found particularly intriguing. A music academy."

"A music academy?" Gwinnie set down her teacup.

"He thought there are probably children with a music talent who have no opportunity to learn. Rather like Robbie Gilgorn and his art talent."

"Possibly," Gwinnie said slowly. "But how would we find them?"

"I don't know, though I'm certain Soothcoor would not have suggested the idea if he didn't have a glimmer of a notion on how to set things in motion.

"True." She nodded and picked up her teacup again.

"Oh, he also told me the Dowager Countess of Harleigh is enjoying spring from Camden House Sanatorium."

"I wonder how they got her to go there?"

"Probably the threat of having me arrest her. No one will cause you any more harm; if someone tried, they wouldn't live long enough to be arrested," Lewis promised.

Gwinnie leaned over and kissed his cheek. "Are you happy here?" she asked. "Do you miss solving crimes and making friends with the mudlarks and other city children?"

"I am extremely happy being with you. I could never have imagined our life now, to live as we please."

"Mr. and Mrs. Martin of Rosevale," Gwinnie declared. Then she grew solemn. "The only thing that will make me happier is to bear your child."

"I know you are disappointed that you have not conceived yet. I, however, am not," admitted Lewis.

"You're not? Don't you want children?" She ran a hand through his blond waves.

"I do. I want children with you," he said, capturing her wayward hand in his and brought it to his lips. "But right now, I want to be selfish and not share you with anyone."

Gwinnie smiled softly. "There is merit in that. Like enjoying the activities that may lead to a child," she said coyly.

Lewis laughed. "Yes, like those activities."

"I'm done playing the violin for the day. Are you done with your accounts and ledgers?" she asked.

He grinned. "I am. Are you suggesting, Mrs. Martin, you'd like to indulge in that activity?" he asked, as he rose from his chair and pulled her up beside him.

"I'm tingling at the thought."

He laughed, his clear blue eyes sparkling at her. "Never let it be said I let tingles go to waste."

"Never," she said, as he hooked her arm through his. She laid her head against his as they made their way to the stairs. At the base of the stairs, Gwinnie gently pulled her arm from his.

"Race you!" she suddenly declared. She grabbed her skirts and took off running up the stairs.

Surprise held Lewis's feet momentarily, giving Gwinnie her head start.

"Vixen!" he declared. He took off after her.

She beat him to their room and threw herself backward onto the bed. "I won!" she crowed with delight.

Lewis raised one blond eyebrow, his lips curving into a stalking smile as he closed the bedroom door behind him.

SCRIBBLINGS BY HOLLY NEWMAN

A Chance Inquiry series
The Waylaid Heart
Rarer Than Gold
Heart of a Tiger
Murder of a Dead Man
And coming soon
Murder on the Downs

The Art of Love series
An Artful Deceit
An Artful Compromise
An Artful Lie
An Artful Secret
An Artful Decision
And coming soon
An Artful Practice
An Artful Trade

Flowers and Thorns series
A Grand Gesture
Honor's Players
A Heart in Jeopardy
Heart's Companion

Other works
Gentleman's Trade
Reckless Hearts
A Lady Follows

The Rocking Horse (novella)
Perchance to Dream (short story)

ABOUT HOLLY NEWMAN

I decided to be a writer when I was in the fifth grade. I filled notebooks with stories—until a mean-spirited high school teacher told me I had no talent for writing. Crushed, for several years I stopped writing, but writing was an itch that wouldn't go away.

My interest in the Regency period came while in high school when I volunteered to re-shelve returned books at the community library. Every week there were Georgette Heyer novels to be shelved. I finally checked one out and became immersed in the world of the Regency.

Fast forward ten years. When attending Science Fiction Conventions, I met people who read science fiction, but also enjoyed the works of Jane Austen and Georgette Heyer, just as I did! They liked these books so much that they wore Regency costumes at the science fiction conventions. They even had Regency era dancing on the convention program. These science fiction readers and writers knew a lot about the Regency era. Intrigued, I did research on the era and quickly went from casual Regency reader to a Regency history buff. Woo-hoo!

After that, with encouragement from science fiction authors, it was just a small step to writing Regencies.

After living thirty years in the Arizona desert, I now live in Florida, seven miles from the Gulf Coast, with my husband, Ken, and our *clowder* of cats. (I don't dare say a number of cats. My husband has developed a habit of collecting strays.)

Subscribe to my newsletter to learn about books and other writings I'm working on. You can sign up here to subscribe and get *Perchance to Dream*, a Georgian fantasy short story.

And be sure to follow me on Bookbub, to be notified about new books and book sales.

Here are other ways to connect!

Website: hollynewman.com
Etsy: etsy.com/shop/readercomforts

- facebook.com/HollyNewmanAuthor
- instagram.com/hollynewman1811
- pinterest.com/holly2658
- goodreads.com/Holly_Newman

Milton Keynes UK
Ingram Content Group UK Ltd.
UKHW041405191024
449759UK00009B/28

9 781648 397400